5/30/23

HILL COUNTRY SIREN

HILL COUNTRY SIREN

A Joe Robbins Financial Thriller (Book 3)

PATRICK KELLY

May your path be replete
with wonders!
Patrick Kelly

CHAPARRAL PRESS, LLC

Published in paperback and eBook versions by Chaparral Press, LLC.

Cover designed by Derek Murphy.

ISBN 978-0-9911033-5-5 (pbk.)
ISBN 978-0-9911033-4-8 (ebk.)

To Mom and Dad, my everlasting love.

PROLOGUE

November 2, 2003

I LOVED SOPHIE TYLER long before she hired me.

She was a hometown hero, a musician who grew up in Austin and made the big time. Sophie got her start in the midseventies working live venues with a band called the Texas Strangers. She worked the southwest circuit until she got her break as a solo artist in the early eighties.

In high school I couldn't afford the ticket for a live performance, but I bought her albums and played them over and over, studying the covers and the liner notes, mesmerized by her voice. I would put her album on the record player in my upstairs bedroom and climb onto the roof to look at the stars.

When an incident affects me profoundly enough to invade my dreams, I write about it. The setting down of words on paper helps me think through the events, the role I played, the gains and losses, and the lessons learned, if any. I've been writing this story for weeks now, typing away in solitude, earbuds in, listening to Sophie's music.

Though my journey began with a simple investigation it eventually meandered, step by avoidable step, onto a path both replete with wonders and laden with perils. To the wonders I contributed nothing, but as for the perils . . . I don't know. Perhaps you should be the judge.

CHAPTER 1

LATE IN THE SUMMER OF 2003 I met Rico Carrillo and Adrian Williams at Austin Java on Barton Springs Road. The place was only a mile from the condo so I rode my bicycle, an old Schwinn I bought for thirty dollars at a pawnshop.

We sat at an outdoor table about twenty feet from the road. Saturday traffic was light. The sun had warmed the morning air in a hurry, and sweat made the polo shirt cling to my back. I reached around to pull it free.

Adrian was African-American and about six feet tall. He looked like a stereotypical security professional: conservative attire and grooming, great physical condition, watchful eyes, and a neutral expression. The two of them had served in the Marines together, and Rico had referred Adrian to me.

Adrian's big hands rested on the table. He wore a navy-blue golf shirt decorated with small white sailboats.

"So . . . you believe someone has scammed Sophie Tyler," I said, my voice rough, dry, and to my ears at least, a tad giddy. I sipped coffee, hoping the liquid would allow my next words to emerge normally. Ever since Rico mentioned the gig to me I'd had trouble relaxing, my blood pressure elevated.

"It has to do with a two-million-dollar investment she made in an independent film," Adrian said. "Sophie and I use the same accountant. He told me that he had related some concerns about the investment to Sophie, and when I mentioned it to her she asked for my help."

I had finished my latest project a few weeks earlier, taken a short break, and was now ready for the next thing. Generally I made money working interim CFO roles, but I was good at ferreting out fraud schemes. I'd done that kind of work before but never for a rock star.

"Why did she ask you for help?" said Rico. "Why not go to the police?"

"She wants to keep this low-profile," said Adrian. "Her ex-boyfriend, Bryan Slater, brought her into the movie, and if it turns out bad, she only wants her money back. No publicity."

"Okay," I said.

"Sophie asked me to look for someone from out of town."

"Sounds like you and Ms. Tyler are on a first-name basis," said Rico. He lifted a large mug to his lips and narrowed his eyes slightly. As the head of Austin's Homicide Division, Lieutenant Rico Carrillo had a suspicious nature.

"As far as I can tell," said Adrian, "she's on a first-name basis with everybody. Anyway, the accountant also told me Sophie's not doing well financially. If this investment goes bad she might lose her house."

"Where does she live?" said Rico.

"Beverly Hills."

"Not exactly a middle-class neighborhood."

"She's had that house for fifteen years, ever since the *Ancient Spirits* album."

I must have played that album a hundred times, eventually had to replace it, twice.

"Who manages her money?" I asked.

"Johnson Sagebrush. He's her manager. He handles everything from Sophie's schedule to her diet, but I have no idea if he's good with numbers."

"You seem sort of overinvested in this thing," said Rico. "It's not your responsibility. You're her security consultant, not her bookkeeper."

"She's my best client. I don't want to lose her. Plus, there's something about being around her that's . . . I don't know . . . it's different, special."

Adrian stammered the words and looked down. Had he become starstruck by his client? If so, he had picked the right star. With one look at a photo of Sophie my eyes became entranced, locked onto her face, and her hair, which she wore long, straight, and draped carelessly about her shoulders.

"Anyway," Adrian continued, "I was coming to Austin to scout security for the festival next weekend, so I asked Rico if he knew anyone, and he mentioned you. I understand you have some security experience as well."

"That was a long time ago," I said.

"Joe's a boxer, too," said Rico, with a half smile. "He can handle himself in tough situations."

"What does that have to do with a fraud investigation?" I said.

Rico was medium height and in good shape, his hair and mustache speckled with gray. His left eye had a curious flaw, a black sectoral heterochromia that grew in size with his blood pressure. He was calm, and the wedge-shaped flaw covered only an eighth of his otherwise almond iris.

He'd asked me to take this meeting as a favor, said he didn't think I'd make much money on it, but he'd like to help out a friend. I owed Rico many favors. He had saved my life the year before.

"I thought we'd bring you on as part of my security team," said Adrian. "You could help out with security at the festival and look into this investment at the same time. That would camouflage your investigation. I suggested the idea to Sophie. She loved it."

My pulse jumped. "You already talked to her about me?" The words *about me* came out wrong, almost a squeak.

Adrian nodded. "Rico gave you a strong recommendation."

Rico lifted his eyebrows, and his smile grew wider.

"Could you fly out Tuesday to meet Sophie?" said Adrian. "She'll give you all the background."

Meet Sophie Tyler?

That was the only real question I had for the meeting. Would I meet her in person? Some of my projects made watching paint dry seem like an action movie, but not this one.

I would have done the job for free.

Just then our waitress walked up. She had spiked hair, dark lipstick, and a pierced eyebrow. "Anything else, guys?"

We asked for touchups on the coffee as she cleared the dishes. She leaned her hip against the table. "You all going to ACL?"

Rico shook his head. "Live music's not really my thing."

"I had to beg my manager to get two days off," she said. "Sunday's the best lineup, but I couldn't miss Saturday. Sophie Tyler's playing."

"That's right," I said.

"It's gonna be awesome. You don't want to miss it." She turned and walked back into the restaurant.

"Okay," I said. "I'll fly out Tuesday."

• • •

On the way out, Rico stopped by the bike rack. The top of his head came to the top of my shoulder. He wore sunglasses, a short-sleeved buttoned shirt, jeans, and cowboy boots. The pecan trees around us created merciful shade.

"Thanks for meeting with Adrian."

"You bet." I reached down to open the cheap combination lock.

"It sounds like an interesting assignment."

"Sure does."

Rico held out a package of gum and I took a piece. He popped one into his mouth and took a few big chews on it. "So . . . how's Missy?"

I wrapped the cable around the seat pole and closed the lock to hold it in place. Every so often Rico asked about my love life. I think he worried about me since Rose and I had been apart for so long, or maybe Alma, his wife, forced him to ask me.

"You're behind the times. I haven't dated Missy in four months."

"Let me guess. Commitment issues."

"I'm dating a new woman. Alyssa Stavros."

"Alyssa Stavros." He said the name in a flat tone.

"Yep. Nice Greek girl. Her father owns a restaurant on South Congress."

Rico bobbed his head slightly, like he found the whole conversation a little surreal. His raised his eyebrows. "Did you help her out of some trouble or anything?"

"Not really."

That wasn't completely true. When I first met Alyssa at the Saxon Pub on South Lamar she had just broken up with a macho boyfriend named George. Alyssa and I had gone out only a few times when we ran across George outside Threadgill's. He wanted to fight me. I stood away from him in a boxing stance, and every time he came too close I popped him with a light jab. At the same time Alyssa yelled at him, constantly. Soon enough he gave up, cried a little, hugged Alyssa, and went home with his friends.

"Not really?" said Rico. "What's that mean?"

"It means she didn't really need any help."

"It's too bad about Missy. Alma hoped that you and she would settle down."

Bing. I called that right. I liked Alma, a lot, but she believed in a rigid formula: Every man should find a woman, settle down, and start a family. But I already had a family.

"Alma wants me to marry again?"

"It's not too late. What are you? Thirty-eight?"

"Thirty-seven."

Rico was about to get on a roll. When I first met him, three-and-a-half years before, he had me down in his notebook as a murder suspect, but since then we had become friends. Every once in a while he would ask me a financial question related to one of his investigations. I had become an on-call subject matter expert, unpaid, of course.

"You and Rose split three years ago. That's long enough. Let's say you and . . . was it Alice?"

"Alyssa."

"Say you and Alyssa got married now; you could have two kids before you're forty. Alma would love that."

"I have two kids."

Two wonderful kids: Chandler (twelve) and Callie (ten). They had reached the age when they formed their own opinions, a time when parents needed to double-down, to focus thought and energy into achieving the right balance between being there for the kids and allowing them to grow. Rose and I worked together to achieve that balance. We never fought over the kids; in fact, we didn't fight at all anymore.

Rico shook his head. "You'd better watch out. You could wind up alone."

"Maybe so, but for now I've got enough on my plate. I'm not looking for anything long-term."

"Like I said, commitment issues." But he nodded acceptance and turned to go. "Thanks again for meeting Adrian. Let me know how the fraud thing works out."

"Will do."

* * *

PEDALING BACK TO THE CONDO I stopped in Zilker Park to observe preparations for the festival. A temporary chain-link fence surrounded the fifty-acre site. An electric drill sounded as workers erected a stage. The sun burned my neck, and a drop of sweat slid down my back.

I had planned to invite Alyssa to join me for the three-day festival, but with the new assignment, maybe I'd better not. I might end up working security for a rock star, a weird turn of events. Working security, like back in college. Was I regressing? What was next? Beer pong?

CHAPTER 2

THE NEXT MORNING, sitting at the breakfast table in my condo, Alyssa wore one of my T-shirts and nothing else. I wore boxers.

Over the past couple months we'd settled into a routine on Sundays. We'd have breakfast and then make love and lounge in bed for an extra hour. But that morning I sensed uncertainty on Alyssa's part, a lack of sparkle in her eyes, so I didn't press for the normal routine.

She took a last sip of coffee, placed her cup on the table, and looked at me with amber eyes. She gave me a half smile that revealed perfect teeth.

"What do you want to do now?" I asked.

"Brush my teeth."

"Sounds good. What next?"

Alyssa shrugged. "Use your imagination." She stood and walked toward the master bedroom, the T-shirt barely covering her butt. She was tall and fit, and I followed her.

I hurried through the teeth brushing and kissed her neck from behind, my hands on the front of her thighs, pulling her to me. I lifted the T-shirt. She giggled and raised her arms. As I tossed the shirt to the side she turned around, grabbed the sides of my boxers, and tugged on them.

"Let's get rid of these, too."

She pressed full breasts against my chest and tiptoed as I leaned to kiss her. She reached her arms around my neck and pulled me toward her. My hands crept down to the small of her back.

One of her hands slipped off my shoulder and traversed my chest and stomach. The hand ventured lower.

I lifted her, and she wrapped her long legs around me. Still kissing, I walked us into the room and laid her on the bed.

We did it the traditional way, her on the bottom with legs spread, me on top lying between them. We took our time. Her eyes watched me intensely.

Even as she grew more excited, she still watched me, as if she were trying to capture the moment. Her expression seemed out of place, but she lifted her knees higher and pulled at me with her hands.

I increased the pace. I reached behind her upper back, trying to bring her even closer. I grew frantic.

"That's it, baby," she said.

I began to feel light-headed, my face buried in her hair, my chest mashed against her breasts.

The pressure dissipated. I regained awareness slowly, still breathing heavily. A thin film of perspiration covered my chest. She ran her fingers across my back and blew cool air at my shoulder.

I leaned up and saw her staring at me with the same expression, a look of reluctant closure.

"What?" I said.

"I love you."

I was stunned.

"I love you," she repeated.

"I . . ."

"You don't have to say it. Don't think you have to say it, but I had to say it."

Lying on top of Alyssa, having just made love to her, I felt like a damn fool.

"It's not your fault," she said. A smile of kindness came to her lips.

I put my hands to the bed and pushed away to see her clearly. Her fine dark hair framed her beautiful face. Her creamy breasts lay in sharp contrast to her tanned skin.

"I'm sorry," I said.

"I'm the one who changed," she said. "We agreed on the rules upfront, no commitments. I was happy to agree. After George, I would have sooner said 'good-bye' than 'I love you.'"

I rolled off and lay on my side, my hand on her lower torso. She turned toward me and leaned on her elbow.

"With George things were so hard. We argued all the time. He called it love, but I found it stressful. With you it's all so easy. We hang out, we talk, we laugh, and we make love. Life is good." She smiled. "Right?"

"Right."

"Then I realized I could be happy with a man for my whole life."

"Oh."

"I'm thirty-three and have just now realized I want the same thing all the other women want. I want to get married. I want to have kids and a house. I want to live happily ever after."

Sooner or later most women wanted to know where they stood, but with Alyssa I hadn't seen it coming. I knew how the conversation would end and it made me feel hollow, like a tree felled by a storm and left on the ground to rot.

"Isn't it sad?" she said.

"No."

"I'm pathetic. When we first dated I knew exactly what I wanted. I wanted control. I wanted to have a good time without chains. But then one day we were in the park, and I saw them."

"Who?"

"A young couple, late twenties, early thirties. They were in love, and she was very pregnant. In an instant I knew. I wanted to be her."

When Rose was pregnant with the girls we lived in a starter home in a suburb of Dallas. I had an image I kept in back of my mind, to be drawn out at special times. In the image Rose was standing at the kitchen counter, eight-and-a-half months pregnant with Callie. I stood close behind her, my hands on her hard belly, her hands on mine. Chandler, a toddler, stood next to us with her arms wrapped around my leg, our first group hug.

But that was just an image, a moment I could never recreate; we'd have no more group hugs. My own behavior had seen to that.

Perhaps Alma was right. Perhaps I should forget my past, find someone new and settle down. I had enjoyed every minute with Alyssa, the talking, the laughing, and everything else.

"Well," I said, "maybe . . . You just surprised me."

"No. We can't. I hate to admit that, because I've grown to love you, but we can't."

"Maybe we could. Give me some time to get used to the idea."

"No, time won't do any good." She rolled away from me, put her feet on the floor, and sat straight. She had perfect posture. I had never seen a back so strong and beautiful.

"Why do you say that?"

She stood and turned toward me, arms folded across her breasts. Her eyes gave me that same look of closure.

"Because you're still in love with Rose."

CHAPTER 3

"SOPHIE TYLER. YOU'RE GOING TO meet Sophie Tyler?" Chandler's voice climbed into a shriek with her second mention of the name.

"Actually, it looks like I'll be working with her."

Chandler's eyes opened wide. "You're going to work with Sophie Tyler?" She wore shorts, a T-shirt, and flip-flops. She had inherited Rose's dark complexion and hair, while Callie, her younger sister, had my sandy-blond hair and golden eyes.

Chandler body's changed every week. Her arms and legs grew fuller, there was a slight curve to her hips, and she now wore a bra. If I could have my way, she wouldn't grow into a woman; she'd stay my little girl. But I couldn't have my way, and the realization that the changes would continue created a haunting sensation that I tried, without success, to ignore.

I had come to the house to watch the girls while Rose went to a charity function. Chandler claimed she no longer needed a babysitter, but she didn't mind if I came over to "hang out" with her and Callie.

We sat at the island counter in the kitchen of the great room. The girls snacked on graham crackers and milk. I swiped a cracker from

Chandler's plate and looked at the pool through the picture window. Lake Austin lay a quarter mile down the hill.

"Who's Sophie Tyler?" Callie asked.

"You dummy," said Chandler. "She's the most famous rock star to ever come from Austin."

"Oh . . ."

Chandler sang a couple lines from one of Sophie Tyler's tunes. She monitored the celebrity scene closely, whereas Callie, only ten years old, was more into sports.

"Don't worry," I said to Callie. "It's not like she's Mia Hamm or anything."

"Yeah. It's not like she's Mia Hamm."

Rose walked in from the bedroom wing. She wore a black cocktail skirt, a pink sleeveless top, and a matching gold necklace and bracelet. Her hair was shoulder-length and touched with highlights. A thousand yoga sessions had strengthened her arms and legs and core.

I felt as I always felt when Rose walked into a room; I wanted to touch her. When we lived together I could touch her at any moment, and the memory of my lost privilege created another ache that I tried to ignore.

"Mommy," said Callie, "can we go swimming with Daddy?"

"Is your homework done?"

"No."

"You have to get your homework done first. After that it's up to your father."

The girls gobbled the last bites of snack and ran back to their rooms.

Rose got a glass down from a cabinet and filled it with water from the refrigerator. While her back was turned I scanned every inch of her. She had a red-and-green yin-yang tattoo high between her shoulder blades. About half of the tattoo showed above the back of her top.

She wore peep-toe black shoes with modest heels that accentuated her calves. An eyeful of bare thigh showed above her knee.

"Did you know your tattoo is showing?" I said.

"What?" Rose shot me a questioning look.

I touched my own upper back to indicate the spot.

"Damn," she said. "I thought this top covered it. Dave never notices those things. I'll have to change." She sipped from the water glass and looked across the counter at me. "So, how's Alyssa?"

I wanted to interpret her question as proof that Rose still had feelings for me, but that seemed naive. Sometimes I overanalyzed her words, examined each one for hidden meaning. I saved them for later when time would allow careful scrutiny.

"We're not dating anymore."

"No?" Rose walked closer, concern on her face. "That didn't last long."

"She told me just this morning."

"That's too bad. What happened?"

"She wanted to get serious."

"Oh . . . and you're not ready."

Rose stepped to the inside edge of the island. She stood three feet from me, brown eyes holding mine. Her hands rested on the countertop, a bigger diamond on her ring finger than she'd worn when we were together, just one more sign that she'd found a better man.

"She didn't give me a chance . . . said it wouldn't work."

"Why not?"

"She said I was still in love with you."

Rose took a sharp breath and stood straight. "Are you . . . still . . . in love with me?"

Dave's footsteps came down the hall and into the kitchen. He looked brilliant in khakis and a white cotton short-sleeved shirt. He was freshly shaven and wore his brown hair cut short. With quick and graceful steps he walked straight to me, a smile on his face, and shook my hand.

I found it hard to hate him even though he slept in my old room with my former wife and spent time with my kids every day. He treated the girls well, a little distant at times, but he cared about them. In plain truth Rose had picked Dave over me, and that part still hurt, but I couldn't hate her, either.

"Joe," said Dave, "it's great to see you. Thanks for coming over."

"It's nothing. I enjoy it."

"You about ready?" he asked Rose.

She was still looking at me, but now turned to Dave. "No, I've got to change my top. My tattoo is showing." Rose turned to walk back toward the bedrooms and then stopped. "Joey?"

"Yes."

"The Polaris is acting up. It scoots around the pool all day but never vacuums any debris. Can you look at it?"

"You bet."

Dave turned back to me with his eyebrows scrunched down, his head shaking slightly. "She's not thinking straight. You don't have to do that. The pool guy will service the Polaris."

"I don't mind. It'll give me something to do while the kids watch television."

* * *

After Rose and Dave left and the kids had finished their homework, the three of us swam in the pool. We took turns jumping in from the boulders along the back edge to see who could make the biggest splash. I had a significant weight advantage, but Callie, fearless in the water, put up stiff competition. I gave up after a few tries and sat on the side of the pool to watch. They kept going, inventing new techniques, both serious and playful at the same time. After each entry Callie swam to the steps, climbed out, and scampered across the top of the boulders for another try. I warned her not to run.

When at last they'd had enough I bundled them up in beach towels and sent them back to their rooms to shower and change while I made the pasta that Rose had set aside. Over dinner they wanted to discuss vacation plans.

"You remember that time we went to Disney World for Thanksgiving?" said Callie. She spun her fork against the plate until she had the spaghetti in a tight enough bunch to lift to her mouth.

That was four years earlier, a lifetime in the past. Callie had been six, Chandler eight. We'd escaped the usual family drill for a long weekend of running between theme parks in Orlando. They'd been the perfect age for the trip. I had a momentary flashback: Rose and I stood watching, my arm around her waist, as the girls waited patiently for Snow White's autograph.

"Oh my gosh," said Chandler, her eyes bright. "That was so fun."

"Let's do it again this year," said Callie.

Callie's enthusiasm sometimes ran away with her. She focused so hard on the positive that she couldn't see the downside, the difficulties. Chandler looked pensive, perhaps working through the challenges.

"That sounds great, honey," I said, "but I'm not sure we can work it out."

"Why not?"

"Well, your mom and Dave might have other plans. He might want to visit his family for Thanksgiving."

"That's okay," said Chandler, a smirk on her face. "He doesn't have to come."

Callie put her fork down and looked at Chandler; then she looked at me, still silent, and the three of us burst out laughing.

* * *

LATER, AS THE GIRLS watched television, I took the Polaris down to the freestanding workshop and disassembled it with a Phillips-head screwdriver. Dave had no gift for handyman chores, but I kept a basic tool kit on-site for ten-cent jobs. The channels for the water jets were clogged with fine bits of leaves and dirt, and I cleaned them out with a straightened paper clip. While working I thought about Rico's wife, Alma, and her formula.

I never understood the concept of a second family. The men left me puzzled, the ones who got divorced, played the field for a year or two, married a younger woman, and sired more children. I had a hard enough time giving Chandler and Callie the attention they deserved.

I pictured myself wandering in romantic limbo with the freedom to date other women but no right to hope for more. I had my chance. I married Rose, had two beautiful daughters, and lived a fabulous life for eleven years. Then one night, on a drunken trip to Vegas, I made the biggest mistake of my life and cheated on her. Events soon spun out of control, and I wound up like this.

The absurdity of the moment struck me like a clap on the back. I stood hunched over in my ex-wife's husband's workshop, sweating slightly, laboring to mend a device for their pool. But I didn't care. Any excuse to be around her, to pretend at usefulness, to accede to a specific request, no matter how small, was good enough for me.

Alyssa was right. I still loved Rose.

CHAPTER 4

On Tuesday morning I woke up early, left the condo early, and arrived at the airport two hours before my flight, my stomach tight with nervous energy. I would meet Sophie Tyler that day. An appointment I had never imagined, or even hoped for, had appeared out of nowhere. I had won the lottery without buying a ticket.

I landed at LAX with a couple hours to spare and drove to Santa Monica to look at the ocean and calm down. I sat on a bench to enjoy the mild temperature and the breeze on my face. The air carried a scent of seawater. The palm trees swayed. Tropical flowers bloomed. I watched Californians through my sunglasses as they walked their dogs and played volleyball and lay in the sun.

I strolled through hundreds of tourists on the pier to chat with fishermen at the far end. The fishing was slow, a few small perch and mackerel, but the anglers didn't seem to mind. I bought a hot dog and leaned on the side rail to eat and watch the surfers.

Sophie Tyler had left Austin to live in the land of glitter. Southern California had many advantages: ideal climate, beautiful scenery, and access to the right people. Of course, the congestion and cost of living were bothersome, but if you had enough money it could feel like paradise. For the past two decades Sophie Tyler had plenty of money.

My knowledge of her background, while fresh in high school, had atrophied over the years, so the day before I had spent two hours on the Internet to catch up on her life, my eager eyes consuming every page.

After she left the Texas Strangers she played a hundred small venues and made low-budget albums before finding her own style, a funky mix of rock and country reminiscent of Bonnie Raitt with hints of Joni Mitchell. Her career broke out, and from 1985 to 1995 she made twelve albums, three of which went platinum. She landed a few movie roles and toured every year.

She had high-profile romantic encounters, most of them brief. An article in *People* magazine chronicled her known liaisons, over twenty, including a couple other rock stars, a few actors, a high-tech entrepreneur, a politician, and a baseball player. She dated regular folks as well: a policeman, a schoolteacher, and a real-estate agent in Mexico. The article made a passing comparison to the dating habits of Cher. The paparazzi captured her and her men on the move, ducking into a nightclub in New York, dining on a sidewalk in Barcelona, sunbathing on a luxury yacht. There were no marriages and no children. She was forty-six and had recently broken up with an actor, Bryan Slater, age twenty-eight.

I drove to Adrian Williams's office on the outskirts of Beverly Hills and arrived with thirty minutes to spare.

* * *

ADRIAN DROVE THE ESCALADE on Canon Drive. Tall date palms lined each side of the street. The size of the homes and the perfect landscaping told the story: Living in that zip code demanded affluence. Big money creates headaches. A host of new decisions must be made, anonymity slips away, and one day the rich man discovers he's unhappy. If given the opportunity and the money required to live on that street, I would have stayed in my two-bedroom condo.

"So you were a boxer," said Adrian.

I sized him up for the third time. He had the quiet confidence of a well-trained professional. Despite my years of training and sparring I knew he'd be a tough opponent to face in the ring.

"Long time ago," I said. "Golden Glove stuff, a few bouts in college."

"Judo, too?"

"A little, couple years."

"Tell me about the security company you ran in school."

"Not that much to tell. We did small jobs to earn extra money—bouncer work and live-show security at small venues. I focused on the Fort Worth market."

"We should compare notes." Adrian crossed through the intersection with Sunset Boulevard and kept driving north on Benedict Canyon Drive.

"Oh, no. You're well beyond my expertise already."

His eyes scanned oncoming traffic, glanced at parked vehicles, and assessed anything that moved on the bordering lawns.

"The basics never change," he said. "It's all about situational awareness."

A few minutes later he made a right turn on a side street and pulled into a driveway on the left. He stopped at an intercom box, rolled down the window, and pressed the button.

So this was Sophie Tyler's house, just a regular everyday mansion in Beverly Hills. Behind the hedge was a stone wall eight feet high. Through the wrought-iron gate the driveway curved between palm and laurel trees as it climbed a small incline. A white stucco wall and red-tiled roof were visible through the trees.

A deep voice emanated from the intercom speaker. "Tyler residence. Johnson speaking."

"Hey, Johnson. It's Adrian. Can you buzz me in?"

"Certainly. See you in a minute."

A click sounded and the gates swung to allow us passage. I sat up straight, checked my shirt collar, and resisted the urge to turn the visor mirror my way. Adrian drove through the lush landscaping and into an open circular drive with a fountain in the middle. A gray Porsche sat parked on the opposite side of the fountain.

We walked up three stone stairs, but as Adrian reached for the bell the door opened. A bald man of indeterminate age stood in the doorway. He wore a bright yellow collared shirt and white slacks.

"Adrian," he said, "it's good to see you."

"Johnson, this is Joe Robbins."

"It's a pleasure," said Johnson as he reached to shake my hand. "I'm Johnson Sagebrush. Sophie's manager." His handshake was firm, genuine.

"Nice to meet you."

I detected a fragrance. It took me a moment to realize Johnson wore cologne. It smelled masculine and expensive.

"I'm bringing Joe on to help with security," Adrian explained. "There will be fifty to sixty thousand at ACL, and you know how she likes to walk the crowd the day before the show. I thought we needed more coverage."

"Absolutely. Couldn't agree more."

"I emailed to tell her I was bringing him over. She said to come by at two."

"Sophie told me to expect you. She always likes to meet the security team." Johnson looked at me, making direct eye contact. He stood a few inches shorter than me but was built solid, strong hands and forearms. He smiled confidently, at ease with his position.

Just then another man came from behind Johnson and stepped onto the porch. He looked about fifty and wore a denim shirt and stylish jeans. Gray chest hair sprouted from his open collar.

Johnson turned to him. "Leaving already?"

"Yeah, I have another meeting. She just wanted my thoughts on the set list."

Johnson introduced me to Halet Blevins, Sophie's talent agent. From my research I knew that Halet booked all of her live appearances.

He had a relaxed feel about him, happy eyes, and an easy smile. He was medium height, the smallest man on the porch by a fair margin. He looked from me to Adrian, then back to me. "From the size of you two," he said, "I'd say Sophie's in good hands." He glanced back at Johnson. "Sorry to run out on you, but I'm late already." After promising to meet us in Austin he hurried down the stairs and half trotted to the gray Porsche.

"Come in, guys," said Johnson. "Sorry for all the commotion. We're busy getting ready for this trip. Sophie's upstairs with Keri but should be down in a few minutes."

Sophie Tyler, rock star, would be down in a few minutes. Walking through the foyer we passed a convenient mirror, and I checked quickly for mustard splashes or other disasters. All looked good, but my palms perspired.

The walls were white plaster. A room on the right had the vibe of a museum exhibit, with dark wooden flooring, an iron chandelier, and modern art. A display of classical string instruments stood arranged against the far wall.

Johnson walked straight into the main room of the ground floor and turned left into a kitchen, which had the same wood floors and stainless-steel appliances. A large kitchen island with a butcher-block top dominated the center of the room. Expensive pots with copper bottoms hung from a rack above the island. I got the feeling the pots were for show, and if I lived in that place, I'd have to dress up to go to the kitchen.

"Can I offer you something to drink?" said Johnson. "We have lemonade, filtered water, raspberry hibiscus tea."

Adrian declined, and I opted for the tea. Johnson's hands moved surely as he pulled down a glass and filled it with ice from the refrigerator. As he handed me the tea the fragrance of his cologne drifted near, and I recognized it as sandalwood.

"You know," he said, "it's so nice today we might as well meet outside."

"Great idea," said Adrian.

"Oh, by the way," said Johnson, "I noticed one of the security cameras isn't working."

"Really? Which one?"

"I'm not sure. Let me show you."

They walked over to a side door and stepped into the next room. I sipped the tea and looked out the rear window. The drink tickled my taste buds: a light sweetness perfectly balanced with the flavor of raspberries. Californians make everything fancy, not like Texans, not simple, but somehow it works—except with the people. Sometimes fancy doesn't work with people. More than a few Californians I'd met looked good on the surface but faded into nothing when you tried to grab ahold of them.

The open window overlooked a huge pool. Ornamental palm trees graced the outside edges of the patio. Lounge chairs and round tables with umbrellas were placed at various spots around the pool. Bamboo wind chimes rang softly with the light breeze. It reminded me of a high-end boutique hotel.

A man with dark hair paced the patio while talking on his cell phone. He wore jeans and an untucked short-sleeved shirt. He carried a document in his right hand that was about an inch thick.

Adrian talked as he reentered the room with Johnson. "I'm going back there now to check that camera. I might have to replace it."

"You want me to go with?" said Johnson.

"No. It should be simple enough."

Johnson led us back through the main room to a sliding door that opened onto a covered porch, the patio, and the pool deck. A second building stood off the back edge of the pool, perhaps a guesthouse. Untamed woods, thick with various pines and shrubs, began where the lawn ended. Somewhere beyond the woods stood the eight-foot wall. An occasional car drove by outside the wall on the left.

Fat bumblebees bobbled their way through richly mulched flower beds filled with sunflowers and lilies. Cumulus clouds floated in an azure sky, and the air felt good on my skin. I could learn to enjoy California during the hot Texas summer, fancy people and all.

Adrian walked around the pool, past flowering oleanders and down a path that led into the trees.

The man with the cell phone looked at us briefly but then turned and walked away.

"That's Bryan Slater," said Johnson, "an acquaintance of Sophie's. He came by today to drop off a movie script. I'm sure he'll say hello in a minute."

So this was the guy who'd brought Sophie Tyler into the questionable movie investment—her latest ex. His shoulders slumped and he stopped pacing. He bowed his head and looked at his feet.

"He's an actor," said Johnson. "Maybe you recognize him."

"Wasn't he on a television show?"

"He's had a lot of small parts. He played a boyfriend once on *Beverly Hills 90210.* Since then he's had parts in *Alias*, *Witchblade*, and a number of others."

"I don't watch a lot of television."

"Good for you."

It was hard to gauge Johnson's height because he slumped his shoulders; he might reach six feet if he stood straight. The yellow shirt was buttoned up the middle and hung loose about him. He was overweight and waddled slightly when he walked, but his hands were quick to the task at hand. He had brown eyes, a welcoming smile, and a big nose.

"Have you worked a lot of celebrity security details?" he asked.

"A few. Adrian found me through a mutual friend in Austin."

"You're certainly big enough. What are you? Six-five?"

"Six-four."

"Like to sit down?"

"Actually, it feels good to stand in the sun and not sweat. We're still hitting a hundred degrees on a regular basis in Texas."

"I'll bet."

I took advantage of the break in conversation to look around the property again. Tall fan palms ringed the edge of the landscaped area, their fronds rustling in the wind. The wind made me think of Johnson's last name, the same as that of a hardy plant from the Southwest forced to survive in windy, arid conditions.

"You know," I said, "I don't think I've ever heard the name Sagebrush before."

"Oh, look, Bryan's off his call." Johnson waved him over and introduced us.

I stepped toward Bryan and put out my hand. He looked a little stunned from his phone call, but tried to recover by offering me a firm grip.

"Sorry," he said, "I'm distracted. An audition."

He stood nearly as tall as me and weighed a few more pounds, his body sculpted from working out. He had strong chest muscles, bulging biceps, and snug jeans, his hair carefully unkempt.

"Joe lives in Austin," said Johnson.

"Awesome," said Bryan. He gave me an infectious smile. "I hear great things about Austin these days. It's on fire."

"Don't tell anyone," I said. "We're trying to keep it a secret."

"I'm looking forward to attending the festival."

"You got your own room, right?" said Johnson.

"Yes." Bryan rocked his head from side to side, as if he weren't sure where he stood. "But if Sophie doesn't want me there I won't come."

"No, no," said Johnson. "I talked to her yesterday. The invitation stands; just make sure you have your own room."

"Of course."

Bryan didn't seem the least put out by Johnson's insistence. The exchange struck me as odd. Where I come from a breakup cancels all previously made plans, but maybe celebrities played by different rules: Once a boyfriend, always a friend. Or maybe the relationship had lingering life, potential to bloom again.

"I'm not sure how much time she'll have today," said Johnson.

"Fine," said Bryan. "If she's too busy, that's okay. I really just wanted to give her the latest draft of *Galveston Lost*." Bryan held the script up in his hand.

Johnson looked at his watch and then to the upstairs balcony, which extended the full width of the house. "You guys sit tight here a minute. I'm going to see if I can hurry things along."

While Johnson hustled back to the house, Bryan and I sat at one of the round tables. He continued to watch Johnson.

"It would be nice to have a manager to keep me on schedule," he said, a touch of envy in his voice.

I had just thought the opposite. What a pain to have someone herd you around.

It's time to meet the new security guy. Your hair appointment is at four. That new promoter in New Orleans wants to talk later.

But I didn't mention those thoughts to Bryan. Instead I said, "Maybe you'll have your own manager someday."

He looked at me and nodded slightly, his face brightening. "Every failed audition is an opportunity to learn." He said the line as if he'd read it in a self-help book for budding actors.

Bryan held the script on his leg. It bounced with his nervous energy.

I might as well get to work.

"What's the title of the movie again?" I asked.

"*Galveston Lost.*" He said it with confidence, a big smile on his face, barely able to contain his excitement. The script bounced faster. Bryan was a rocket on the launch pad.

"What's it about?"

"*Galveston Lost* has everything: Civil War—everyone loves a movie set in the Civil War—naval battles, and a great love story. It's awesome."

"So tell me the story."

He looked grateful, as if I'd done him a favor by asking about his movie.

"Okay. Here's the elevator pitch. A single mother, widowed by the war, manages a tavern in the port. At the start of the story a Confederate officer tries to win her heart, without success. Then the port is attacked and taken by the North. For the next three months a ship's captain from the North seeks the woman's affections, and she begins to fall for him despite her loyalties to the South. Then the South retakes the city in a harrowing battle, and the first officer returns."

As he reached the end of his pitch I nodded, trying to signal my approval. "Lots of conflict."

"It's awesome. I like Sophie in the heroine role, personally."

"What about you?"

"One of the leading men. I can't decide if I want to wear blue or gray."

"At least you know which side wins."

Bryan shrugged. "The final decision rests with the director. I'm a coproducer, so I certainly get a vote, but we have to give him a free hand."

Bryan looked at the house. Two women walked with Johnson from the mansion onto the covered porch. My throat felt tight. I breathed deeply through my nose to still the buzzing in my chest.

The taller woman, whom I recognized as Sophie Tyler, had long hair the color of golden sand. The second woman, who I guessed was Keri, stood a few inches shorter and wore yoga pants and a workout top. Sophie turned to look at us.

"Hey, Bryan," called Johnson. He waved Bryan over.

I discretely wiped my hands on my pants to dry them.

As Bryan hurried to the patio, Sophie and Keri came together to touch cheeks. Keri put her hand on Sophie's back to pull them closer and then turned into the house. By that time Bryan had reached Sophie, and they shared a perfunctory kiss. Bryan talked fast as he handed her the script. She listened politely and then said something. They talked for another thirty seconds, no more, and then Johnson touched Bryan's elbow. The two of them turned toward the house, and Sophie came down the stairs toward me.

I stood and walked to meet her halfway. She took long strides, her hips moving gracefully, her hair wandering freely with her motion. She wore flat sandals, blue slacks, and a sleeveless white top. Her arms were long and tan.

As we drew closer I studied her face. She had high cheekbones and a straight nose. Her teeth bucked slightly in a way I had always found alluring.

"And who might you be?" she asked.

Her words, though simple, were carried by her voice, a voice crisp and cool, like the air of a spring morning.

I stood silent for a moment, mute, and then summoned the courage to speak. "Uh . . . Joe Robbins."

"Joe Robbins?"

She continued walking toward the table, and I fell in step beside her.

"Yes . . . I . . . ah . . . I'm here with Adrian Williams. He asked me to meet with you about a fraud investigation?"

"Oh . . . right."

"Although I guess that's sort of a secret, so we told Johnson and Bryan I'm part of the security detail."

"You're the guy from Austin."

"That's right."

"I never thought Adrian would find someone so fast." She seemed genuinely surprised at Adrian's efficiency. "Sorry for the secret-agent routine. Should we sit?"

I sat to her right. As I came to rest my knee bounced as fast as Bryan's had a few minutes earlier, so I put my hand down to hold it steady.

"Where's Adrian?" she asked.

"Checking on a faulty security camera."

Her eyes settled onto mine and remained steady. She had big eyes. Were the irises blue, or green? Mostly blue, with a tinge of green. My study of her eyes caused a lull in the conversation, but she didn't seem to mind.

"My daughter, Chandler, is a huge fan of yours. Me, too," I said. "She thinks it's cool that I get to meet you."

"Is she coming to ACL?"

"Probably. Her mother and I haven't worked out the specifics."

"Maybe I'll get a chance to meet her."

"Oh . . . she would go crazy."

Sophie was silent, just smiled pleasantly and continued to look right at me. I was happy to stare all day, but it occurred to me that she would grow impatient soon.

"Gosh . . . here I am babbling, wasting your time. How can I help you?"

She pressed her lips together. "Honestly, when my accountant, Marco Ruffini, first mentioned his concerns I thought he was imagining things. He sits in that office all day with nothing better to do . . . sometimes he sees demons that don't exist. You know these finance types."

"Yeah, we're a dull crew."

She realized the faux pas and laughed at herself. "Oh, I didn't mean you, of course." She reached to touch my arm.

My skin tingled where she touched me, and the tingle travelled down to the tips of my fingers.

"Anyway," she said, "when Adrian said something about it I thought we'd better do some checking on the side."

"Sure."

"I still don't believe fraud is involved. You met Bryan just now, right? How did he strike you?"

"Seems nice enough."

"Exactly. He's a good guy. We dated for a while. Did you know that?"

"Adrian told me."

"He may not be the brightest bulb on the marquee, but Bryan doesn't have a dishonest bone in his body. And he's *so* excited about this project, his first as a producer. Still, a thousand people vie for indie money in this town, and I'm sure some of those deals are crooked. If someone is trying to steal from me, I want my money back."

"You deserve that."

"But I don't want any publicity. I don't want tabloids dragging up the relationship with Bryan and confusing everyone with rumors about fraud and money problems. That's the nightmare scenario. Make sense?"

"Perfectly."

She sat with legs crossed at the knee, hands in her lap. My mind kept wandering, relishing her voice, soaking in her physical presence, but I controlled it, forced myself to focus on the business at hand.

"Mind if I ask a few questions?" I said.

"Please do."

"Who manages your money now?"

"Johnson. He pays all the bills. He negotiates with the record companies and the promoters. He invests all the money, although it was my decision to invest in the film." She turned her gaze to the mansion. Small crow's feet sprouted from the corners of her eyes. "Johnson's a terrific manager. He takes care of everything and only charges me ten percent. He's basically on call twenty-four-seven, lives right here in the guesthouse."

"Right."

"It's not his fault I've made bad investments. I told him what I wanted to do each time."

"What sort of investments?"

"Real estate. High-tech. What is the opposite of the golden touch?"

"Bad luck?"

"I have *beaucoup* bad luck when it comes to investing."

"Do you trust Johnson?"

I always roll out the trust question in a fraud interview. It tells you as much about the person you ask as the target of the question.

"Yes. He's been with me for ten years. I trust Johnson as much as anyone, except Keri. Keri and I were best friends in high school."

"Who brought you the film?"

"Bryan. I also know his coproducer, Toby Wycliff. They might have a part in the film for me. I guess that's partly why I invested, but I'm sure the movie is real." She took the script from the table and handed it to me. "It's a good story. You should read it."

I flipped the pages, lots of white space around the lines of dialogue. I glanced at her. She continued to smile. I had the backstory but what I really needed to do the job was data.

"Investment fraud can be hard to detect," I said. "I need to review the financial accounts in some detail. How do I manage that without tipping off Bryan?"

"Hmmm. Good question." She paused for a few seconds. "I'll call Toby Wycliff to tell him we're doing an 'accounting review' and that I don't want Bryan involved. He'll go for that."

"Okay. I also need to talk with your accountant, and I want to go through your personal books to trace the money."

"Marco's easy. I'll let him know to expect your call. Johnson keeps my personal books on a laptop. Let's see. How do I get you access to that . . . ?"

Her voice drifted off at the end of the question. She absently put a hand to her face, as if it would help her think, and then she reached to touch my forearm. I looked at her fingers. Her touch kindled a warm comfort that spread to my shoulder and settled in my chest. She stared into the distance, not looking at me, perhaps unaware that she touched me. Her hands were finely crafted with long fingers that skimmed the top of my arm while her thumb traced the underside to my wrist.

I inhaled deeply and studied the skin on her face, smooth, natural, unblemished. She had eight years on me but appeared to be midthirties. I wanted to caress her cheek and put my hand on the back of her neck.

"I have an idea," she said. "Can you come back at seven?"

"Yes."

I could come back anytime.

"Johnson and I will be out for drinks at a friend's house. Keri will let you in."

Shoot. For a moment I thought she intended to meet me again, but she was only arranging confidential access to the data.

"Does Keri know about the investigation?" I said.

Sophie nodded quickly. "I tell her everything. We're like sisters. She can show you the laptop."

"Do you know the password?" I asked.

She chuckled. "We're not very secure. All the passwords are on three-by-fives taped to the drawer of the desk."

"How will I reach you to share my findings?"

"Call my cell now. That way I'll have your number, too." She recited her number, and I entered it into my phone. She let her phone ring once, then hung up and tapped on the keys.

I had just entered Sophie Tyler's number into my phone. What did she label me? "Joe R"? "Finance dude"? "Awkward"? Would she answer if I called?

"I should ask how much you charge," she said. A little smile appeared on her face. She didn't often deal with vendors. That was Johnson's job. Perhaps she smiled at her chance to deal with the working class.

"Three hundred per hour with a cap of two thousand a day. It shouldn't take more than a couple days. I'll work the security gig throughout the festival to preserve confidentiality."

"Good. Then I'll see you in Austin."

With our business settled we talked for a few minutes until Adrian returned. She told me about old Austin clubs she played in the early eighties. She laughed easily. I felt comfortable talking with her, like we had known each other a long time, and I realized later that she worked to create that impression. I kept wishing she'd touch me again.

When Adrian came back Sophie walked us to the front door, and as we parted she took my hand in both of hers, her left lightly grasping my wrist. I thought she held my hand for an extra moment while we made eye contact, but I might have imagined that part.

CHAPTER 5

I PARKED IN A MANHATTAN BEACH public garage, fed the meter, and hurried to Highland Avenue. The surf pounded the beach from two blocks down the hill. People in sunglasses strolled by me.

I spotted Gwen Raleigh from half a block away sitting at a sidewalk table on the other side of a waist-high brick barrier. She had changed her hair; the dark brunette was almost gold. Her sunglasses rested on top of her head. As I drew closer I walked faster. My attraction to Gwen had always been strong.

She and I had worked together at Connection Software before the whole thing went to hell in 2000. It was a crazy time, a time of great stress, a time of stock markets that climbed for years and then crashed in a single week, a time of collapsing companies, and in the middle of all that mess Gwen and I wound up in bed together at the MGM in Las Vegas. It was tempting to blame it all on her, but I had made the key decisions, the bad decisions, and I bore the responsibility. And after all the dust had settled Gwen and I had remained friends.

After the crash she had grown weary of software and moved to L.A. to learn the film business. I hadn't seen her in nearly three years and had called the day before to see if we could get together.

She saw me, smiled her crooked smile, and stood to give me a warm hug and a kiss on the cheek. She smelled natural, clean.

"It's good to see you," she said. "God, it's been so long."

"You look great. Still swimming every day?"

"Afraid so. It's an addiction."

I sat at the two-top opposite Gwen and studied her face. A few crinkles had made their way to the corners of her eyes; otherwise, she looked the same. She reached across the table to grab my hands, and I rubbed my thumbs across the tops of her fingers.

"I still wish you had moved out with me," she said, never one to waste time.

"I couldn't. The kids."

"You're so predictable." She sipped from a glass of white wine. "Seeing anyone?"

"I was. She left me recently. What about you?"

Gwen placed her hand to the side of her neck, her skin smooth there. "No. No time. I'm focused on work."

"Tell me all about it."

The conversation wandered for about an hour, touched on Austin briefly, but stayed mostly on the subject of the entertainment business. In Los Angeles success required the right connections, and Gwen was a great networker. She had worked as a freelance assistant to learn the trade, always cultivating new relationships.

"It's fiercely competitive," she said, "but I've made progress. I'm raising capital for a documentary."

"Good for you."

"What brings you to L.A.?"

"I'm doing a small project for Sophie Tyler." The words slipped out. I didn't even think about it, my guard down.

"Really? That's so cool. I know her talent agent."

Sophie's talent agent?

I had just met him a couple hours earlier as he walked out of her mansion; he had salt-and-pepper hair tucked behind his ears, a tan face, and thin lips.

"Halet Blevins?" I said.

"That's him. He's one of my best networking contacts. Halet knows everyone in this town. I can't believe you're working for Sophie Tyler."

"It's a small project. Won't take more than a couple days." I tried to downplay the engagement. My legs felt restless, as if they wanted to walk away from my slip in confidentiality.

"Halet's been with Sophie forever," Gwen said, "since she first struck it big. Sophie was a huge deal ten years ago, but she doesn't draw the same crowd these days."

"Sounds like you know Halet well."

"I met him at a party. A lot of business gets done at parties. We went out for dinner a couple times, and he wanted to take the relationship further, but I couldn't get past the age difference. Plus . . ."

"Plus what?"

She hesitated, not sure whether to tell me the next part. She took another sip of wine and told me anyway. "I wasn't exaggerating before. Halet knows everyone in this town, but everyone knows him, too. Someone warned me that Halet had, or has, a bit of a coke problem."

"Oh."

"Also, he's apparently gone a few rounds with the IRS."

People with money and expensive habits, like cocaine, often find themselves upside down with the Internal Revenue Service. They spend and spend, forgetting that the federal government always wants their cut.

"Yeah," she said, with a bit of a smirk. "A wise CFO once told me, 'Don't fuck with the IRS.'"

I had given that advice at a company meeting when asked a naive question about cheating on taxes. I tell anyone who asks about the IRS the same thing.

My phone showed six o'clock. I wanted to spend more time with Gwen, learn more about her struggles in Hollywood, but I needed to leave then to make Beverly Hills by seven.

"I'm sorry, but I have to go. I have an unexpected appointment."

Gwen frowned. "Shoot. I hoped we could have dinner."

"I'd love to, but it might be nine or ten o'clock."

"I'll wait."

CHAPTER 6

I PARKED ON ANGELO DRIVE, two blocks from Sophie's mansion, and walked purposefully to her front gate. I wasn't sure how much time I needed on Johnson's laptop, and I didn't want him to return and find my rental car parked in the circular drive. Close-set Italian cypress trees created a tall hedge between the curb and the perimeter wall of her property. The wall was made of rough stone pieces secured with mortar.

I pressed the button on the intercom.

After a few seconds a female voice answered noncommittally. "Yes?"

"It's Joe Robbins."

I speed-walked up the driveway to find Keri waiting at the open door. She wore her hair in a simple pixie and leaned against the frame in capri pants and a purple T-shirt. Her right arm was behind her back, perhaps tucked in a pocket.

"Hey," she said.

"You must be Keri."

She stepped aside to let me in. "You know, this whole approach seems sketchy to me." Her right arm stayed behind her back. "But I suppose Sophie knows what she's doing."

Keri had a small voice, on the quiet side, timid. She spoke of Sophie in the same tone of respect a younger girl gives her oldest sibling. Her eyes flitted about my face while her fingers played with a gold chain at her neck; then she gestured me into the room on the right with her left arm, which seemed odd. It was as if she didn't want me to see behind her back.

"If you don't mind my asking," I said, "what's your role in the Tyler business? Are you a personal assistant?"

"I'm whatever Sophie needs me to be . . . whenever she needs me to be it." She said the words simply, as if her position were as commonplace as a fireman or schoolteacher.

"That sort of sounds like Johnson's role."

"Johnson manages. I . . . assuage."

"I see." But I wasn't sure I did. I gave up trying to understand and mentally categorized her as a personal assistant. "And you met Sophie in high school?"

She nodded. "She was a sophomore; I was a freshman."

The left side of the room was dedicated to a seating area, with a comfortable sectional, side chairs, and a black wooden table. The other side of the room exhibited the array of string instruments: violin, cello, stand-up bass, and an acoustic guitar. They were finely constructed and polished to a high sheen. Spotlights illuminated each one.

Keri noticed me staring. "Beautiful, aren't they?"

"Very."

"She can play each instrument at an accomplished level. It's taken her fifteen years of lessons to achieve that goal. A true artist never stops growing." She strolled to the cello and lightly touched the neck. Keri turned to me with a tight smile on her face. "You asked about my role. Sophie has a gift to share. Her music brings civilization to an otherwise savage world. My true purpose, and Johnson's as well, is to ensure that Sophie can pursue her destiny unhindered by life's irksome realities."

It sounded like a well-rehearsed speech, but I detected an undertone of tension. Keri had been serving that purpose for twenty years. Could she do that forever without wanting something of her own?

"Where's the laptop?"

"It's in the office to the side," she said, and pointed.

The office was about twelve feet square and tastefully furnished with a sofa, a few Andrew Wyeth prints, a bookcase filled with movie scripts, and a desk. The laptop sat open on the desk in hibernation mode.

I sat in the swivel office chair.

Keri still held her right arm behind her back.

"Have you brought me flowers or something?" I asked, nodding at her arm.

She gave me a sheepish look and then pulled her arm out to reveal a pistol.

Damn.

I didn't blink. My eyes watched her carefully, my adrenaline rushing. She pointed the gun at the floor. She was only four feet away, a distance from which she could hardly miss. Keri didn't seem like the violent type, but a nervous finger on a trigger could kill me as easily as an angry one.

"Did you plan on shooting me?"

"Sorry. I get anxious being alone with a strange man in the house. You can never be too careful."

I looked closely at the weapon, a small-caliber semiautomatic. "Is that a twenty-two?"

"Yes."

"Do you know how to use it?"

"I took the safety course."

"Please put it down. I'll concentrate better if it's pointed away from me."

Keri shrugged, sat on the sofa, and placed the gun at her side.

I opened the drawer to take a look. Sure enough, two three-by-five cards were taped to the side. Each card contained usernames and passwords for bank accounts, email, and other services. I took a portable hard drive, connector cable, and a notepad from a small backpack. I jotted down the information and typed in the password to get into the laptop.

"This is going to take a while."

"Fine. I'll wait here. Do you need anything?"

"Please don't shoot me."

I plugged the hard drive into a USB port and followed the prompts to load the backup manager software. After that I ran the full backup process to grab all the user files on Johnson's laptop.

I checked the time. Seven thirty. How long did it take to have drinks with friends? At least a couple of hours.

I looked through Johnson's file directory. He was well organized and had created folders labeled by purpose and date. There was a folder labeled "Finances" and subfolders for "Business," "Personal," "Taxes," and "Investments." I quickly scanned each subfolder.

The Business folder contained profit statements from Sophie's accountant, Marco Ruffini. In the Investments folder Johnson had saved three years' worth of statements from Schwab, Vanguard, and Morgan Stanley. The Personal folder contained scanned copies of various receipts but no bank statements. I wanted to find the transaction for the investment in the independent film. Johnson might have moved the money directly from one of the investment accounts.

I started with the most recent statements. She owned a mixture of stock, bond, and commodity funds in the Schwab and Vanguard accounts, and a real estate fund with Morgan Stanley. The sum total was just short of three million dollars, a fortune for most people, but it didn't seem like much for a rock star in the second half of her career. Of course, she might own other assets I didn't know about, and there was the house in Beverly Hills.

I looked at the one-year returns. The Morgan Stanley fund had done well, up twenty percent. The Vanguard fund was up almost seven percent, but the Schwab balance had fallen over two million dollars.

I dove more deeply into the Schwab files. The detailed transaction reports showed a steady pattern of withdrawals for the past two years. Every two or three months Johnson sold some shares and transferred the proceeds to an account at Bank of America. That must be the operating account. The transfers averaged about thirty thousand a month.

And three weeks earlier, on August 26, Johnson had sold a large fund and moved two million dollars to B of A.

I looked at the time again. Eight o'clock.

One three-by-five card contained a password for Bank of America. I tried logging in and ran into a delay. A small arrow on the screen spun in circles. An error message reported the log-in page unavailable and suggested I return later.

"How long will they stay?" I asked.

"No telling." Keri fidgeted on the sofa. "Did you get what you need?"

"Not quite. I want a couple more pieces of data."

I'd give the B of A system fifteen minutes to come back up. In the meantime I examined the folder Johnson had labeled "Personal." He'd saved credit card statements for the prior three years.

I opened one of Sophie's AmEx Centurion Card statements, and then a second, and a third. I'd never seen anyone spend so much money. The bills averaged over thirty thousand a month, with huge entries for restaurants, catering, first-class airline tickets, and endless retail. I recognized several brand names from Rodeo Drive. She was spending eight or ten thousand a month on fashion, which struck me as wasteful, even for a celebrity.

I retried logging into Bank of America and got the same message. I leaned back in the chair to look at the intricate molding where the wall met the ceiling. How much would it cost to own a place like this? Adrian had said something about Sophie possibly losing the mansion. Even if she owned the house outright, she'd have real estate taxes, utilities, housekeeping, landscaping, and maintenance bills. I wondered whether Johnson kept a personal budget for Sophie.

"What are you doing?" asked Keri.

"Thinking."

"You should wrap this up. It's almost eight thirty."

"I just need one more thing. The system's slow." I turned to Keri. "Will she call before they come home?"

"Maybe."

"How far away are they?"

"A few minutes."

My fingers tapped mindlessly on my leg, nervous from the time pressure. I closed my eyes for a moment to calm my thoughts, and then tried the B of A system again. It accepted the password and slowly loaded the first page. The account balance was just over twenty-one thousand. I clicked for detailed transactions and waited some more.

Keri's cell phone rang.

"Hey. What's that? Already? But he's still here." Keri listened a few moments and then said, "Don't worry. I'll get rid of him." She hung up. "They're on the way. You have to get out of here now."

"Two minutes," I said. "No more."

The transactions on the first page went back only a week. I clicked for the next page.

"No . . . now."

"Make it one minute."

The two million came in from Schwab on August 26 and was wired out the same day. I clicked on the outgoing wire to get detailed information. The wire went to a Houston branch of Wells Fargo with further credit to Second Chances Production, LLC, the production company for *Galveston Lost*. I clicked to capture a screenshot and wondered why they chose a bank in Houston, but then I remembered the Galveston location. Houston was a short drive from Galveston and had more to offer in the way of infrastructure.

"Damn it," said Keri. "If Johnson sees you, it'll screw up her plan."

"I'm not a miracle worker."

"No, you're a slow worker."

I ignored her dig, my fingers keying as fast as they could, my mind double-checking the work to avoid clumsy mistakes. After copying the screenshot to the backup disk I unplugged the hard drive and began closing windows on the laptop. With a last look at the screen I pressed the Function and F4 keys to put the machine back to sleep and took a deep breath.

"Okay, I'm done."

Keri walked quickly to the hallway and the front door. With her hand on the knob she stopped. "Wait, let's double-check." She led me back through the kitchen and opened the door to the security room. A rack above the desk displayed eight monitors. After a second they blinked and the upper right screen showed a Mercedes pulling up to the gate. "Shit. They're already here. I'll have to try hiding you."

"No, I'll go out the back way." My heart pumped blood to my arms and legs to ready them for flight mode.

"There is no back way."

"I'll make one."

Keri followed me as I walked through the kitchen to the main room and opened the sliding door to the back patio.

"Maybe I'll see you in Austin," I said.

"My hands are shaking." Her left eye twitched.

"Don't forget to put your pistol away."

She looked at the gun in her hand. "Damn. I forgot about it. Bye."

She scampered across the main room to the staircase on the opposite side. As she ran up the stairs I stepped outside and pulled the door closed.

The sun had fully set, and the patio was well lit. I ran around the pool, pulled a penlight from my back pocket, and followed the path Adrian had used to cut into the woods. Ferns and shrubs created dense foliage on either side. The air was moist. About forty feet into the woods I found the wall, jumped to get a handhold, and scrambled up to the flat stone cap. After scanning the road for headlights I dropped behind the line of Italian cypresses and stepped out to the street. Two minutes later I drove the rental away from Beverly Hills, my throat dry.

I needed a drink.

* * *

GWEN AND I RELAXED over dinner and wine in Marina del Rey. Afterward I drove back and parked the rental in front of her condo building in West Hollywood. She wore a strapless auburn sundress, white sandals, and onyx teardrop earrings. She unbuckled the seat belt and turned toward me.

"Oh," she said, as if remembering a matter of little consequence. "I talked to Halet Blevins earlier."

I leaned away to watch her facial expression. "Really?"

"He was surprised to hear you and I had worked together at the Connection. He said you were on Sophie's security team. What's that about?"

It felt as if I'd sent an important email to the wrong address. I scrambled for an explanation.

"Yeah, sounds weird, I know. My friend manages her security and needed an extra guy for the ACL festival this weekend. I've been a Sophie Tyler fan for ages; I'm doing this as a lark."

She smiled. "That's so fun. What a cool hobby. Celebrity security."

Tension melted from my shoulders. Nothing would come of my slip in confidentiality. It didn't matter much anyway, because Halet's work as talent agent was not in the scope of the investigation.

"Do you want to come up?" she said. "I have a terrific view."

The tip of her tongue touched her upper lip. The sundress fit tight across her breasts, and I felt a tingle of excitement. I almost reached for her, but in that instant I recalled the moment when Sophie caressed my arm. The warm sensation returned to my chest. I closed my eyes for a second and saw Sophie laughing beside the pool, her hair arranged lazily about her shoulders.

"It's kind of late," I said. "I have an early start tomorrow."

Gwen sighed and looked away to reach for her purse. "Well, in that case you can kiss me good night."

I leaned toward her until our lips nearly touched. Her eyes sparkled, and she closed the remaining gap. Through parted lips her tongue ventured out to touch mine. My hand moved to her waist on its own accord.

"Are you sure?" she said.

"Rain check?"

"You didn't used to be such a killjoy."

CHAPTER 7

Marco Ruffini's office was a one-room affair in a small building on Santa Monica Boulevard in Beverly Hills. I took the elevator to the second floor, walked down a white-walled hall to suite 203, and pressed the button outside.

"Come in," said a man's voice.

I turned the knob, pushed, and the door took over, opening to the inside at a precisely measured pace. It had been modified for disabled access.

Marco's office was twenty feet square, with a couch and coffee table to one side, an enormous flat-topped desk in the middle, and an array of filing cabinets occupying most of the rest of the space. Windows across the back afforded a nice view of a small, palm-lined park.

He sat hunched in a high-backed webbed chair, a mobile scooter parked behind him against the window. He contorted his back and shoulders to look at me, a pained smile on his face.

"You must be Joe Robbins."

"Yes."

"Happy to meet you." He lifted his hand from his lap and extended it across the table. I stepped forward and leaned to shake it. "Please take a seat. If you don't mind, I'll finish this email. Won't take a minute."

"Sure."

His disability appeared to affect his legs and posture but little else. He hunched over terribly in the chair but moved his arms and hands without constraint. His fingers flew across the keys as he transcribed his thoughts into a message. Marco finished the email, turned toward me, and struggled to straighten his shoulders.

"How long have you had the practice?" I asked.

"Twenty-five years."

"I'll bet you've seen some crazy stuff."

He made a raspy noise that I took for a laugh. "I could write a book, but my clients would sue me."

He wore a white shirt and tie. His shoulders hunched over so far, and his head inclined at such an angle, that it was difficult to determine whether he looked at me or something else. Periodically he straightened his back and lifted his shoulders six inches, which allowed his face to angle toward me without twisting, but the longer he sat the more his shoulders sank, and soon he had that kink in his neck again.

His eyes shone intensely, the lids open wide. They studied me carefully at first, taking in every detail, and from then onward they flitted between the monitor and me.

"I gather Sophie's hired you to look into the movie investment," he said.

"That's right."

"I can tell you right now it's a bad idea. Any investment in an independent film is a bad idea. Most of them lose money."

"Why is that?"

"Lack of distribution. The big studios spread their risk across many projects, and a few winners make enough to support all the rest. But independent films don't have that luxury. Most of them never achieve theatrical release, so they lose money. I think that's why Sophie got defensive when I expressed concern about this deal. She's lost money on investments before."

"She mentioned that."

"She's not alone. A lot of celebrities have lost money on bad investments: hotels, restaurants, real estate, and so on. You name it, they find a way to lose money on it."

Marco straightened up and looked at me with clear eyes. He seemed to be on a roll, so I waited to see what he'd say next. His shoulders began their slow decline.

"Sophie can't afford financial risk now. Johnson shares all her numbers with me, everything on the business side and the personal side, so I can find tax deductions. The data shows that she spends a lot more than she makes. I see two kinds of celebrities in my work: those who manage their money well, and those who end up playing on cruise ships. Sophie falls in the second category."

I recalled the regular withdrawals Johnson made from Sophie's savings. At the current rate of negative cash flow she'd run out of money in less than ten years, sooner if her earning power declined. My statement of work didn't include providing financial advice, but perhaps I could shoehorn some in, help Sophie avoid the cruise-ship scenario.

Marco's shoulders had sunk so low his head was level with the desk. I felt an urge to lower my shoulders, too, but resisted.

I said, "Adrian mentioned you had concerns about a potential fraud scheme."

His eyes shifted from the monitor to my face, and he straightened his shoulders again.

"I don't know that fraud is involved, but I get nervous with independent films. Unscrupulous producers use investors' money to pay themselves knowing full well the movie will never earn a profit.

I picked up a few warning signs with this deal. First, Bryan Slater is coproducer, and he's never done this before. That increases risk."

Bryan had not struck me as a savvy businessman, but my Internet research into Toby Wycliff showed he had more relevant experience, and I made that point to Marco.

He nodded. "Fair enough. My second concern . . . Bryan gave me the name of their accountant, more of a bookkeeper, actually. I needed to contact him for tax records. Anyway, I never heard of the guy, and I know every outfit in Hollywood."

Marco sounded a little offended; perhaps he wished he had a chance to bid on the project. Did he know every reputable accounting firm in L.A. or did jealousy influence his perception? I made a mental note to check on the bookkeeper.

"Okay. Anything else?"

"Two million up front is a big number for one investor. On an indie film I'd expect a schedule of drawdowns dependent on hitting certain milestones."

That struck me as odd, too, but as Marco said at the outset, his concerns didn't prove fraud. Many people would have ignored those wrinkles—first-time producer, unknown bookkeeper, big upfront investment—but I respected his concerns. Marco viewed the world through a skeptic's lens, and so did I.

"I would have poked around on my own," he said, "but this kind of thing requires legwork." Marco paused to look down at his lap. "My legs don't work for shit anymore."

"No worries. Sophie hired me to do the poking around, but you could help me in a couple ways."

"How?"

"First, don't tell anyone I'm involved. Sophie wants to keep this low profile."

"Sure. I would have done that anyway."

"Second, I want to tell people I'm working for you to perform diligence verifications. That way they might be more open to talking with me. Is that all right?"

"Absolutely. It's a good idea."

"Great. Thanks."

As I stepped out of Marco's building the sun warmed my face. Soon enough the project would demand that I sit behind a computer and study numbers, like Marco, but I was in the meet-the-players stage, a critical step in any fraud investigation, and that allowed me to smell the junipers on the walk back to my car.

* * *

INSIDE THE CAR I PICKED UP the script to study the one-page informational sheet. It gave a brief synopsis and summary credentials for the executive producers and the director. The address, phone number, and website address for Second Chance Productions were listed across the bottom of the page.

I called the number, got a voice recording from Toby Wycliff, and hung up without leaving a message. The office was on Western Avenue about four miles east of Beverly Hills.

Twenty minutes later I looked at an old three-story building with surface parking. Inside the lobby a young receptionist sat at a modest desk in the corner; she didn't look up from her magazine. A glass display case indicated the Second Chance office was in suite 305.

The single elevator made lots of noise, and I had to wait ten seconds for the doors to open. A few stains soiled the carpet, and the walls needed a fresh coat of paint. The vertical windowpane next to the door of suite 305 was dark. I knocked on the door but received no answer. After half a minute I retraced my steps to the lobby and the receptionist.

"Hey, how's it going?" I said.

She looked up from the magazine. "Oh, I'm sorry. So few people stop at my desk . . . sometimes I don't speak to a soul all day."

"No problem. I went up to see the producers at Second Chance Productions, but the door's locked and the office is dark. Do you have any information on them?"

She looked surprised. "Yes. Yes, I do. I can help you." She opened a thin drawer at the top of the desk. I could see the sparse contents: a few pens, a roll of tape, a paper-clip dispenser, and a couple notepads. She picked up a notepad and read aloud. "'Toby Wycliff is in Europe on a road show for the independent film *Galveston Lost*. He will return on September twenty-fourth.' And they left a phone number."

She read the number, the same one I'd called earlier.

Back in the rental car I phoned the office again and left a message for Toby Wycliff to say I was working for Marco Ruffini to perform due diligence on *Galveston Lost*.

After that I returned to the Beverly Hilton and got on my laptop. The website for the production company had some nice photos but no more detailed information than the one-pager on the script.

Next I pulled up California's state government website and did a public records search on Second Chance Productions, LLC. They had created the company four months earlier, and the address matched that of the business office.

The company was real, but that didn't verify the existence of the film. Thousands of hungry writers lived in Los Angeles. A fraud perpetrator could option a decent script for a few thousand dollars.

Back at the computer, I turned my attention to Gregory Ackerman, the director. The search on his name produced stronger results. He had his own website, presented in both German and English, with links to trailers for a couple films and a television series. The website provided contact information in Germany.

I scanned the trailers. The television series and most of the films were in German. One film was shot in England using English-speaking actors. I'd never heard of it.

By then it was noon. I had a flight to Austin at three fifteen. A time zone check told me it was nine p.m. in Germany. I pulled up my checklist, studied the questions for Ackerman, and dialed the number. After four rings, a man answered.

"Ackerman."

"Excuse me, do you speak English?"

"*Ja* . . . I mean, yes."

"Thank you. My name is Joe Robbins. I'm calling from Los Angeles. Do you have a few minutes?"

"Yes. I'm waiting for a table."

The line was so clear he sounded like he stood next to me.

"Great. I'm with Marco Ruffini and Associates, an accounting firm. We're conducting due diligence for our client's investment in the film *Galveston Lost*."

"Yes. *Galveston Lost*."

So far, so good. At least he knew of the project. I looked at my next question.

"Have you committed to direct the film?"

"Yes, I have. Well, my commitment has a condition. I told Toby I would do the picture if he could raise twenty million dollars. I don't want to start a project that can't be finished."

The film certainly seemed like a real project. Fraud was still possible in various forms, but I doubted that Ackerman, an experienced director with a career, would play a part in it.

"Do you know how they're progressing with the fundraising?"

"No, I'm afraid not. I haven't spoken to Toby in a week, but I'll see him on Friday in Berlin. I'm introducing him to some people. Who is your client?"

"I'm not at liberty to say, but I will tell you my client was introduced to the project by Bryan Slater."

"Oh, yes. Slater."

I got the impression Ackerman didn't think much of Slater. "Will he be in the movie?"

"Perhaps. We haven't made any final casting decisions."

"What drew you to the film?"

He took a few minutes to outline the elements of the story that made for a good film. His answers convinced me the film was legitimate. To test for sophisticated fraud schemes I'd have to examine the books of Second Chance Productions, but before hanging up I couldn't resist asking a question that was not on my list.

"Do you think *Galveston Lost* will make a profit?"

Ackerman took his time formulating a response. A smattering of restaurant noises came through the earpiece.

"It's difficult to say. We can make a good movie, I know that, but to generate a return Toby and Bryan will have to sell it."

I ended the call with Ackerman and rolled the chair back from the desk to look through the window at the pool downstairs. White lounge chairs lined the outer perimeter. About ten people lay on chairs enjoying the sun. It was tempting to stay in paradise for a bit longer, but Callie had a soccer game the next day that I didn't want to miss.

I concluded the movie was real, but I also agreed with Marco's observation: Investing two million in *Galveston Lost* was a bad idea.

"*Beaucoup* bad luck," Sophie had said, but maybe her losses were simply driven by bad decisions.

CHAPTER 8

On the flight back to Austin I got upgraded and sat next to a salesman who slept most of the way. I had a wealth of information from Johnson's laptop and started with the profit statements for Sophie's business. She received quarterly royalties from two record labels and a variety of other sources. Concert earnings came from a few different promoters and fluctuated from month to month.

Over the preceding twelve months she had grossed one million seven hundred and seventy-nine thousand dollars. In the year before she had received eight percent more, visible evidence of her gradual decline in earnings.

The business expenses were straightforward. As her manager Johnson earned ten percent of everything, whereas Halet Blevins earned fifteen percent of concert revenues only. On top of those commissions she had touring expenses, Keri's salary, Marco Ruffini's fees, and three thousand a month to the public relations agency. On the bottom line the business netted Sophie a little less than a hundred thousand a month.

Next I reviewed her tax filings for the past two years. Marco had deducted her mortgage interest from first and second loans on the mansion and other business expenses for travel, entertainment, and so forth. Still, she would have had to pay income tax except for the carry-forward of prior-year losses. The silver lining of her investment losses, as Marco's tax filing demonstrated, was lower taxes.

Sophie was following the typical formula for a celebrity's financial ruin: a combination of bad investments and living beyond her means. Unless she had other assets I didn't know about, she needed to make lifestyle changes or she'd wind up broke.

I recalled again the feel of her hand on my arm. Why had she touched me? In retrospect the gesture seemed out of place, odd, but at the time it felt natural. Perhaps she reached out by instinct, lost in thought, craving human contact for nourishment. Different people have more finely developed senses. Some have sharper vision, while others hear distant sounds. Sophie might have a heightened sense of touch. Perhaps she needed to touch a person to understand them, to read them. What had she found in me?

I spent the rest of the flight reading *Galveston Lost*. When we began our descent into Austin I put the script away and looked out the window. As the plane tilted to align for approach, the September landscape came into view, a few patches of green and lots of brown where the Texas sun had fried all the grass.

* * *

By the time I got home it was almost nine o'clock, seven on the West Coast. I fixed a glass of ice water and walked out on my balcony to watch the last rays of sun filter through the live oaks. When darkness had descended I called Sophie to check in, wondering whether she would answer. The phone rang four times before she picked up.

"Hello."

"It's Joe Robbins."

"So my phone told me. How are you?"

My mind drew a blank and my heart jumped a step. For an instant I felt acutely aware of my own circumstances; I was talking with Sophie again.

"Hello?" she said. "Are you there?"

I gulped water, hoping the wetness would inspire my tongue.

"Yes. I'm fine. I called to give you an update. Is this a bad time?"

"I'm out for dinner with Johnson and Keri, but I just stepped away."

"Do you want to talk later? Or tomorrow?"

"No, let's talk now. They can wait a couple minutes. What have you found out?" Her words bounced happily, as if my call had provided a welcome distraction.

"From what I can tell, despite Marco Ruffini's misgivings, the investment is legitimate. They have an office, a legal entity, and a website. Toby Wycliff is in Europe raising money. Did you reach him?"

I breathed easier. After the rough start I had found my voice.

"Yes, I caught him last night. He was in Paris, and I told him to expect your call."

"Do you have his mobile number? I left a voicemail at his office but don't know how often he'll check that line."

"Sure. I'll text you the number as soon as we hang up."

"I also talked to the director, Gregory Ackerman. He's real, although he says he won't do the picture if they can't raise twenty million."

She paused, and through the phone I heard what sounded like traffic noise. A car honked its horn.

"What happens in that scenario?" she said. She asked the question flatly, as if indifferent to Ackerman's condition.

"I don't know. Maybe they get another director, or maybe they fold the tent and refund your money."

Sophie didn't say anything. Was she concerned? Disappointed?

I glanced at my notes and continued. "I still want to look at the production company's books. When I get ahold of Toby I'll ask for that data. That's about it. Oh, I read the script."

"Really? What did you think?"

Okay. We'd moved beyond the numbers to the movie script, from the left brain to the right. Was she being polite or did she honestly care for my opinion?

"I liked it," I said, "nice balance of conflict, romance, drama, and irony."

"What's the irony?"

"Well, the way I see it, you have the South fighting the war to protect their way of life, which is personified by the heroine. The Southern officer wins the naval battle for Galveston but loses the romantic battle for the woman, so even though he wins in combat, he loses what he was fighting for."

"Wow. For a finance guy you go pretty deep. Can you see me in the lead role?"

"I'd like to see you in the role, but I don't think you should have invested in the film."

I held my breath as silence came across the phone: five seconds . . . six seconds . . . I had strayed from the fraud investigation to provide financial advice.

"Why not?" she said in a neutral tone.

"Before answering, let me ask *you* a question. Do you have assets beyond the accounts with Schwab, Morgan Stanley, Vanguard, and Bank of America?"

Another long pause. "No, I don't think so. Johnson has done a good job of simplifying things."

"You need a solid financial cushion, and independent films are risky. Even if they make a great movie you could still lose your money."

"Now you sound like a finance guy again."

"Sorry. Comes with the territory."

While waiting for her next response I sat in a chair but got up again a few seconds later. I walked to the rail and leaned over the side. Perhaps I'd given too much unsolicited advice.

She said, "Maybe we can discuss your philosophy about movies and money further, in Austin."

A slow smile crept across my face. I tried to sound calm and professional.

"I look forward to it."

After we hung up I spent a few minutes reviewing the conversation. I'd handled myself well, covered the fraud business first, tossed in some color commentary on the film, and didn't lose my train of thought. While waiting for her text of Toby's mobile number, I allowed myself a moment of self-praise. When her text came I called Toby and left him another voice message.

By then I was hungry. I made pasta and opened a medium-priced Tempranillo. After dinner I sat on the balcony with a second glass of wine.

Rose and I had seen Sophie perform live once, in Dallas, years ago, soon after we married. We had gone to the Cotton Bowl for a rock band's reunion concert. Sophie was the opener, and she stole the show. I stood on the arena floor a hundred feet from her, oblivious of my surroundings, drawn in by the music, particularly her voice. I remember feeling as if every sound I'd ever heard until that moment was muffled, dull, toneless, and that now, for the first time, hearing had become my dominant sense.

I tried to picture her playing to the geriatric crowd on the Neptune Lounge of Deck Three. I couldn't see it, or maybe I just didn't want to see it. With sensible cost trimming Sophie could avoid the cruise-ship scenario. That was my skillset, my specialty. I could help her with that process.

* * *

I LOOKED AT THE CLOCK: five fifty-three a.m.

I splashed my face, put on running gear, and ran down to the greenbelt. I took the path to Zilker Park and then to Barton Springs Road to check the festival grounds. Fencing ringed the perimeter, the main stages stood tall, and hundreds of Port-a-Potties waited side by side. It was Thursday. Sophie and her entourage would arrive around noon to play a warm-up show that night at Antone's. The festival would start Friday. I ran the fence perimeter to the lake and did a short loop.

I had little to do on the investigation except wait for a call from Toby Wycliff. He would provide the financial data I needed to verify the integrity of the production company. I also wanted to ask Bryan Slater some questions to get a better feel for him. How could I do that without blowing my cover as a security guard? I remembered Bryan's enthusiasm for the movie project and got an idea.

* * *

THAT AFTERNOON I WAITED for Adrian in the lobby lounge of the Four Seasons. An excited buzz filled the room. The well-heeled crowd had begun to arrive for the festival weekend. Beautiful people sat all around me, dressed in expensive casual clothes: designer cutoffs with hundred-dollar T-shirts and embroidered ball caps, khakis with polo shirts and straw fedoras, linen skirts with breezy tops and floppy hats.

Adrian approached from the elevators. He wore black cargo pants, black running shoes, and a green short-sleeved collared shirt. His jaw muscles flexed as he surveyed the room. Once he'd settled in a chair next to me I gave him a summary of my findings.

"So you think it's legitimate," he said.

"I want to examine their financial books, but yeah, so far it looks good."

I sipped my coffee and glanced across the room. Lyle Lovett walked into the lobby lounge. A middle-aged blonde jumped from her chair to give him a hug.

Adrian took me through the security detail for the weekend. We had the show that night at Antone's, a walk-around of the festival the next day with Sophie incognito, and her festival show on Saturday afternoon.

"The truth is I don't need a team for the show at Antone's or her concert at ACL," said Adrian. "Antone's has bouncers and ACL has its own security. The trick is her self-guided tour of the festival tomorrow. She'll be on the ground surrounded by tens of thousands of people. If one fan recognizes her she'll be mobbed for autographs and photo ops. Those scenes get dicey fast. I must have a three-person team for that walk-around, including you and me, but my other guy called in sick, and I can't find anyone available in Austin. Do you know someone?"

I thought of my friend Sanjay Kumar. He was a genius with computers, an amateur hacker, and a gambling addict. I had first hired Sanjay when he needed money to pay off a debt. He had since recovered financially but had grown to like doing one-off jobs for me. He found it a welcome distraction from staring at a computer screen.

"Yes. He's not beefy, but he's observant."

"I don't need muscle, just a good pair of eyes."

"I'll call him."

I looked at Lyle Lovett as he stood and walked toward the hotel entrance with the woman.

"Lyle Lovett's leaving."

Adrian peeked over his shoulder. "Yeah, this place is crawling with celebrities. Ray Benson came to Sophie's suite for lunch."

"Heck of a job."

"My wife can't stand it. She's worried one of these stars will seduce me."

I looked him over. Adrian had a strong physique and a handsome face. I could see an errant star taking a run at him.

"Every job carries risks," I said with a hint of sarcasm, but Adrian didn't respond. He was all business.

"By the way," I said, "do you know if Bryan Slater will be at Antone's tonight?"

"I'm sure he will. He flew out with us this morning."

"Good. I want to ask him some questions about his movie."

CHAPTER 9

SOPHIE WAS TO ARRIVE at Antone's by limo and enter the club through a side entrance on Lavaca. I arrived early and parked my car on the top level of a garage across Fifth Street from the club. From there I could watch both the club and the intersection with Lavaca. At ten thirty my cell phone rang.

"Two minutes," said Adrian.

"I'm ready."

I hurried downstairs, crossed Fifth Street to the corner, and fast-walked down Lavaca. My phone rang again.

"We're almost there," Adrian said. "Hang on."

About twenty people milled around the side entrance. They must have known Sophie would arrive there. A limo turned from Fourth Street onto Lavaca and cruised toward the club.

"I see you," I said.

"Anything to worry about?" he asked.

"Nothing. Some autograph seekers."

"Okay. Stay close."

Two seconds later the side door to the club opened. A large man with dark hair and a handlebar mustache emerged and looked toward the limo. He wore a black dress shirt with the sleeves rolled up.

Fans saw the limo and bunched together. Several held their cameras ready to take pictures. I edged my way through the crowd to get closer to the curb.

"Hey man, not cool cutting in."

"I'm with Ms. Tyler," I said.

"Sure you are."

The limo pulled to the curb, and Adrian got out on the opposite side. The streetlights created an eerie glow. Adrian gave me a nod and moved around the car to open the sidewalk door. I took a close look at the cluster of people, all with smiling faces, low tension. My pulse quickened.

"There she is."

"Sophie."

I studied her closely. Her shoulders and arms were uncovered, her hair parted in the middle and brushed to frame her face. She wore a flower-print sleeveless top, jeans, and cowboy boots. I moved closer, within reach.

"You folks ready to party?" she called.

Cheers rose from the small crowd, and Sophie stepped into them. Adrian and I walked on either side to create some space.

Sophie noticed me and leaned to speak in my ear. "So in a pinch you *are* a security guy." Her breath grazed my cheek, ratcheting my pulse to a higher rate.

"I try to be flexible."

"I feel safer already." She gave me a soft elbow in the side.

My hand rose instinctively. I held her upper arm with a light touch to keep us connected as we walked through the crowd.

A small blonde with tight curls thrust a notebook at her, and Sophie reached to sign it. Cameras flashed around us, and we walked slowly toward the door, with Sophie continuing to sign autographs and chat up the crowd.

"*Hill Country Siren* is my favorite album ever," said a fan.

"Thanks. I have a few tunes from that album on tonight's set list."

"Play 'Misty Eyed', please. Play 'Misty Eyed'."

"You bet."

By then we had reached the door. Adrian pointed out Sophie's entourage, including me, to the man in the black shirt and then led Sophie inside. I paused at the door to let the rest of the entourage through. Johnson Sagebrush paused to shake my hand. As he did the light trace of sandalwood brightened the smells of the street.

"Good to see you, Joe."

"Thanks."

Keri let Johnson get a few steps ahead and then leaned toward me. "I hope you got what you came for the other night. You almost gave me a heart attack." She smiled and her eyes twinkled in a conspiratorial way.

Did she expect a response? I couldn't tell whether she was proud of our mission's success or pumping me for information.

"Yeah. It's all good."

She walked past me, and Bryan Slater stepped up.

"Hey, Bryan."

He didn't recognize me at first, but then he pointed a finger at me and nodded. "I met you at Sophie's . . . on the patio. Sorry, I've forgotten your name."

"Joe Robbins."

"Good to see you again." He started to step to the door.

"Sophie loaned me the script for *Galveston Lost*."

His eyebrows squished together. "She did?"

"I'm kind of a movie buff. Great story. Love to chat about it. I didn't follow part of the second act."

Bryan didn't expect to hear this from a security guy, but after a moment's hesitation he nodded. "Yeah, sure. Maybe when the band's on break or something we can grab a few minutes."

"Awesome."

The word *awesome* made Bryan smile, an automated response.

Inside the club it was dark and loud. As we entered a narrow passageway, the opening act, the Swamp Rats, played a cover of Marshall Tucker's "Fire on the Mountain". The stage was on our left and above us. The guy with the black shirt stood by a narrow hallway on the right. He let Keri and Bryan through but moved to block me.

"Sorry, dude. It's a mob scene in the green room. The band members each brought a friend, and it's a small space. Can you wait out here?"

"Do me a favor," I said. "Tell Adrian I'm scouting the crowd."

"You got it."

I walked out front to watch the band. The patrons drank their beers and cocktails and looked to the stage, their feet tapping to the music. A cowboy and his girl swing danced. Ten tables occupied a space off to the side of the stage, but the area in front was for standing only.

Antone's was bigger than I remembered, and crowded, too, with room for several hundred, but the stage stood six feet high, so an overzealous fan would find it difficult to reach the musicians.

Ten minutes later, as the Swamp Rats' two guitarists played dueling solos, I noticed Bryan Slater at the bar. I walked over just as he turned around with a glass of whiskey and ice. He held the glass in the air and spoke up so I could hear him.

"All they have is beer in the green room. I wanted something stronger."

"Good idea."

"I'd buy you one but I guess that's a no-no."

"Not when I'm working."

He looked at the stage and around the bar. "Seems like a peaceful crowd."

"Antone's is generally a laid-back scene."

"So you read the script."

A young woman with curly black hair and a red halter top approached us with a smile on her face. She wore jeans stretched tight over curvy hips. Two similarly dressed women, both blondes, watched her from ten feet away. I guessed they were her friends.

"Aren't you Bryan Slater? From *Witchblade*?"

"Yes."

She turned on her heel and gave a thumbs-up sign to her friends. They laughed. "Can I have your autograph?"

"Sure thing. Do you have something to sign?"

"Oh, shit. Wait right here. I'll be back."

Bryan wore his infectious grin as she left. "Honestly, I wish it happened more often, particularly with girls who look like that." He winked. "So you said something about the second act?"

The Swamp Rats wound down the song, giving us a few moments of relative quiet.

I had spent two hours earlier devising an idea for the script in hopes of engaging Bryan long enough to ask him a question relevant to my investigation. When I finished pitching my idea Bryan stood with an elbow cupped in one hand. He tapped his lips with two fingers and then nodded his appreciation.

"It has potential," he said. "Lots of tension there. Let me give it some thought."

The woman with the black curls and red halter top returned with a blank bar receipt and a cheap pen. As Bryan signed the paper the woman and her two friends clustered around him, twittering away.

I surveyed the crowd again and saw nothing of concern from a security standpoint. The Swamp Rats would wind up their set soon.

Bryan shook the girls' hands and walked back to my side. Before he could say anything I returned to the movie discussion.

"Are you guys going to shoot the movie in Galveston?"

Bryan watched the girls walk away. The one with the black curls continued to steal glances at him, but he turned from her to answer my question.

"We'd like to, but we don't have to. It comes down to incentives, and some states are getting aggressive. We need a port city with off-shore islands and the ability to set up period scenes. I like Galveston, but we could easily use Charleston or Savannah."

"I thought maybe Houston being so close would sway the decision."

Bryan frowned. "Why?"

"They have good film production capabilities and a low cost structure."

"Really? I didn't know that."

"Didn't Sophie say something about you setting up shop in Houston?"

He scratched his temple. "Did she? I don't know why she'd say that."

I worried about blowing my cover. "Maybe I got that wrong. I talked to someone about a different film last week."

The noise from the Swamp Rats rose again, and our conversation died.

Bryan's ignorance of the Houston location struck me as odd. The money had gone to a bank account with Wells Fargo in Houston. Why would a California production company have a bank account in Houston unless they needed it for operations?

After a few minutes Bryan turned to me. He still looked a little puzzled. "I'm heading back to the green room. Nice talking with you, Joe. Thanks for the script idea."

"You bet."

On the way he stopped to chat some more with the woman in the black curls and her friends. As the Swamp Rats began their last tune, Bryan left the girls and walked toward the green room.

When the song ended customers swarmed the bar for fresh drinks. A few minutes later Adrian stopped by.

"Sophie will start soon," he said. "Have you seen anything of concern?"

"No, just a happy crowd so far . . . no unruly drunks or anything like that."

"Good. I'll stay in the offstage shadows to the left. You watch from out here."

"Got it."

Even though I stood toward the back I could see Sophie clearly, the concentration on her face, the smiles she gave to her band mates.

The drummer was in the back on an elevated platform; the piano player sat on the drummer's right at the same level. The bass guitar player stood on Sophie's left, and the lead guitarist was on her right. She sang every song with occasional backup from various others. She played a wide array of instruments: acoustic, electric, and slide guitar; mandolin; fiddle; even harmonica. The band played anything and everything: blues, rock, country, and bluegrass.

Her vocals enchanted the crowd, the high notes crazy high, and the soulful sounds impossibly real. The lyrical structure varied widely, sometimes metered verse, and at other times lengthy prose strung across multiple octaves. Sophie's talent enabled a sound as natural as leaves blowing on a windy day.

I found it difficult to focus on the security detail. Her voice captured me. I looked away from the stage, or more accurately, away from Sophie, and tried to concentrate on simple tasks. I estimated the size of the crowd: three-twenty to three-forty. I looked for the biggest man in the room, then the drunkest. I played these games of concentration for her entire performance, sometimes succeeding, but often failing.

When she sang "Wounded Heart" I found the task near impossible. Sophie didn't know me well, but it felt like she sang only for me, that she knew about my divorce, the loss of my soulmate, and my wounded heart.

> Never mind your wounded heart, my friend
>
> The jagged pain you feel will someday end.
>
> Though love's quick cruelty stabs you like a knife
>
> New love breathes into willing hearts new life.

After the song I went back to playing games to avoid distraction, but I felt different, my mood elevated. And when she finished the final encore and the lights came up and she had left the stage, the warm comfort that had come when she first touched me returned.

Adrian had told me they'd make a quick exit, and by the time I walked to the green room they were gone. Only the man in the black shirt remained.

• • •

BACK AT HOME I HAD shed my clothes and was brushing my teeth when my cell phone rang in the main room. Who would call at two thirty a.m.? I jogged in to look at the screen but didn't recognize the area code.

"Hello."

The fuzzy sound of a poor connection came through the earpiece. After a moment of hesitation a man spoke over static.

"Joe Robbins?"

"Yes."

"Toby Wycliff from Second Chance Productions."

"Oh, hi."

I stood next to the sectional dressed in my boxers and nothing else. Two thirty in Austin meant nine thirty in Western Europe.

"Sorry to call so late. I expected to get your voicemail. I received your message days ago but we're in Paris now, and our schedule's been crazy hectic. Every time I get a free moment it's the middle of the night for you."

"That's okay. I wasn't asleep."

"Good. Anyway, I'm glad to hear Sophie considered investing. It means a lot."

"Yeah." I blinked. My brain had already begun the shutdown process. I struggled to re-engage. Something about what he just said didn't make sense.

I yawned and turned back to the bedroom. My bed looked so good I couldn't resist lying down. I rested my head on the pillow and willed my eyes to remain open.

"You mentioned due diligence," he said. "At this point I don't think that's necessary."

"Why not?"

I guessed that he didn't want to share the data. Some entrepreneurs treat confidentiality like a religion. I'd have to talk him into it.

"I haven't had a chance to talk to Bryan about it yet," he said, "but we've had a setback on fundraising."

"What's that?"

"It's the Civil War subject. Another Civil War film, *Cold Mountain*, is premiering in December. Everyone wants to see how that does first. In the last week two verbal commitments withdrew, and I'm getting zero traction in Europe. We'll have to shutter this."

My eyes opened wide. "Really?"

"Yes. These projects only work when the planets come into alignment. The *Cold Mountain* issue sets us back six months. By then

Ackerman, Bryan, and I will each be doing something completely different. This film may never come back."

"What will you do with the production company?"

"I'll shut down the office, but probably keep the legal entity in case things come alive again soon."

"What about investors' money?"

"We'll return it, what little we've actually raised. Costs so far have been minimal. Bryan and I will cover those out of pocket."

Okay. That sounded good. Perhaps after a bit of reflection Sophie would decide to invest more conservatively.

"So you see," he continued, "there's no point in Sophie investing now."

I sat up, my mind clearing fast, my muscles tense. "She already invested," I said, standing up at the same time.

A silence of several seconds followed. I strode into the bathroom and stared at the mirror, my eyes hard.

"Really?" he said. "How much?"

"Two million dollars. You haven't received it?"

"No, I . . . uh . . . I'm sure we have. I haven't spoken to my bookkeeper in a week."

"Her manager wired the money ten days ago."

"Really?" he said again. "I'm surprised our bookkeeper didn't mention it, but we had a long list to cover. Maybe it slipped his mind."

Maybe, but that sounded strange. A two-million cash infusion for a startup would hardly go unnoticed. Alarms rang in my head. The sleep I'd cherished moments before had vanished with a few words.

"Look, Toby, do me a favor. Get in touch with your bookkeeper and call me the second you have news on that wire one way or the other."

"Sure."

"If that wire got hung up I need to know immediately."

"I'll try him now, but it's late, and truthfully, he hasn't been as reliable as Bryan suggested."

"What do you mean?"

"Bryan brought in the bookkeeper . . . said he came highly recommended. I'd never heard of the guy."

At this point the silent alarms were screaming at me.

"But I'll check with him about the wire," said Toby. "I'm sure it came through, and we'll return it later today."

We ended the call soon thereafter, and I paced the great room: in front of the sectional, around the kitchen table, and back again. What happened to that wire? Banks don't misplace two million dollars, and bookkeepers don't neglect to mention investments to anxious bosses.

The fact that Bryan brought in the bookkeeper sounded wrong. He didn't strike me as the type to have those kinds of connections.

I got on the computer to recheck the screenshot of the wire instructions. They hadn't changed. Ten days before, two million dollars were wired to Wells Fargo Bank in Houston, with forwarding credit to Second Chances Production, LLC.

I stared at the details of the transaction. The Houston location had already sent me a warning. Now I looked at the receiving party again. Second Chances Production, LLC.

Second Chances.

Plural.

I grabbed the script from the kitchen table and flipped to the information page. Second Chance Production Company, LLC.

Singular.

A typo was possible, but the warning signs kept piling up.

Corporate fraud came in two varieties: salami and whole-hog. In the salami approach the perpetrator took a thin slice at a time and worked the scheme over a long period, hoping to never get caught. In the whole-hog approach he stole a big chunk all at once and skipped town.

I called Toby back to ask where they banked their money, but the call went straight to voicemail.

I feared that someone had given Johnson Sagebrush bogus wiring instructions. Several suspects immediately came to mind: the bookkeeper, Bryan Slater, or Toby Wycliff. Any of them could have provided the wiring instructions.

Now the Houston angle bothered me again. A fraudster might have an account with that bank already, making it easier to move the money downstream.

I pulled up the Texas government website and searched public records for Second Chances Productions.

Damn.

Second Chances Productions, LLC, had been formed in Texas a month ago, and the president of the company was Bryan Slater.

His acting skills had fooled me, but the scam struck me as dumb. He left a trail so visible I had discovered it in a couple days.

By then it was three o'clock. No one would be awake for hours, and I needed instructions from Sophie. Did she still want to keep a low profile or should we involve the police?

I lay down in bed again and tried to sleep, my mind swirling.

CHAPTER 10

I WAS SOUND ASLEEP when the phone rang.

Three thirty-seven a.m.

I rubbed my eyes and cleared my throat.

"Hello."

"It's Rico."

"What . . . what is it?"

"Do you know a man named Bryan Slater?"

"Um . . ." My mind grappled with sleep, fighting its way to awareness. Bryan Slater . . . "Sure. Yes, I saw him tonight at Antone's. He used to date Sophie Tyler."

"He's not dating anyone now. He's dead."

"What?"

I sat up so fast my head grew dizzy. Bryan Slater was dead, but I'd seen him only a few hours before.

"I'm looking at him. Someone caved in his skull. Wasn't he involved somehow in that fraud thing you're doing for Adrian?"

"Yes."

Involved? He was absolutely involved. I'd pinned him as guilty an hour earlier, and now he was dead. I reached for the light switch on the bedside lamp, my head clear now.

"Can you come over here? Maybe you can give me some facts on this thing."

"Where are you?"

"Red River Street. A half block north of Cesar Chavez."

"Give me twenty minutes."

* * *

THE POLICE FLASHERS swept the brick building with red and blue lights. I pulled the Jeep to the side of Red River Street and walked to the taped-off area at the corner of a parking lot. Bryan was behind a Dumpster at the farthest point from the street. The police had erected two light stands to illuminate the scene.

He lay on his back with one leg straight down and the other bent awkwardly. His face appeared untouched, but his forehead looked wrong, concave instead of convex, and his ear was misaligned with his face, the lobe pointed toward his nose. His head rested flat against the asphalt, and the blood had flowed in a thin stream to the edge of the lot a few feet away.

His eyes were closed, and his mouth formed a wry smile. He had always worn his hair carefully disheveled, but now it just looked weird, ugly clumps matted with blood. I stared at him, my eyes locked on his hardening shape, lifeless on the pavement. He looked calm, as if he had lain on the parking lot to take a nap.

I thought of his still heart, pumping only a few hours earlier, perhaps skipping a beat when the sexy woman asked for his autograph. His brain had processed her looks and her request, sent signals through complex networks to trigger the response of his infectious grin. All that wonderful machinery was now shut down, in darkness. Bryan Slater was a fellow human being with thoughts and problems and aspirations, and someone had brought his unique attributes to an abrupt and permanent end.

I don't hate many things in life, but I do hate murderers.

Why had someone killed Bryan? It was Rico's job to find out, but I had already tried Bryan Slater for the crime of fraud against Sophie Tyler and found him guilty. He was a good actor after all. He knew about the bank account in Houston because he had opened it himself. He had created a second company in Texas with a similar name and given Johnson Sagebrush bogus wiring instructions. Once the money had hit the account all he had to do was grab it and run.

But several flaws with that logic demanded explanation. How did Bryan Slater—not a huge star but still recognized by many—hope to disappear? And if his plan was to run, why had he not done so already? The money cleared his account ten days earlier. Why stick around?

A photographer took endless shots, his white flash causing me to blink. Rico talked to two men. One of them saw me and alerted Rico to my presence.

"Hang on, Joe. Be there in a minute."

I stood outside the tape and watched the photographer do his work. Off to the side a uniformed policeman talked with two men dressed in shabby clothes. I guessed they were homeless. It was the quietest time of the night, and I saw no other person in any direction.

"Tell me about Bryan Slater."

I jumped a little and then recovered. Rico had sneaked up on me with his notebook.

"I don't know him well. I met him twice: once in California at Sophie Tyler's house and then tonight at her show at Antone's."

"What time did he leave Antone's?"

"I'm not sure. Bryan came with the band as Sophie's guest. I last saw him about eleven thirty, but the band didn't leave until after one.

I watched the show from the crowd, and after the last song the band immediately left by the back door. Bryan might have gone with them."

"Did he talk with anyone else?"

I described for Rico the interaction with the autograph seeker and her friends.

"Did you see him again?"

"No. Not until now."

Rico looked at Slater's corpse. "What a mess. The murderer beat him with some sort of club. He knew what he was doing, too. It's not easy to destroy a man's head like that. He has no wallet, no money, and no ID, which suggests a robbery, but muggers rarely murder their victims. Certainly not with a blunt instrument."

"How did you know to call me?" I said.

Rico looked over to the uniformed policeman. "Pearson there is a Hollywood buff. One of the homeless guys found the corpse, and Pearson got the call. He recognized Slater. When I heard the name I remembered Adrian mentioned him as part of that fraud investigation."

"You have a sharp memory."

"That's why I'm a lieutenant. I called Adrian also, but he wouldn't come. When he heard Slater was dead he went to Ms. Tyler's suite. I want to go over there now and talk to both of them. Can you walk with me?"

"Sure."

Bryan Slater was killed two long blocks from the Four Seasons. As we walked I considered the available facts. A mugging gone wrong occurring in the same week that Bryan defrauded Sophie was too convenient. Bryan had gone to the parking lot with someone, or to meet someone, and the ensuing conversation had ended with his murder.

Unlike me, Rico tended to think out loud, but he didn't say a word for the first full block. As we passed under a streetlight I saw his face. His jaw muscles flexed as he ground his molars.

"Everything okay?" I said.

"Some days I hate this fucking job."

"What's up?"

Rico stopped. "Adrian told me one thing . . . Bryan Slater was a marine. Not many marines make it to Hollywood, but Bryan did."

"I'm sorry."

"This one is personal. I understand active duty marines dying in Iraq or Afghanistan, but I can't tolerate a tweaker, or anyone else, killing a jarhead in my town. We're going to catch this fucker."

"Maybe I can help."

Rico looked at me closely. "How's that?" His left pupil had turned solid black with his blood pressure, which made for an unnerving match with the almond pupil in his right eye.

"I don't think a tweaker killed Bryan Slater."

As we continued the walk I brought Rico up to speed on my investigation and explained my theory that Bryan's murder resulted from a disagreement between thieves or an argument with someone who had discovered the scam. When we reached the entrance to the hotel Rico looked at me under the bright lights of the portico, his expression all business now.

"So how do we find this bookkeeper?"

"Toby Wycliff will have his contact information. Also, Marco Ruffini."

"Okay. We'll check it out."

• • •

Sophie had a suite on the seventh floor. Rico and I exited the elevator and walked on the plush carpet. When we reached the suite Rico knocked.

Adrian opened the door about halfway. He looked fresh despite the hour, always the professional. He glanced back into the room and turned to Rico. "Do you have to do this now? She's upset."

"That's why I came myself instead of sending a detective. I'll go easy, but I need to ask a few questions so we can get the investigation started."

Adrian stepped back to let us in. I looked for her but didn't see Sophie right away. A kitchenette was on our right as we walked into the suite. On the left sliding doors opened into a darkened bedroom. The seating area occupied most of the main room, with a beige sofa for three, two matching armchairs, and a glass-topped coffee table. All the lights were on: electric candles in the chandelier, a lamp next to the indoor plants, and fluorescent overheads in the kitchenette.

Sophie sat still on the far end of the sofa, staring at the coffee table with her shoulders slumped. She wore jeans and a T-shirt and did not acknowledge we had entered the room. I felt an urge to move closer.

Johnson Sagebrush sat next to her on the sofa and talked softly. When he saw us he walked over, and Adrian introduced him to Rico. Johnson had changed clothes from earlier; he wore old khakis, running shoes, and a wrinkled T-shirt.

He shook his head, circles under his eyes. "Jesus Christ, this is unbelievable. When Adrian called me . . ." He looked at Rico with a question on his face. "He's really dead? Murdered?"

"I'm afraid so."

Johnson closed his eyes and brought a shaky hand to his temple. He took a deep breath. "I've got to keep my shit together. She's fucking devastated. Look at her."

Sophie hadn't moved. She continued to stare at a fixed point in space above the coffee table.

Johnson whispered, "She hasn't said a word since I told her, keeps staring at nothing."

"Where is Keri?" I asked.

"At her parents' place," said Johnson. "She left the club after Sophie went on."

"Who's Keri?" said Rico.

"Sophie's personal assistant," said Adrian.

"All right," said Rico. "Introduce me."

The four of us walked into the sitting area. Johnson retook his seat to Sophie's right on the sofa, while Rico and Adrian sat in the facing chairs. I remained standing about six feet from the others, my torso and feet pointed toward Sophie.

She didn't move when they sat down.

Rico studied Sophie's face, trying to read her; then he looked at Johnson, his eyebrows furrowed, and then he looked back to Sophie and rubbed his cheek. Adrian sat stock-still in the chair, his shoulders straight, head erect.

"Sophie?" said Johnson.

Her head turned slowly toward him, eyes wide open. "I don't understand. What has happened?"

"Bryan Slater was murdered."

"You said that before, but it doesn't make sense. I saw him tonight at the show."

Adrian said, "Sophie . . . this is Lieutenant Carrillo of the Austin Police Department."

She turned her eyes to me. "I thought your name was Joe."

"My name *is* Joe . . . Joe Robbins." I gestured toward Rico. "This is Lieutenant Carrillo. His job is to find the person who murdered Bryan. He needs to ask you a few questions."

"I don't know anything." She barely opened her mouth, the words slipping out quietly, just above a whisper. Her hands gripped each other tightly. She seemed lost, like a child in a shopping mall who wandered away from her parents. I wanted to help her find them.

"Ms. Tyler, I'm terribly sorry this happened," said Rico. "It must be a shock." He spoke in a soft, flat monotone. He had used the same voice many times, polished it with care to help him solicit information from damaged sources.

"A shock . . . yes . . . that's what it is, a shock."

"I apologize for seeing you so late, and so soon after Mr. Slater's passing, but the faster we begin the investigation, the better chance we have of finding the murderer."

Sophie blinked and looked from Rico to me to Johnson. She adjusted her posture, straightened her shoulders and head.

"Of course. How can I help?" She sounded better, more alert.

"Did you see Mr. Slater after the show tonight?"

"After the show? Let me think. After the show I got in the limo with Johnson and . . ." She turned toward Adrian. "You were in the limo."

"That's right."

"I didn't see Bryan. He must have left early. It was late . . . nearly two o'clock. We came straight to the hotel, and Johnson dropped me at my room."

"Did you talk with anyone else?"

"No. I got ready for bed, but I didn't sleep well. I never sleep well alone."

Adrian looked up from his hands to glance at me for a moment and then looked down again. Did he know something I didn't know?

"What about you, Mr. Sagebrush?" asked Rico.

Johnson turned to Rico, his face thoughtful. "Let's see. I went to my room and watched a little television to wind down, maybe thirty minutes. Then I went to bed."

"Did you talk to anyone else?"

Johnson shook his head. "No. I was sound asleep when Adrian called."

"Did you see Bryan Slater after the show?"

"No."

"Can either of you think of anyone who might have reason to harm Mr. Slater?"

Johnson answered for both of them. "Harm Bryan? No. He told me this was his first visit to Austin. I don't think he knew a soul in town."

"Was he staying here at the hotel?"

"Yes," said Johnson. "We all drove to the show together."

"Why didn't he come back with you?"

"I don't know. We were all in the green room while the Swamp Rats played. Bryan left for a while and then came back."

Rico glanced over, and I nodded. This was likely when Bryan came out and talked to me.

Johnson continued. "When Sophie went on and Bryan went out to watch, Keri took off, and I stayed in the green room. I've seen her play so many times I don't always watch the show. Bryan never returned to the green room, and we left the club immediately after the encore."

"You didn't look for Bryan?"

"I glanced around for him, but we didn't wait. I like to leave as soon as we can. You can waste an hour chatting with random people."

Rico asked them a few more questions without learning anything of consequence. After he wrapped up, Sophie remained seated while Johnson walked us to the door. As we got to the door Rico paused for a moment.

"Mr. Sagebrush . . . just one more question. I understand Ms. Tyler recently invested in an independent film being produced by Bryan Slater. Adrian tells me her accountant had some concerns about that investment. He suspected a potential fraud. What do you know about that?"

Johnson's lips drew tight, and then he blew a skeptical puff of air from the side of his mouth. "I think Marco Ruffini's concerns were unfounded. In any case, the two million was returned to Sophie's account yesterday. I understand they're putting the film on hold."

The money had been returned? I shifted my weight as my face grew warm. The data didn't square with what I had heard from Toby Wycliff just a couple of hours ago. Toby and his bookkeeper must be out of sync. I wanted to ask Johnson a question but couldn't; so far as he knew I was a security guard.

Rico looked at me laterally through narrowed eyes.

Johnson touched both Adrian and me on the upper arms.

"Can one of you guys stay here with her?" he said. "I don't think she should be alone."

I glanced at Sophie, the money forgotten, my heart rate accelerating. She sat in the same spot as before, motionless.

"I'd do it," he said, "but I need to wake up the PR folks in L.A. and talk them through this. Once the press find out about Bryan's murder, and that he was here as Sophie's guest, they'll try to make a story of it."

Adrian blinked several times and cleared his throat.

"I'll do it," I blurted.

"Oh, good," said Adrian. He let out a sigh. "I . . . I could use a couple more hours of sleep to be ready for later."

His excuse sounded lame, but I didn't care. I turned to Johnson. "What do you want me to do?"

"Make sure she doesn't do anything silly, like start drinking. She's got the walk-around tomorrow and the show on Saturday. She needs to be on her game."

"Sure," I said. "I can do that."

"Thanks. I'll go tell her."

As Johnson walked to her, I stood taller, my senses on high alert.

Rico watched me with interest, half smiling, and then he spoke to Adrian. "Hey, can you give me some time later? I need to connect with the LAPD, and you know a lot of those guys."

"I can't do it today. I'm running security for Sophie."

"I just need a couple hours."

Adrian looked at me. "What about your buddy? Did he agree to help out?"

"Yes."

"Okay. The two of you can bring Sophie to the festival. I'll help Rico in the morning and meet you at the VIP entrance."

* * *

ONCE EVERYONE LEFT I SAT in the chair across from her and didn't speak for ten minutes, figuring she could use some quiet time. The air felt still, and I opened the last button on my polo. She continued to stare at nothing, dressed in her jeans and T-shirt. I longed to stare at *her* but resisted the temptation. I looked at my hands for a while, and then examined the drapes, the carpet, and the framed pictures on the walls.

I thought about Bryan Slater lying on the ground with his skull crushed. Maybe a thief had murdered him after all. Or maybe something else happened. Maybe he had a drug problem and met someone recommended by the girls at the club. Maybe that went wrong and the dealer bludgeoned him and took all his valuables. There were a hundred possibilities, but the money wire still bothered me. Something about that whole setup felt wrong, but I needed sleep to figure it out.

I glanced at Sophie and moistened my lips.

The bluish-green eyes remained stationary, staring at a spot in empty space. With no makeup and little sleep her face looked older.

She sat suspended in concentration. Every once in a while her eyes squeezed closer together, as if in reaction to an unpleasant memory.

When ten minutes had passed I cleared my throat, and she looked at me.

"Can I get you some water?"

"Yes, please."

I filled two glasses with ice and water and handed her one. She drank deeply, her throat muscles moving as she swallowed. She set the half-empty glass onto the table.

"Adrian refused to stay with me. Didn't he?"

"I . . . uh . . ."

"He doesn't trust himself around me, or maybe he just doesn't trust me."

"You don't have to tell me a thing."

But she kept talking anyway. "I made a pass at him when he first started working for me, about six months ago. It was thoughtless. I knew he was married. Anyway, he rejected me."

"Johnson is working with your PR team but didn't want you to be alone. Adrian is helping Lieutenant Carrillo, so that left me."

"Alone." She leaned back on the sofa and studied my face. "I don't do alone well."

I didn't know what to say. Sophie's pass at Adrian explained his hesitation about staying with her one-on-one. Her words—*I don't do alone well*—suggested that she always had people around her, the closer the better. Perhaps that was why Bryan had been invited on the trip. Maybe she'd expected him to visit her suite after the show.

She picked the glass up and drank it empty, then placed it firmly on the table.

"Do you want me to call Keri?" I said.

"What time is it?"

"Almost five."

"No. Let her spend the morning with her family. Things will get hectic soon enough."

"You should try to get some more sleep."

She rubbed her forehead with the back of her hand, her eyes closed. "Yes, I think I will."

We both stood. She took two steps toward the bedroom and then stopped, unsteady on her feet. I moved closer. Her eyes blinked, and she shook her head once. Her shoulders swayed and her upper body went off balance. I reached for her elbow. Sophie turned and leaned on me. With arms folded against her chest she tucked her face into my neck.

She sobbed once and said, "Hold me. Just hold me, please."

I wrapped my arms around her back and pulled her close, feeling the warmth of her body. She smelled of clean skin mixed with a flowery lotion, and her hair was damp from an earlier washing. In that moment she didn't seem like a rock star—she was only a woman in shock.

"It's just so awful," she said. "I can't believe he's dead."

We stood like that for a few more moments, and then I helped her walk into the bedroom. She unzipped the jeans, let them drop to the floor, and climbed in bed in T-shirt and cotton panties. My breath came quick, and the nerves in my hands tingled. She pulled the comforter to her shoulder. I stood still next to the bed, and touched her shoulder.

"You won't leave me, will you?" she said.

"No, I'll be in the other room."

"Good."

I turned out all the lights in the suite and opened the shade to the balcony. Streetlights reflected off the surface of Town Lake. I closed the shade, took off my shoes, and stretched out on the long sofa. When I closed my eyes I saw Sophie lying in bed, the comforter tucked beneath her chin.

If I thought about Sophie, or Bryan's death, or the mystery of the money, my mind would churn and I'd never sleep, so I focused on listening to distract my thoughts. Air swooshed steadily from the vent in the ceiling. Ice cubes dropped from the automaker in the freezer. Soft lights from the thermostat and smoke detector kept the black of night at bay.

Sleep stealthily approached, pulling me into the world where no one controls his thoughts.

* * *

THE MOVEMENT OF THE CUSHION edged into my semiconscious state. It must be Alyssa, returning to bed after an early-morning trip to the bathroom. A light hand touched my shoulder.

No, it wasn't Alyssa. She had left me. I was on the sofa in Sophie Tyler's suite.

I opened my eyes to see Keri. She sat on the sofa with her hip nudged against my side and gave me a weak smile.

Sunlight streamed in around the edges of the wooden shades. A radio clock on a side table read nine fifteen. I yawned and felt the stubble on my face, my mouth dry. It took me a moment to recall the events of the night before.

"Thank you for staying with Sophie," she said. She wore a pink crew-neck shirt with long sleeves.

"Sure. You must have heard about Bryan."

She nodded. "Adrian called to fill me in. It's awful."

That was all she said. She sighed and her smile turned tight. I sat up and rubbed my eyes.

"Is Sophie still asleep?" I asked.

"Yes, I'll let her rest as long as I can."

That seemed a good idea. She'd looked hammered the night before. After four hours of sleep I felt groggy, but movement would serve to wake me.

Keri bit the nail of her pinkie, then caught herself and placed her hand in her lap. She had chewed all her nails short. She owned a gun, but despite that fact, she struck me as a reluctant person, unsure of herself, walking through life as if in a minefield.

"Maybe she should skip the festival today," I said.

Keri frowned. "She won't want to miss it. She wears a disguise and walks from stage to stage, listening to the other bands. She calls it market research. And frankly, she could use a distraction."

"Have you spoken with Johnson this morning?"

"Not yet. I talked to Halet twice, but Johnson didn't answer his phone. I thought maybe he was here."

I stood, stretched, and looked for my shoes. "Well, I'd better go so I can change and be back in time to pick up Sophie."

A knock came at the door to the suite.

"That's probably Johnson," she said. "I'll get it."

While Keri walked toward the door I slipped on my shoes and then opened the wooden blinds. Sunshine lit the entire room. I walked to the entryway and was surprised to find Keri talking with Rico Carrillo. Two big men stood behind him in the hall. I recognized one of them as a detective from his team.

"Did you leave your parents' home last night?" asked Rico.

"No," said Keri.

"What about Johnson Sagebrush? Have you seen him?"

"Not since last night."

"What about you, Joe? Seen Sagebrush today?" He hurried through his questions, not bothering with the soft approach he'd used with Sophie earlier.

"No," I said, "he's probably still in his room."

I looked at Keri, her forehead pulled down in worry.

"He's not in his room," said Rico. "Did he call?"

"No," I said.

Rico stared at me; his shoulders and neck were tense. "I don't think he's in the hotel."

"What's happening?" said Keri, an edge of panic entering her voice. "Where do you think he is?"

"I can't say."

"Has he been hurt?" said Keri.

"We don't know much at this point." Rico spoke sharply, and then handed Keri his card. "If you hear from Mr. Sagebrush please call this number immediately." Without another word he turned to leave.

As he stepped out the door I looked at Keri again. Her right hand clutched her left arm at the elbow. "What the fuck?" she said.

"Hang on," I said.

I caught the door from closing and stepped out. Rico had walked a couple steps.

"Hey, wait a second. What's going on?"

He half turned, his colleagues a couple steps ahead of him. "I can't share details. You know that."

"Rico, these people are going to freak out."

He stepped toward me, inside my personal space. The sectoral heterochromia had grown to cover half his iris. He spoke low so his colleagues couldn't hear.

"You know I'm not supposed to tell you anything, but hey, we're friends, and you said you wanted to help. Sagebrush called Slater's cell number at two thirty this morning; then he used his key card to enter his own room a half hour later. Now all his belongings are gone from the room."

"Damn." Sagebrush was gone. What an odd time for him to leave, unless . . . "You think he's involved in Bryan's murder."

Rico's lip twitched. He kept his voice low. "The motherfucker was *right here* in the room with us, and I let him slip away." But Rico was a professional; he might lose his cool for a second in front of me, but he wouldn't show that side to his team. He stood straight and spoke in a normal voice. "One of my guys is going through the hotel video now. We'll learn a lot more this morning."

"Why would he come back here if he murdered Slater?"

He shrugged. "I don't know. One possibility is that he wanted more time. If he skipped last night we'd have spent the last five hours looking for him."

"Yeah. Time to get away." I tried to think. Something nagged at me. I struggled to extract the thought before Rico left.

"I have to get to work. If anything comes up let me know." He turned to go.

"The money," I said.

"What?"

"Johnson said Sophie's money had been returned, but maybe it hasn't. Maybe Johnson and Bryan scammed Sophie and then had a falling-out. Maybe Johnson lied when he said the money had been returned."

Rico turned back to face me again and reached in his shirt pocket for a package of gum. He jammed a piece in his mouth but didn't offer me any, chewing as he thought. "Okay. We'll check that, too."

CHAPTER 11

BACK AT THE CONDO the first thing I did was check Sophie's account balance at Bank of America. Sure enough, the two million had been returned on Wednesday and then transferred to the Schwab account on Thursday.

Sophie had hired me to investigate a potential fraud. With the investment unwound and Sophie's money safely returned I had to conclude there was no fraud. My engagement was complete, except for the security cover.

But if Johnson murdered Bryan Slater, he did it for a reason. Money? Not from the Second Chance investment. Another reason perhaps?

The thought that kept nagging me while I showered, got dressed, and made breakfast, was the strangeness of the money trail: the account in Houston, the Texas company formed by Bryan Slater, and Toby Wycliff's purported lack of knowledge of Sophie's investment.

What if Johnson and Bryan had planned to steal the money but something went wrong, something that caused them to unwind the scam?

Then a troubling thought hit me: What if *I* was the something that went wrong, my questions, or perhaps just my presence? What if someone told Bryan or Johnson that I was investigating? Bryan panics and sends the money back. Johnson gets mad at Bryan and kills him. Kills him? With a blunt instrument? It seemed an extreme reaction to a fraud gone wrong.

But what if Johnson had schemed to commit the fraud, learned of my investigation from someone else, and decided to unwind the fraud on his own? Then Bryan got suspicious because of my questions at Antone's and challenged Johnson. The conversation between them got out of control and Bryan was killed.

The speculations turned around and around and I got nowhere. Finally I gave up and took a second cup of coffee out to the balcony. Overcast skies kept the temperature in the high eighties. Sound-check noises came from the park a half mile away. The first bands would begin to play in thirty minutes.

I called Rose's cell phone.

"Hey Joey, what's up?" She spoke fast, her words bright. She and I had planned to share the kids' time at the festival, but given my temporary role on Sophie's security detail, Rose had agreed to take them full-time.

"Everyone all set?" I said.

"We're ready to boogie. Have you arranged what we talked about?"

"Not yet. Things have gotten hectic with Sophie Tyler's schedule."

I didn't want Rose to worry about Bryan Slater's murder. She had this perception, which I had somehow created during a couple of my previous engagements, that whenever trouble was afoot I couldn't resist getting involved. In this case Bryan Slater's murder might have nothing to do with my investigation. And even if it did the murderer would have no reason to care about me. But I could explain all those facts to Rose and she would still worry, so I didn't tell her any of it.

I had told her the day before that I would try to arrange for the girls and her to meet Sophie at the festival. If I could pull it off, my status with the girls, particularly Chandler, would rise to "hero". But now that I knew Sophie would walk the festival in disguise the prospects for a personal autograph session seemed remote.

"Tell you what," I said. "If I can make it happen I'll try to call you, but phone reception will suck at the park. Bring the girls to the food tent at five o'clock. If it seems appropriate I'll ask Sophie to come by for a few minutes."

"Okay. It's certainly worth trying."

After we hung up I got dressed in clothes suitable for the Texas heat: light shorts, a maroon quick-dry tee, sunglasses, a ball cap, and Merrell sandals with hiking soles.

I had already arranged to meet Sanjay on the way to the hotel.

* * *

"I NEED YOUR ADVICE with Mandi," Sanjay said.

I steered the Jeep out of his complex and turned onto South Lamar toward town.

Sanjay grew up in Hyderabad, India, but had studied and worked in the States for more than a decade. He was six feet, skinny, with thick black hair combed roughly left to right. He wore glasses, khaki shorts, and a royal blue polo shirt.

We had known each other for years and had worked together on half a dozen projects. We shared common interests: outdoor activities, enjoying a beer or glass of wine with a good meal, and a strong preference for conclusions based on logic rather than intuition. We had discussed our families in great detail. I met his brother when he visited from Seattle, and Sanjay joined me on outings with Chandler and Callie.

Although a brilliant engineer, Sanjay often spent hours without talking, observing the world in silence, analyzing the data. He once told me, after several many beers, that he suspected he would remain a bachelor forever. He had said the words with a quiet acceptance, his tone attempting to mask an ocean of disappointment. I had protested his statement at the time ("Never say never. It could happen any day.") and certainly hoped he was wrong, but secretly, I had thought he might be right.

Then one day he showed up at a sports bar with Mandi, a tiny but energetic Texan. They made a most unlikely couple, nearly a foot different in height and polar opposites in cultural background, but Sanjay had blossomed under Mandi's care. She possessed a gift of spontaneity that overcame his analytical tendencies and forced him to have more fun.

During their time together Sanjay had undergone a marvelous transformation: he was more relaxed, smiled frequently, and even tried his hand at telling jokes. He had little experience with women, and in the early days of their relationship, he often called me with minor questions, afraid that he'd do something wrong. Since then he had grown confident, but on rare occasions he still asked for my advice.

"Okay, what's the issue?" I said.

"She wants to have kids."

"Oh."

Sanjay didn't believe people should have children. He had studied the global-warming debate carefully and concluded that the only long-term solution was a dramatic decline in human population.

"I've laid out all the facts," he said, "proved to her the problems of overconsumption. She smiles and nods and says, 'But they're so cute. How can you not want kids?' I don't know what to do."

He slumped in the seat with downcast eyes. Even his normally well-groomed mustache looked droopy.

What could I tell him? I would sooner live without the sun than without Chandler and Callie, but children weren't for everyone.

"Logic won't bail you out this time," I said.

Sanjay stared at his hands in his lap.

The air conditioner struggled against the heat, so I turned it up another notch, making my own small contribution to global warming.

"Some women," I said, "and some men, too, feel an overwhelming need to procreate. They're driven by instinct—the instinct to bequeath their DNA to the future. You just can't change their minds."

Sanjay shook his head at that, but he had no response. He sat silent in his seat for the rest of the drive into town. I wished for better advice to help him grapple with the question, but no wiser words came. Every couple had to make that decision for themselves.

I drove the Jeep up the Four Seasons driveway and under the portico. A young woman with short cutoff jeans and black jackboots waited next to the drive. She had black lips, a nose piercing, and pink hair. Two valet attendants stood to the side. The tall one poked the other in the ribs and tilted his head toward the girl. They both laughed, and the short one came to my window.

"Are you staying at the Four Seasons?"

"No, I'm picking someone up."

"Very good, sir."

Adrian had given me a two-way radio kit with wireless headsets. The festival crowds would jam cell phone signals, so we needed the radio for short-range communication. While we waited, Sanjay and I sorted out how they worked. We had just finished when the girl in the cutoffs opened the Jeep door.

"Hey, man, can you give me a ride to ACL?" Her voice squeaked as she leaned her head in the Jeep. Her face looked unwell, pale, like a vampire. An arrow protruded from her nose piercing, and skulls hung from her ears. Her eyes were hidden behind sunglasses with bright red frames, but the high cheekbones looked familiar, and I sensed something else about her, a vibe, or perhaps an attitude, an informal invitation for me to get to know her.

But I ignored that sensation and said, "Sorry. I'm waiting for someone."

"Are you sure?" The squeaky sound was gone, replaced by a velvety voice I recognized. I leaned closer. The air seemed lighter. She smiled.

"That's excellent," I said. "Just excellent. Sanjay, meet Sophie Tyler."

"Nice to make your acquaintance," she said.

He shook her hand weakly.

"I . . . uh . . . I . . . you . . ."

Sanjay rarely stumbled for words. He froze, staring at the punk girl before us, a woman he knew was a rock star, a celebrity.

"Sanjay," I said. "Climb in the back."

He scrambled. Once he was situated, Sophie sat in the front passenger seat.

At first I couldn't look away. She wore a black short-sleeved tee with blink-182 on the back. When she sat the short shorts rode higher, showing miles of bare leg. I swallowed hard. Her skin was pale all over, as if it had never seen the sun.

"Keri's good with makeup," she said. "I think she could do it professionally if she applied herself."

"How did she do that to your skin?"

"It's all about the foundation. You can't use the cheap stuff. Once that's blended in she layers on a colorless loose powder. I'm good for two hours of walking around. After that you'd better find me some shade, or I'll melt like icing on a cake."

I watched her lips move and then focused on the white perfection of her neck. I heard the words *melt like icing on a cake* and tried to imagine how they applied to Sophie, then I realized that several moments of silence had transpired.

"Where's Keri?" I said.

"I told her not to come. She can spend the day with her family. Anyway, fans recognize Keri, so she would blow my disguise." She turned and pushed my shoulder. "*You* will be my handler today. None of my fans will recognize you." She laughed. "By the way, thanks for staying last night. It gave me comfort to know a friend was nearby."

"It was nothing."

I had risen to the status of "friend". I sat up straight. She grinned at me, and I felt myself grinning back at her. Something tugged at the back of my mind. Oh, right, the murder, and the money.

"Any word from Johnson?" I asked.

"No—and it's very strange. One of Lieutenant Carrillo's men came by to check on us. The police seem to believe Johnson may know something about Bryan's murder."

"Has he gone missing before?"

"No, he's reliable. Keri and I talked about it. At first we thought a mugger or thief must have killed Bryan, but Johnson disappearing at the same time is so strange. They must be connected somehow."

I put the Jeep in gear and pulled out.

"By the way," she said. "I love the color of your Jeep."

Sanjay leaned forward between the seats and said in a loud tone, "It's marigold."

Sophie wiggled her eyebrows and offered a bemused smile.

"I promise," I said. "He's normally an intelligent person."

We made it a hundred yards before stopping at the light at Cesar Chavez, where I stole another look at her. I sensed everything from three feet away: her smell, her voice, her arms, and the thousand tiny gestures she made.

I stared too long.

"What?" she said.

"Nothing. It's your makeup. I can't stop looking at it."

She gave me a knowing smile that said she didn't mind.

* * *

We parked at the condo and walked on a dirt path along the MoPac bypass to a point where a VIP cart could pick us up. The air was hot and sticky. Long blades of wild grass waved gently on both sides of the path. Sophie held her hands out to skim the tops of the grass while I gave her an update on the fraud investigation.

"So there's no problem," she said.

"I still want to talk to the bookkeeper. I can't understand why they set up the account in Houston or how the bookkeeper got word to refund the money."

"But the money's back in my account?"

"Yes."

"Good. That's the important thing."

Yes, that was important; however, there was also Johnson's disappearance, which reeked of guilt. But he had worked for Sophie for ten years, and I didn't want to badmouth him without proof. Rico would have solid facts soon.

About halfway to the park Sophie stopped on the path and took off her sunglasses. Reaching up, she removed mine as well and looked into my eyes, concentration on her face, as if she struggled with a decision.

I turned to face her directly, my heart pumping warmth to my torso and limbs. I almost touched her arm but resisted; instead I focused on her blue-green irises.

What was she thinking? She seemed on the verge of asking a question, but then she changed her mind, put the words to the side. After a few moments she gave me a quick nod.

"Is everything okay?" I asked.

In the makeup she looked young, early twenties.

"I'm not sure. Everything's gone weird on me: Bryan's murder, Johnson's disappearance. I feel adrift."

Sanjay walked ahead of us. He noticed we'd stopped, so he stopped. Sophie stood still and kept looking at me, like perhaps I had some sort of answer.

"Maybe the music will help," I offered, puzzled now, not sure what to say.

She smiled at that. "It always does."

At the VIP entrance, Sophie chatted with a promoter's assistant while Adrian scanned Sanjay and me from head to toe; then he looked at Sophie. "Okay, here's what we're going to do. In that disguise Sophie fits in with the Austin crowd. On the other hand, I do not."

With his super-short hair, muscular chest and arms, creased shorts, and tucked in polo, Adrian still looked like a security professional.

"If I walk next to Sophie it will attract attention," he said. "We'll look like the Odd Couple. Joe, you walk with Sophie and stay close at all times. I'll keep a distance of about ten yards, and Sanjay will rotate counterclockwise from farther out."

Sanjay and I nodded. I resisted the temptation to smile. I had just pulled the long straw, my blind-squirrel moment for the year.

"And keep a close eye out for a big, baldheaded white guy," said Adrian.

"You think Johnson might come here?" I said.

"No, but it bothers me that he's gone missing, so watch for him just in case."

"Big like overweight?" asked Sanjay. "Or big like tall and strong?"

"He has a few extra pounds but plenty of muscle. About six feet, broad shoulders, and barrel-chested."

When we first entered the festival grounds Sanjay observed us from too short a distance; then he over-adjusted and lost sight of

Sophie, but he soon learned to balance the extremes. After a half hour he became nearly invisible; I had to actively search the crowd to find him, but I knew he was there, because the reports kept coming in.

"Nothing exciting up front," he said. Five minutes later he'd moved around us. "Clear in the back."

Adrian had a gift for the work, moving naturally. I often lost track of him, but he was never far away.

As we walked, I swung my arms and took long relaxed strides. Part of my job was to relay Sophie's wishes to the rest of the team.

"Sophie wants to see Tupelo Train at the Austin Ventures stage."

"Confirmed," said Sanjay. "Moving left now."

The festival occupied fifty acres of Zilker Park. The grass was brown and dry and smashed flat, the crowd trampling what the summer had not yet burned away. Fifty thousand fans listened to music or strolled between the eight stages and the dozens of bar booths. Everyone seemed to smile.

At the Austin Ventures stage a couple thousand people waited for Tupelo Train to play. Some stood, while others sat in chairs or on the ground. We stayed at the outer edge of the crowd. I had brought a blanket and spread it out.

Sophie sat comfortably, her long, pale legs crossed, one jackboot resting on top of the other. She seemed content to people-watch from behind the sunglasses.

A half dozen fifty-somethings passed a marijuana cigarette among themselves, and the pungent odor drifted over, hanging in the air. A roadie came onstage to tune the guitars. The stage was a hundred and fifty feet from us. I watched the crowd constantly but casually, at ease with my assignment.

Tupelo Train came on and launched into a funky cover of Little Feat's "Dixie Chicken." Sophie smiled and leaned toward me. "Nobody will ever top Lowell George's vocals on that song, but Penelope gives it a great run." Sophie moved her head to the beat while lightly tapping her thighs. She pointed to the bass player as if to cue him for his solo.

I surveyed the crowd again. No one paid us the slightest attention. Several of the pot smokers stood and began to boogie.

Sophie's eyes sparkled as she watched them.

"You like music, don't you?" she said.

"Yes, I always have."

"You bop your head." She laughed, teasing me.

"Do I?"

"Come. Dance with me."

I stretched my legs and stood, then reached for her hand. "There's nothing I'd like better, but Adrian would have a heart attack. You go ahead."

She stood and danced in place, moving her upper body and arms. I stood beside her in a wide stance, swaying slightly to the music, focused on surveillance. Occasionally I succumbed to the urge to glance at her.

After *Dixie Chicken*, Tupelo Train played original songs, a blend of Southern rock and blues. Penelope Lane made the group special. She belted tunes to get the crowd moving and then slowed the pace to stir their hearts.

"She reminds me of me fifteen years ago," Sophie said. "Back then I could drink and smoke and hit all the notes at will. These days I can get the job done, but it takes a lot more preparation."

She said the words wistfully, not complaining, but aware of the age difference, aware that the peak had come and gone. Her smile grew strained, but she kept dancing, and from where I stood, on her left and a foot behind her, Sophie appeared immortal.

"Bald guy coming in from the right," said Sanjay over the radio.

Adrenaline coursed through me. My muscles tensed, and I turned to look.

After two seconds' delay Adrian responded. "I'm coming."

"I don't see him," I said.

"What's the matter?" said Sophie.

"Maybe nothing."

"He's fat," said Sanjay, "wearing a yellow shirt and drinking a can of beer."

Then I saw him, facing away from me, with sweat stains under his arms and Che Guevara on his back. His neck was too thick to be Sagebrush. I took a deep breath.

"Not him," said Adrian. "But good spot. Keep it up."

Sophie stepped close and touched my arm. "What was it?"

"Nothing. Sanjay saw someone who looked a little like Johnson."

Sophie turned her head in that direction. "Johnson? Here?"

"No . . . it wasn't him."

"Why is Sanjay looking for Johnson?"

"It's just a precaution."

"You think Johnson might be at the festival?"

Sophie's voice had pitched up. I scanned the nearby people and saw that a man and woman had stopped listening to look at us. The woman nudged the man and said something. If we stayed a moment longer someone might recognize her, so I reached for the blanket.

Ten minutes later we stood under live oaks at a corner of the festival grounds and drank ice-cold sodas. Sanjay and Adrian stayed at a distance. Sophie drank half the soda and then sat on the ground and hugged herself. I sat next to her and watched closely. She turned to me, her chin trembling.

"You think Johnson killed Bryan, don't you? You think they had some sort of fight . . . something to do with me."

She rocked in place and shook her head.

I wasn't sure how to respond. My first impression of Johnson—the business manager who served raspberry hibiscus tea—didn't square with the image of Bryan Slater lying with his skull crushed. I had few facts and couldn't see the point in sharing random conjecture with Sophie.

"The police will find him soon," I said. "And we'll know the truth."

"Jesus Christ. What the fuck is happening?" She started to lose it then, little sobs that shook her shoulders. She crunched forward into her knees, trying to get smaller. I reached for her shoulder and pulled her to me, let her lean hard into my chest.

Adrian stood fifty feet away. He took a deep breath and shook his head.

"Can you get us some tissues or something?" I asked over the radio.

"Sanjay, you do that," said Adrian. "I'll stay here."

She cried softly for a short while and then settled against me, not moving. I rubbed her back.

Sanjay returned a few minutes later with a handful of napkins.

Sophie's body grew hot against me and she sat straight, her eyes wide. Tears had formed rivulets in the makeup. She blew her nose and then pulled a mirror from a pocket and dabbed at her face.

"What do you want to do next?" I said, squeezing her shoulder. "Do you want to sit here awhile longer?"

She pushed off the ground to stand. "No, I'm ready. I had my cry."

"You sure?" I stood next to her.

She made strong eye contact and gave me a quick nod. "Yes. Let's check out some more acts."

I marveled at her strength. She continued to push through the tragedy of Bryan's murder and the mystery of Johnson's disappearance. Occasionally the turmoil won, as it had with the crying jag, but she would not collapse in the face of crisis.

I pulled out the festival schedule and we looked at it together, her shoulder brushing against mine. She pointed out a few bands she'd like to see. We roughed out an itinerary and walked toward the main stage at the east end of the park.

"Could you do me a favor?" I said. "My kids are coming later. They'd love to meet you."

"Absolutely. I'd like that. How old are they?"

"Chandler's twelve, and Callie's ten."

"What fun." She gave me a thumbs-up sign. "I need to do something fun."

"It will mean the world to them."

After that we strolled the festival with Adrian and Sanjay as our lookouts. At five o'clock we walked under the tent next to the food court. Adrian and Sanjay stayed outside, making slow circles around the tent.

Large picnic tables arranged in rows provided seating for several hundred. I spotted Rose and Chandler and Callie. They ate tacos and chips and drank from water bottles. Despite the heat, I felt wide awake and energized. This was a big deal for Chandler and Callie; they had never met anyone famous.

Rose saw me approach and her eyebrows squished together. Her eyes narrowed.

I leaned to whisper in her ear, "Don't let your mouth drop, but the woman next to me is Sophie Tyler."

"No way."

"Yes." I took a deep breath, stood straight, and turned to Sophie. "You sit next to Rose." I hurried around the end of the table to sit between the girls.

Callie leaned over to ask, "Who is that woman?"

I spoke in her ear. "That's Sophie Tyler. She's in disguise." I quickly repeated the message to Chandler.

The girls sat frozen, staring at the pink-haired woman before them.

"This is Rose," I said by way of introduction, "and this is Chandler and Callie."

"It's a pleasure to meet you all," said Sophie. "Sorry for the disguise, but if I remove this wig, autograph seekers will interrupt us. I don't mind them, but sometimes it's nice to listen to music without having to talk to fans."

"Thank you *so* much for meeting us," said Rose. "The girls love your music."

The man on Sophie's other side looked at her and tilted his head to one side. He sat just out of earshot of our conversation. I stared at him until he saw me and turned away.

"It's great to meet young music lovers like you," said Sophie, looking directly at each of the girls in turn. "I'm afraid most of my fans are aging with me. We're all going out of style."

"I love *Hill Country Siren*," said Chandler, her voice bubbly. "The whole album's great. I listen to it over and over."

"Thank you, Chandler. It's nice of you to say that."

Callie remained silent and held the inside of my arm. She nestled against me.

Sophie removed her sunglasses to reveal her eyes. She smiled so that her teeth showed, which made her face recognizable. "What about you, Callie? Are you enjoying the festival?"

Callie sat straight and let go of my arm. "Oh, yes. We've already seen three bands. The best was Tupelo Train."

"We saw them also."

"Later we'll see Roseanne Cash. She plays country mostly, but Mommy says we should listen to all kinds of music."

"Your mother is a smart woman."

Rose sat with hands in her lap, her shoulders back, and looked at Sophie with steady eyes. "One of the great things about the festival is the broad variety of musical acts." Chandler and Callie relaxed, along with Rose, and the four of them discussed other acts they'd seen.

I felt like running a victory lap around the picnic table, but instead I divided my time between listening to the conversation and watching people around us. I hadn't forgotten Adrian's warning about mob scenes. After ten minutes I reached across the table for the sunglasses. "Here, put these back on."

"Do I have to?" Sophie complained.

"Yes."

"All right. You girls are lucky to have such a nice father. He's been taking care of me." She reached across the table to put her hand on mine and then rubbed her fingers back and forth twice. "I don't know what I would have done without him."

My pulse bounced at the feel of Sophie's touch, but at the same time my stomach twisted. I glanced at Rose.

"We know," said Callie. "He's the best daddy in the world."

Rose studied Sophie's hand, looked at me, and rubbed her forehead. I wanted to tell her, *Don't rush to any conclusions. That touch doesn't mean a thing. Sophie touches everyone. She uses it as a form of communication.* But of course I couldn't say any of that.

Rose's expression changed into a smirk, as if to say, *Wow, really?* I clenched my jaw and pulled my hand back from Sophie.

"There's a man out here with a miniature camera," said Sanjay in my earpiece. "He's circled the tent twice. I think he may have spotted her."

"That's it," said Adrian. "Get her out of there."

"We'd better go," I said to Sophie.

"Can you sign my festival map?" said Chandler. She held the map over the table.

"Honey, that's going to attract a lot of attention," I said.

But Sophie had already reached for it. "Of course I can."

"Mine, too," said Callie.

I was the only one with a pen. As Sophie signed the maps the man next to her looked again. I stared him away but could tell he sensed something out of place.

Before we left Sophie shook Rose's hand and leaned to speak in her ear. She touched Rose on the elbow, and as Sophie stood up, Rose smiled.

What on earth did Sophie say?

As I stood to leave Rose walked to my side. She gave me a peck on the cheek and whispered in my ear, "Thanks for arranging this. It means a lot to Chandler."

All was good with the world. I had earned my "hero" status, if only for a day, thanks in large part to Sophie's charm.

"Which way should we leave the tent?" I asked over the radio.

"Away from the food booths," said Sanjay. "The camera guy's waiting in line for tacos."

"Where to now?" I asked Sophie, as we exited the tent.

"Let's check out Riot On."

I gave the others instructions and turned back to Sophie. "What did you say to Rose?"

She looped her arm around mine and leaned against me for a few steps. "That was a conversation between women, not to be revealed."

Her arm held mine close, and we fell into a graceful rhythm. I tried to notice everything. Her hip nudged against mine at certain points in her stride. Her voice caressed me. I could taste her words, and smell them, and feel them.

Riot On, the angry rapper, brought me back to reality. The crowd extended two hundred feet from the stage, leaving no room for chairs or blankets.

"The cameraman is back," said Sanjay. "He's on your left. He just took a picture of you two."

I flexed my fingers, looked left, and stepped away from Sophie.

"I see him," said Adrian. "I'm moving toward him."

I said to Sophie, "You've drawn the attention of someone with a camera."

"Shit. That sucks," she said in a flat tone. She shook her head. "Won't be long now. I've tried to stonewall them before, but I can't stomach lying to a fan."

"A woman just said something to the cameraman," said Adrian. "He's shaking his head. Now he's pointing his camera again."

I turned my shoulders, trying to spot the cameraman.

"Don't look," she said. "It will only make the photos more sensational."

"The woman is walking toward you now," said Adrian.

"Damn," I said through my teeth.

"She's almost to you," said Adrian. "Sanjay, move in closer. I'll join Joe at Sophie's side so we can move her quickly."

"Excuse me. Aren't you Sophie Tyler?" asked the woman.

I stepped in, hoping to cut her off, but two others were only yards away.

Sophie shrugged and made a face to me, as if to say, *See?* Then she turned to the fan. "Yes. I'm incognito today."

The woman was in her midthirties and rail-thin. She wore a forest-green tank top. "Would you sign this for me?" She held a hand fan from a vendor.

"Of course."

"Camera dude is still taking pictures," said Sanjay. "A man just tapped him on the shoulder. Another woman hears them talking. They're both headed your way."

"You're Sophie Tyler, aren't you?" asked a man I hadn't seen approach.

"Yes." She reached for the paper the man held and signed it with a strong hand. She said to me in a low tone, "Hold my arm to guide me away. I'll sign as we go."

Adrian walked on her other side, his size creating some breathing room. I pulled her gently, smiling at the increasing fan base around her. Within a minute they were two deep. She signed as fast as she could. People nudged against me, eager to get close. I pushed back a bit but kept smiling. What a nightmare. Dozens of people pressed us from all sides. Someone elbowed me. Adrian's mob had descended.

Sophie greeted every fan. "Thank you. You're too kind. See you at the show tomorrow."

A man stepped forward. "There's a rumor on the Web that Bryan Slater was murdered last night. Is that true?"

Everything stopped. Sophie looked at him. Her lips turned down and began to tremble. She dropped the pen.

"Sorry, folks," Adrian said. "Sophie has to leave. Thank you."

He pulled her hard with no consideration for fans. I stayed close on her other side. A few of them tried to keep up, including the one who asked the question about Bryan, but we didn't say anything more. After a couple hundred feet we were alone again, and Adrian slowed our pace.

She walked with slumped shoulders and said to me in a low voice, "Can you get me out of here?"

"Yes."

Her eyes were dull. "I don't want to be here anymore. I don't want to be anywhere."

At the VIP entrance the four of us came together briefly. Sophie faced Adrian and said in a deadpan voice, "Joe is taking me to his place to cool off."

Adrian's eyes shot open. I stopped breathing. Adrian shuffled back a step. He opened his mouth to say something and then closed it. On the second try he said to me, "Can . . . can you get her back to the hotel safely?"

What else could he say? He provided a service at Sophie's request. She was the rock star, the boss.

My mouth had gone dry. I licked my lips and said, "Yes. Absolutely."

"Okay. We'll get a VIP cart to take you to the edge of the park. I'll head to town to see if Rico needs more help with L.A."

I turned to Sanjay, "Do you want a ride somewhere?"

He gave me a quick smile and shook his head. "No, thanks. Mandi's here at the festival. I'll try to find her."

* * *

RIDING IN THE BACK OF the golf cart I mentally ticked off the list of essentials for guests: Neat condo? Check. Fridge stocked with drinks? Check. Clean towels in the guest bath? Check.

Sophie sat next to me, relaxed, quiet. But why did she invite herself over?

A plausible explanation, considering the crazy events of the day, was that Sophie wanted an hour off the grid, away from her personal assistant and her agent and the public relations folks.

And I was happy to provide sanctuary.

CHAPTER 12

Sweat poured down my back.

During the hot walk back to the condo my energy waned, and Sophie wilted, with the pink wig sagging and the makeup melting. Once inside the condo I invited her to use the guest bath to freshen up. I showered in the master and then took a Diet Coke out to the balcony.

As I walked past the guest room I heard the shower. I imagined the water running from her face, over her breasts, past her waist, and down her bronzed legs to her feet, carrying the white powder to the drain.

On the balcony I relaxed in a chair, my pulse settling, and tried to think of something other than the image of a naked Sophie. A punk band's music floated over from Zilker Park, nearly drowning the calls from a mourning dove in a nearby tree. The pool and patio below were empty.

After a couple minutes my cell phone rang.

"Johnson Sagebrush doesn't exist," said Rico.

"What's that?" I sat up straight, my heart racing again.

"At least he didn't exist before 1993. Sagebrush received no wages under his social security number before he worked for Sophie Tyler.

There's no previous address with that name in the L.A. area, no phone number."

I closed my eyes and tried to think. The words echoed through my head—*Johnson Sagebrush doesn't exist.* No wages. No address. A man from nowhere bashed Bryan Slater's skull.

"What else do you know about him?" said Rico.

"Not much. As Sophie's agent he makes ten percent of everything she earns, so last year he made about a hundred and eighty thousand. He's worked as her manager for ten years and lives in the guesthouse of her mansion."

"The IRS income also shows interest from a Wells Fargo account in Houston. The account is with the same branch as the Second Chances account. He and Slater must have schemed to commit the fraud and then had a falling-out."

"But they didn't commit the fraud. The money is back in Sophie's account."

"Go figure. I tried to freeze Johnson's account in Houston but needed a court order, and by the time I had it in hand, he had already transferred his balance to an account in Belize. That's why he stalled last night. He went to Houston to visit his bank."

I had to respect Johnson's resourcefulness. He murdered Bryan Slater, went back to the Four Seasons for the initial police interview, and then drove to Houston to arrive at his bank when they opened.

"How much did he have in the account?" I said.

"Four hundred thousand dollars. Also, another five hundred and sixty thousand was transferred from a bank in L.A. through the Wells Fargo account and on to Belize. The reigning theory here is that Mr. Sagebrush is about to disappear."

"But who is he?"

"We don't know. The L.A. police did some local work for us and found a phone registered in his name for an apartment in 1992. The complex is close to the bad section of Sunset Boulevard. The police out there will show Johnson's picture around, but eleven years is a lifetime in that neighborhood."

I wanted to review my investigation with the benefit of Rico's new information, but Sophie's nearby presence distracted me. I looked through the balcony door to the condo interior. What would she wear? Would she put the sweaty shorts and shirt back on? I forced myself to focus on the phone conversation.

"We ran into a hassle at the festival today," I said. "Apparently the news of Slater's murder has made the Internet."

"Yeah, we can't keep a high-profile murder a secret for long. We've notified Slater's family and will issue a statement soon."

Sophie appeared in the doorway wrapped in a towel.

My breathing stopped.

Her hair curled inside of a second towel on top of her head. My eyes scanned her carefully, capturing every inch. Her skin had a healthy glow, a warm welcome from the pale disguise. Drops of water clung to her calves. I imagined her without the towel, and my face grew warm. Would she notice? She leaned casually against the doorframe. I inhaled slowly and pressed the mute button on my phone.

"Can I rummage through your stuff for something to wear?"

"Rummage away."

She turned and walked toward the master bedroom.

"Any thoughts on the money?" asked Rico. "The four hundred in the account or the stash he moved from L.A.?"

My mind was clouded by the image of Sophie walking away. I had to mentally replay Rico's words to formulate an answer. "The L.A. cash could be his savings. Sophie paid him ten percent for a decade with free room and board. He could have saved a lot of money."

"Any other ideas?" Rico said.

"Let's see . . . Do you know when he opened the account in Houston?"

"Nineteen ninety-one."

"So he opens an account in Houston in 'ninety-one. He lives in an apartment in Hollywood in 'ninety-two, and starts working for Sophie in 'ninety-three. Let me think about it. I'll call you with anything new."

After Rico hung up I wondered again if my investigation had prompted Johnson to change his behavior? After managing Sophie's affairs for ten years, he killed her ex-boyfriend and disappeared. A normal person would never do those things, but Johnson wasn't normal. He didn't exist until 1991.

Sophie walked onto the balcony. She had combed her hair and wore a burgundy polo shirt that hung halfway down her thighs. Rose had bought me that shirt, but I tried to erase that thought so I could focus on present company.

"Would you like something to drink?" I asked. "Diet Coke? Water?"

"Do you have anything stronger?"

* * *

SOPHIE SIPPED WINE WHILE I gave her the update from Rico. She refused to believe that Johnson had killed Bryan Slater.

"Do the police have proof of that?" she said. "An eyewitness or video or something?"

"Not that I know of."

"I don't believe it. Why would he murder Bryan? Over money? It's absurd to even think that."

She came up with several hypotheses about who else could have murdered Bryan: thieves, drug dealers, even the girls he'd met at the bar. Her theories struck me as far-fetched, wishful thinking, but I let her carry on because that was what she wanted. She didn't want to believe her manager was a murderer.

"What did Johnson do before he started working for you?"

"Gosh. It's been so long I can't . . . I think he was a manager somewhere." She sat back in the chair, crossed her arms, and ran a finger under her chin. Her eyes stared through the trees as if focused on nothing, as if she used her mind to search through the past.

"I remember now," she said. "My previous manager initially brought Johnson on as an assistant; my manager wanted to reduce his workload before retiring. We gradually transitioned more work to Johnson, and he did such a good job that within a year he had taken on the whole gig."

"Did you run a background check?"

"No, I didn't. He sort of grew into the role, and he's good at it. He makes everything proceed without friction."

"Ever meet his family?"

"No. Johnson had no family."

"What about old friends?"

She shook her head. "He kept to himself outside of work. He took little time off, the odd day once in a while, and he vacationed in Mexico a few times a year."

A man from nowhere starts as a gopher to a rock star and grows that into the fulltime job. There had to be more history, but apparently Sophie knew nothing of it. What a chilling thought: she had lived with an imposter in her guesthouse, a man with homicidal potential, for ten years. But she had not yet accepted that possibility, and Johnson was probably maneuvering his way to Belize. I suspected she would never see him again.

We chatted about the festival for a while and the conversation hit a lull. I still wanted to steer Sophie from the cruise-ship path, so I told her I had financial recommendations if she'd care to hear them. For the next few minutes she listened carefully.

"So I can't afford to keep the house," she said. She studied me over the top of the glass of chardonnay.

"I advise you to sell it as soon as you can. You earn plenty, but the mansion consumes all you earn and then some."

Sophie sat in the patio chair with her legs crossed, the hem of the polo shirt in her lap. Her toenails were painted bluish-green to match her eyes. She nibbled the corner of her lip.

"I've known for years that the house was expensive but thought more hard work would earn me enough to keep it. It's a relief, actually, to know I should move out. Now I can look forward to the next thing."

"Do you have a plan for the next thing?"

"I think I'll move back to Austin."

"Move back here?" I said the words too fast and *here* sounded higher, as if I'd lost control of my voice, but she didn't appear to notice.

"Yes. Keri wants to be with her family, and the idea is growing on me as well. I've gotten so wrapped up in the L.A. scene—the clothes, the parties, and the stuff—but none of it makes me happy. I was happiest here in the early days, struggling to get gigs, living on nothing."

I didn't say a word, my mind wrestling with the possibilities.

"A fresh start," she said. "While I play the local clubs, Keri can spend time with her folks. It would reduce the pressure to maintain this image—I'm not sure how it became my image. It crept up on me in small steps across the years. I don't even like it."

Sophie leaned back and stretched her arms above her head. The move pulled the cotton mesh tight across her breasts. The shirt never looked that good on me. If she had been Alyssa, I would have suggested we retire to the bedroom to explore her hidden treasures.

But Sophie lived in a different world, in L.A, among the elite of global entertainers. She operated on a level far above me. To imagine us as a couple smacked of reaching, of a boy dreaming he'd become a football star or president. Then again, if she moved to Austin, downsized her living arrangements, and spent her time in approachable settings, then maybe . . .

"I love your condo," she said.

"It meets my needs."

She walked to the balcony rail to take in the view of downtown and then looked at the pool and the clubhouse. "All these live oaks," she said. "I've lived in L.A. a long time. I've enjoyed it, but still, when I come back to Austin it feels like home."

I stood and stepped toward her, a little lightheaded. My hand touched the railing.

"Do you drive into the hill country often?" she said.

"Sometimes. To take the kids camping or on some other adventure."

"I'd like to do that. Go someplace where time slows down, a place like Krause Springs. Do you know it?"

"I've heard of it but never been. Out Highway Seventy-one?"

"That's it. My daddy took us there for a picnic when we were kids. We swam in the natural pools." She looked off to the side, and her eyes brightened. "And then later, in high school, we'd skip class and drive out to sunbathe on the rocks. I haven't had that much fun in a long time."

She stood two feet from me, with wet hair, smiling at the recollection of a fond memory. I wanted to take Sophie to Krause Springs myself. We'd have lunch under the trees, and I'd hold her weight in the pool and watch her laugh as I threatened to dunk her.

Our hands held the rail six inches apart. Sophie's index finger reached over and traced a light circle on the back of my hand, tickling the fine hairs. I turned toward her as her face lifted, lips moist and full, and leaned close to kiss her, a slow kiss. She moaned softly in the deep part of her throat. I put my hand to her hip and pulled her closer. I felt the small of her back. The front of her leg touched the hem of my shorts.

Her cell phone rang inside the condo, but her lips lingered with mine. I opened my eyes to see her looking at me, searching.

"Your phone's ringing," I said.

She touched the side of my face. "Joe Robbins, where did you come from?"

"You've been out of circulation for an hour."

"Okay," she said with a note of frustration, "I'll get it." She walked into the main room. As she crossed through the doorway she flipped the shirttail to give me a peep shot of her bare ass.

She picked up her cell, still laughing. "Hi . . . Uh-huh. What's that?" She held the phone to the side and whispered, "Keri."

I took the glasses to the sink, my nerves still jittery.

"Christ," she said, "what a pain. Read it to me."

I guessed that the news of Bryan Slater's death had reached the press. Sophie had the ability to switch gears quickly, going from a frivolous gesture to a business discussion in mere seconds. She wasted no time on transitions. I'd known others who possessed that strength, but not many, and only highly successful people.

"No," she said, "don't say 'devastated'. That's too much. 'Distraught' is better. The rest is fine." She turned to me, covered the phone with her hand, and said in a low voice, "They need a statement." She turned back to Keri. "That's good." She walked into the guest room, out of earshot for a couple minutes, and then returned, the phone still at her ear. "Yeah, we were just leaving." She listened a few more moments. "I'm at Joe's condo . . . yep . . . no, no, no. I had to get out of that makeup. It was so hot and icky. Yep . . . yep . . . be there soon. Promise. Love you, too."

Love you, too.

For the first time I wondered whether Keri was more than a personal assistant and friend.

* * *

As we drove on MoPac across Town Lake I wrestled with whether to ask a question, then finally plunged ahead. "It's not really my business, but I'll ask anyway. . . ."

Sophie wore one of my ball caps, her sunglasses, the cutoffs and T-shirt.

"What's that?"

"Are you and Keri . . . uh . . ."

She looked at me with a puzzled expression. "Lovers?" She burst out laughing. "You thought we were lovers?"

"No. I didn't really know what—"

"Keri's not a lesbian. We love each other, no question. No two women could live as we have for twenty years without loving each other, but our love is platonic."

"Does she have relationships with men?"

Sophie tilted her head in a noncommittal way. "Yes . . . sort of . . . some. She's had boyfriends, off and on, but they never seem to last. I think she would say, with some justification, that I have sabotaged her love life. I need Keri. I need her close by, and I think she needs me, too."

If Sophie hadn't been a celebrity I would have asked to see her again right there in the Jeep. But I hesitated.

No. A momentary flirtation had occurred and nothing more. With the fraud investigation complete my brief encounter with fame neared its end. After Sophie's festival show she would return to her world, and I would return to mine.

As we approached the Four Seasons I turned right on Brazos Street a block short of the hotel. Adrian would meet us there so he could escort Sophie via the back way, out of sight of the media. I pulled to a stop and saw him climb toward us on the steps from the lake. Sophie reached for my hand and squeezed.

I squeezed back. Her hand felt small and soft, but also strong.

She said, "You're coming to the show tomorrow, aren't you?"

"Of course. I'm part of your security detail."

"And afterward I'll have a small party at the suite. I want you to come."

"Let's see how things go. Don't feel any obligation."

She looked at me strangely, as if she had no idea what I meant. "Promise me something. Promise you'll take me to Krause Springs someday."

"I'd like that very much."

Very much indeed. Sophie in a simple brown bikini, stretched out beside the springs, the sun warming her skin, no fans, just the two of us out for a day together.

We got out of the Jeep as Adrian reached the top of the stairs. He scanned the cars around us.

Before leaving Sophie looked at me again. "I know what you're thinking. You're saying to yourself, 'After tomorrow, she'll be off to L.A. and I'll never see her again.' But you're wrong." She leaned to kiss me on the cheek. "I'm getting used to having you around, and I don't want it to end now."

Well, I'll be damned.

I didn't say anything for fear of breaking the spell.

Two walkers arrived at the top of the stairs and stopped. One of them stared at Sophie and whispered to the other. Adrian glanced at them and frowned.

"We need to go," he said.

"I'll see you tomorrow," said Sophie.

I watched her descend the stairs, focused on the short cutoffs, and felt a surge of desire. And apparently, at least on some level, the feeling was mutual. Hope sprang forth, but hope for what exactly? A one-night stand? Sophie never committed long-term.

But neither did I, at least not for the last three years.

CHAPTER 13

On my way back to the condo I stopped for a Cobb salad at Panera Bread. The weakened sun cast shadows across the nearly empty parking lot. I carried my dinner to a table on the outside patio and marveled at the light traffic. It was as if the festival had sucked all human life into Zilker Park, draining the nearby areas.

As I ate my cell phone rang, an unknown 512 number.

"Hello."

"Hello, Joe."

Jesus.

"Johnson . . ."

He chuckled.

My stomach roiled as I recalled the sight of Bryan's smashed skull lying flat against the pavement.

"How did you get my number?" I said.

"From Sophie's contact list. I watched as you two swapped numbers on the patio."

"Did you kill Bryan Slater?"

He said nothing for a few moments, but I could hear his breathing. "How's your family?"

A tingle began at the top of my scalp and crawled behind my ears.

"I saw you today with the girls," he said. "Was that your wife? You seemed a little distant. I thought perhaps she was your *ex-wife*."

I shifted in the chair. My right hand balled into a fist.

"Sophie looked hideous in that getup," he said, "but I gather it worked."

"What do you want?"

"Just a chat. Everyone says divorce is tough on children, but a bad parent is worse, much worse if you ask me. So many parents abuse their children, sometimes mentally, sometimes physically, and often both at the same time. My father taught me a lot, but he never took me to a music festival. He never took me anywhere."

Throughout his creepy speech Johnson's voice stayed calm, moderating slightly to provide emphasis at certain points, as if he engaged in a debate. What did he hope to gain from talking with me?

"You should turn yourself in," I said. "A lot of angry police are after you. You may be killed."

"'People do what they want to do.' My father taught me that lesson a thousand times. Most people deny that simple truth. They don't see it. The powerless blame those in charge for everything bad in their lives, when, in fact, the powerless would take the same actions if they could. You're smart, Joe. I know we see things the same way."

If not for his recognizable voice I would have sworn he was someone other than Johnson Sagebrush; a potion had transformed Dr. Jekyll into Mr. Hyde.

"People try to disguise their weakness with fabricated moral codes," he said. "Righteous men condemn adultery between a married man and his mistress, but the truth is they would screw the same woman if the woman would screw them. My father taught me all about fabricated moral codes. He raped my mother frequently, and without mercy, because he knew he could. She never complained to anyone, so he was right."

Hairs raised on my neck. I spoke with a mad dog that must be captured or put down. "You need help," I said. "We can get you help."

A scrawny female grackle walked across the sidewalk to pick at crumbs beneath my table. I moved my foot, and she flew to the next table over.

"Yeah," he said. "People do what they want to do. Like you, for instance, ransacking my computer for two hours the other night."

I sat stiff in the chair, my muscles rigid. He knew about my second visit to the mansion. He knew before he murdered Bryan.

"What did you hope to find?" he said. "Imagine my surprise when I reviewed the surveillance videos and saw Keri watch while you worked. And then you slipped out the back way to scale the wall. Very athletic."

"Sophie hired me," I said.

"No doubt. She's a clever bitch." He paused to take deep breaths. "I'm surprised the police haven't released my photo yet. They'll probably do that tonight, won't they? About time for me to get on down the road."

"What happened with Bryan? Did you two have an argument?"

"Bryan Slater." He said the name with disgust. "What an idiot. Can you believe she dated the guy?"

His tone told me he had murdered Slater. I should try to get something for Rico.

"Where are you?" I said.

"Speaking of Sophie, you'd better watch how she plays you."

"I don't know what you mean."

"Has she told you some things that sound good? Come up with a proposal about a change she'll make or some other offer? That's how she works, you know. She discovers a man's weaknesses and adapts herself to exploit them." He flung the accusations at her. "Don't believe her. Don't fall for it. Like everyone else, Sophie does what she wants to do."

"You have the wrong idea—"

"It disturbs me that she would set her sights on you. Disturbs me greatly. She's not the goddess you imagine."

I shook my head at no one. "There's nothing going on with Sophie and me."

"You're not one of those Hollywood types who deserves to be rolled in the dirt."

"I'm not following you at all."

"Talk to you soon."

He hung up.

I blinked three times and then breathed deeply to clear my head. Johnson had watched from outside the food tent as Sophie and I talked with Rose and Chandler and Callie. He had thwarted Adrian's security measures. My stomach hurt, and I pushed the remains of my salad away.

The grackle walked back to my table and lifted a bit of crust in her beak. She hurried to the side of the patio, out of harm's way, to enjoy her meal in peace.

He had called to probe me for information, but what did I have to give? And why did he warn me about Sophie?

I called Rico and gave him a summary of the conversation. He took the number Johnson had used and said he would call back. I drove the mile to the condo, got a glass of water, and waited.

"It was a pay phone," Rico said after I answered his call. "He was in north Austin on Rundberg Lane."

"That's miles from the festival. How do you think he's moving around?"

"Taxis maybe. He hasn't rented a car in the name of Johnson Sagebrush, that's for sure. We've checked all the clearing systems. Oh, and the bookkeeper was a dead end. His email was fake and the phone number from a disposable."

I walked to the balcony door and looked at the hummingbird feeder that hung on the left above the rail. The feeder was empty.

"You think he's mentally unstable?" said Rico.

"I got that impression, but he never grew angry. He maintained control throughout the conversation and made no demands. He merely explained his philosophy, or rather, his father's philosophy."

"Define the philosophy for me."

"People do what they want to do. There is no morality. Johnson doesn't believe in right and wrong, only action. He will take any action to meet his needs if he can get away with it."

"Why do you think he called you?"

I opened the balcony door and reached for the feeder. "He must have wanted something from me, but he didn't ask for anything."

"You think he was working you?"

"Maybe. But he was obviously at the festival today. Adrian told us to watch for him, but somehow we missed him. He saw us talking with Rose and the kids." I walked back inside the condo and put the phone on speaker so I could rinse out the feeder.

"This fucker is strange," said Rico. "For ten years he manages a celebrity's business and then he goes off the rails: murder, and now this odd phone call."

"I had the same thought. Have you seen guys like this before?"

"Worse. I've seen all kinds of strange. Do you think you're in danger? Could Sagebrush be after you? Or Sophie Tyler?"

Good question. I had felt creepy on the phone call, and Johnson was clearly dangerous. "Well, he said he would leave town."

"But he followed Sophie and he called you." Rico paused, as if thinking. "Okay, I've decided. I'm putting a trace on your phone."

"Wait a minute. You're going to listen to my calls?"

"No. We'll trace incoming calls. Send me a list of numbers that regularly call you so we'll know to ignore those. If Johnson phones you again, try to keep him talking."

"Okay. I can do that. How else can I help?"

Rico didn't answer me directly; instead he spoke as if thinking out loud. "What we need most is to figure out more about his past."

I repeated my question. "Anything I can do?"

"Oh, right." I heard a page turn as he consulted his notebook. "I do have a question for you. My guys went through the bank statements for Johnson's account in Houston. Two-and-a-half years ago, in early 2001, he received the four hundred thousand dollars that he moved to Belize this morning. Can you make any sense of that?"

I thought quietly, ran through all the data I had, and came up empty. "No. I have no idea."

"Maybe the FBI can help. They've expressed an interest. Murder combined with money moving offshore always gets their attention."

* * *

AFTER WE HUNG UP I poured a glass of wine and stepped out to the balcony. The music from two ACL bands converged as it sped through the woods to me, creating a jumbled mess of sound.

I closed my eyes to remember Johnson: bald, bright yellow shirt, and big smile. The call proved—at least to me—that the murder had something to do with my investigation. Someone had told him that Sophie hired me.

I ran through the list of candidates.

Keri? Sophie had shared my role with Keri from the start.

Halet Blevins? He knew I was more than a security guard because of the mistake I made with Gwen.

Or Sophie could have told Johnson by accident, let something slip in the normal course of conversation.

For that matter it could have been Adrian or Marco Ruffini, although they had initiated the investigation, so I pegged them as innocent.

Why had Johnson followed Sophie and me at the festival? Why had he called me? I could think of only one explanation: Johnson had something else to hide, something he was afraid I'd find out, and so he watched me.

Perhaps he hid something from his past, something that would help Rico catch him. Johnson's concern about me meant that I had a chance to discover what he hid, and I resolved then and there to do just that.

This was the point at which Rose would challenge my logic. She had once said, "You go to trouble like a moth to flame, Joey. Like a moth to flame." This was, in fact, the reason she'd chosen Dave Moreland over me, and I had accepted her decision, but we all had to be true to ourselves, to live our lives the best we could.

And I wasn't a rogue vigilante. I was only trying to help.

CHAPTER 14

"JOHNSON WAS THERE yesterday," I said. "You missed him."

"No," said Sanjay. "I didn't miss a bald guy."

We met at the VIP entrance on Barton Springs Road. Thousands of concertgoers passed us on their way to the main gate, their faces bright, rushing to get inside. A woman had to half trot to keep up with her male companion. He urged her to walk faster.

"Then how did he know I met my family in the food tent?"

"Maybe he wore a disguise."

Sanjay had a way of seeing through things, grasping the simple answer. If Sophie could wear a disguise so could Johnson. He smiled slightly, waiting for me to catch up.

"You're right. He could be wearing a hat."

"Or a wig."

"I doubt he'll come again today, but just to be careful we look for a beefy guy four inches shorter than me who is wearing a hat or wig."

"Or both."

The cloud cover persisted, keeping the air warm and sticky, but not scorching. We made our way inside and joined the fans walking toward the stage where Sophie would play.

A man walked near us carrying two folding chairs over his shoulders. His male companion had rainbow hair and smoked a cigar. Aging hippies played Frisbee as a banjo twanged from another stage. I spotted several uniformed policemen in circulation; they wore shorts, dark glasses, and sidearms.

I would be more diligent than the day before, scan every person, and find Johnson if he showed, disguise or no disguise.

Sophie arrived with her band an hour before her five o'clock show. Adrian had accompanied Sophie and stood on the left wing of the stage platform with the VIP guests. I watched from a stationary position a hundred feet in front of the stage, while Sanjay circulated through the crowd and reported in every five minutes.

Ten to twelve thousand people had gathered to hear her play. Guys in red shirts labeled SECURITY stood at the front of the stage.

To warm up the crowd the sound engineer played Sophie's early hits over the giant speakers. Her fans spanned all ages: young girls like Chandler and Callie, older couples, and everyone in between. Rose texted me to say they stood on the right side fifty feet from the stage. I replied that I'd try to find them after the show.

When Sophie walked onstage the crowd greeted her with whoops and whistles and applause. I stared at her for long seconds, the noise around me subsiding. She wore jeans and a light pink top, her hair combed straight and parted in the middle. The cheering continued as she bowed and waved. When the noise subsided she stepped to the microphone to thank the crowd and then quickly turned serious.

"A terrible thing happened two nights ago. . . . My close friend Bryan Slater was murdered." Her voice cracked as she shared the news.

A loud gasp came from the audience. I wanted to help but could think of nothing to do. She carried on.

"No matter how hard we try to make the world a better place, bad things still happen. One of the saddest parts of life is saying goodbye to the ones we love.

"The band talked about canceling today, but honestly, we knew that Bryan would want us to play. He was a showman . . . an actor . . . so we will go on with the show."

She began with "Wish I Could Say Hello", a song of longing for lost loves, for those who'd finished their time on earth. She sat alone on a stool and played acoustic guitar. The breeze pulled at her hair as she opened the song with an instrumental sequence; the crowd quieted and leaned forward.

Her words told the story of a lover killed in an accident, but the specifics didn't matter. The chorus spoke to everyone who'd lost someone they loved.

> Wish I could say hello
>
> Just to see you smile
>
> Watch you turn just so
>
> And stay a while . . .

I didn't know Bryan Slater, but I had lost loved ones along the way: my mother to cancer, my best friend to violence. My mother had a beautiful smile. My best friend had the biggest heart of anyone I ever knew.

She reached with her voice and lyrics to touch each soul and to help them through the pain. After the song she asked for a minute of silence. When the minute was finished the band joined her onstage, and they began a fast rendition of "Me and Bobby McGee".

"I see something strange here," said Sanjay.

"What?" asked Adrian.

"He's not Sagebrush. He's a white guy, tall, with blond hair and a hat. The funny thing is he has a walkie-talkie set like us, and he's watching Joe."

My eyes darted through the crowd, searching for a tall man in a hat. I saw dozens of them.

"At first I wasn't sure," said Sanjay, "but every time Joe moves, he moves. And he's talking with someone."

"Where?" I asked. "Where is he?"

"He's sixty feet behind you and to your right, standing next to a pirate flag. I'm fifty feet behind him."

"Joe, go check it out," said Adrian. "Sanjay, you stay put."

As I turned, my mind ran ahead. Perhaps Johnson hadn't come to the festival at all the day before. Maybe he'd hired someone else to watch Sophie. If we caught the watcher, he could lead us to Johnson.

Ten thousand music lovers sang along with the lyrics.

Rather than walking straight toward him, I weaved through the crowd at a diagonal to his left, hoping to get closer without spooking him. Dozens of portable flags and banners, rendezvous points for friends, flew above the crowd. I saw Texas flags, Homer Simpson, a red blowup doll, but no pirates. I pushed through a throng of women with small children.

"Hey, watch it, we've got kids here."

"Excuse me . . . sorry . . . on your left."

No pirates.

"What color is the flag?" I asked Sanjay.

"White . . . with a black skull and bones."

All the colors of the wheel decorated the airspace twenty feet up: orange, green, purple, light blue, even white. White with a dog, white with Lady Godiva, white with an ice-cream cone, white with a skull. There.

"I've got the pirate flag," I said. "Can you still see him?"

"Yes."

"I'm moving closer."

The skull and bones flew to my left and farther out from the stage. No pathways existed through the crowd. Progress required rapid decisions to move left or right, stepping on discarded cans, and rubbing shoulders with the inebriated. I kept an eye on the pirate flag.

"Where are you exactly?" I asked Sanjay.

"About twenty feet behind the pirate."

"Where is he?"

"He's directly to the left of the flag. He's been watching you move through the crowd."

I spotted him from the corner of my eye—definitely not Johnson: too tall, too thin. He looked toward the stage and wore a straw fedora with a black band. Blond hair curled from the back of the hat, and sunglasses hid his eyes. He had sharp facial features and good posture. Tanned arms protruded from the short white sleeves of his untucked shirt. I could just make out an earplug and the wire that curled inside his collar.

"I see him," I said.

"Joe," said Adrian. "Keep him in sight but don't get closer. I'm coming with two more guys."

Sophie's band had cut into a boogie song, and those around the man danced to the music. They wore tank tops and T-shirts and all varieties of shorts. They clapped and bumped and tapped their feet.

The man stayed in place. He stood flat-footed, large hands at his sides. Every so often he lifted his heels and stood on tiptoe and then came down again. The awkward move bore no resemblance to the rhythm of the song. I could look straight at the band and watch him through the corner of my sunglasses.

"On the way," said Adrian. "We're angling around the crowd from the right side of the stage."

I looked past the man to the far edge of the crowd but didn't see Adrian or any red-shirted big men. I decided to move farther back and turned to step around a couple holding hands.

She sipped red wine from a plastic cup and looked about forty. He smiled and raised his eyebrows. "You're going the wrong way."

"Take my spot."

Once behind them I turned. I stood taller than most of the fans and looked right to see Adrian walking at the edge of the crowd, the two security guys at his side. When I raised my hand to wave they saw me and moved into the crowd.

I cut my eyes left and saw the man looking at me, a weird smile on his face. He turned toward Adrian.

"He saw me looking at him," I said over the radio. Adrian and the security guys pressed through the crowd, still a good way off. When I looked back the man had moved. He walked directly toward the stage, shoving people out of his way.

"He's moving," I said. "I'm following."

My adrenaline kicked in as I jostled by the couple I'd just walked around. "Excuse me. I need to get through. Thanks." I breathed deeply, my nerves on edge, and moved to the next couple. "Sorry. Yep. Thank you."

I saw him. He pushed hard by two women. They glared as he passed.

"Pardon me. Thanks. I need to get closer."

"Hey, man, that's not cool."

"Asshole."

"Sorry."

He had gained five feet on me. How did he get through them so quickly? People stood closer together now. Sophie sang one of her fast-paced country-rock tunes.

"Asshole."

"Jerk."

I couldn't see his head clearly, only the straw fedora. Sophie stood a hundred feet from me. I waved my hands at her, trying to warn her. A thousand hands waved along. I grabbed a man's arm and shoved him to the side.

"Watch it, dude."

"I need to get through."

"Fuck you, man."

"It's an emergency."

The hat was gone. Where? I squeezed through the crowd in the same direction, struggling.

"Shit. Yeah. Someone stole my hat," a man complained to his girlfriend.

She watched the stage without listening to him.

"Where did he go?" I asked.

"I didn't see him. He just stole my hat."

"What does your hat look like?"

"It's a Longhorn cap."

"What color?"

"Black."

The man had switched hats. I pressed ahead, searching for a black cap. I moved through a bunch of teenage girls in skimpy clothes. There . . . a black cap.

I stepped between a blond-haired man on the left and a young woman in an orange T-shirt on the right. The watcher had blond hair, an important fact that slipped my mind, and as I stepped again a metal water bottle swung from the left and struck my forehead.

SSMUUNCK!!

Pain. Sharp pain. No vision. Knees gave out.

I fell onto a small man. He jerked out of the way, and I hit the ground.

I couldn't move. More pain. My ankle throbbed when someone stepped on it.

My vision returned. Legs were all around me, perpendicular to my line of sight. The tempo of the song was wrong, too slow. A woman in boots stepped on my hand, sending swirls of fire up my arm.

"Shit, what was that?" said the woman. "It's a person. Someone's on the ground. Stand back." She pushed at people around me, shouted at them. "Back up. Give him some space."

The crowd spread away from me. I touched my forehead. Blood covered my fingers. I looked up and saw the watcher making his way through the crowd.

"Christ. Look at that blood."

"What happened?"

"Watch out. Stand back now."

A man knelt and studied me with concerned eyes. He put his hand on my shoulder. "Are you okay? Can you stand up?"

CHAPTER 15

Two strangers half-carried me to the aid station. Once there, the attendants laid me on a portable bed. My eyelids kept closing, so heavy. Sophie sang in the distance, but I couldn't make out the song. As the nurse cleaned the cut I fell asleep.

When I woke up Keri Theroux was leaning against the bed studying her phone, while nearby the nurse attended a teenage boy with a flushed face. A different band played from another stage. My brain throbbed with each heartbeat, and I reached to feel a thick bandage on my forehead.

Keri wore yoga pants, lime-green running shoes, and a matching tank top. She frowned as she studied my face.

"Sophie," I said. "Is she all right?"

"She's fine. They finished playing twenty minutes ago. How do *you* feel?"

I raised my head and shoulders to lean on my elbows. "I have a hell of a headache." I touched the bandage again. "And my forehead feels like a scraped knee."

"Ouch." She picked at the sheet on the bed. "I'm sorry this happened. I bet you wish you'd never met any of us."

"I wouldn't say that."

"Sophie wanted to come, but I told her not to. It would have turned into a circus."

I looked around the tent, hoping to see Adrian or Sanjay, but only Keri had come.

"Did Adrian say what happened to the man we chased in the crowd?"

"He got away."

"Damn."

I lay back on the bed and rubbed my temples. We'd lost a good chance to find Johnson. Keri looked as bad as I felt, still picking the sheet, her back curved. She'd been nice enough to check on me. I should try harder to engage.

"Sophie put on a great show," I said. "What I saw of it."

"Her best show in years. She didn't want to stop playing, but ACL has a schedule to keep."

"Where is she now?"

"On the way back to the hotel. The band will party in the suite for a couple of hours, and then she'll kick them out so you two can be alone." She said it matter-of-factly, as if she were announcing the time for the evening news.

I sat up. "Excuse me?" The nurse had covered my legs with a sheet, but I felt warm, so I pulled the sheet away.

"I'm moving back to Austin. My parents are older, in their eighties; they need me here, and . . . it's time anyway." Her voice carried the weight of a final conclusion, as if she had considered the matter for a long time.

"I've been with Sophie for twenty years," she said wistfully. "I keep thinking that someday she'll settle down and I can get a life of my own, but if anything she's getting worse. The affair with Bryan . . . I mean, nice guy and all, but he was eighteen years her junior."

Keri's story seemed genuine, but I had to question the timing. Why decide to leave Sophie now, so soon after Bryan's murder? But I kept those doubts to myself.

"Maybe she *is* ready to settle down," I said. "She told me she might move back to Austin."

Keri shook her head. "She's talked that way a dozen times, but she'll never leave L.A." She looked outside the tent at the people walking by. The whites of her eyes were tinged with pink, and her lip quivered. "I hate concerts . . . so many fucking people." She wiped a tear with the back of her hand. "When we first met, Sophie was a beautiful princess, and her voice . . . a gift from heaven. I *knew* she'd be famous. We had nothing, but we spent all of our time together. She dated more than me, always, but the men didn't mean much to her. That was just sex. *We* were friends forever. I made a conscious decision, knowing full well that each year put me a year behind on my own life. It seemed unimportant . . . my life. But now . . . I can't do it anymore."

"I'm sorry."

She took a tissue from her back pocket and wiped her nose. "I read once that five years next to greatness is worth a lifetime of mediocrity. By that standard I'm way ahead, but sometimes I'm not so sure. Maybe being a housewife in the suburbs would have been just as good."

I had lingering suspicions toward Keri but couldn't resist giving her hand a little squeeze. She blew her nose, put the tissues away, and gave me a quick nod.

"Don't be too late for the after-party," she said. "You should get there around ten o'clock."

"Are you sure?"

"Oh, yes, I'm sure." She put her hand on my shoulder and managed a timid smile. "Don't you get it? It's your turn, buddy boy. It's your turn."

* * *

An hour later, just a few minutes after I arrived home from the festival, Rico Carrillo stood at my front door. He stared at my forehead. The black flaw in his left eye had swollen with anger to cover half of his iris. I got Diet Cokes from the fridge, and we sat at the kitchen table.

"How do you feel?" he said.

"Not that bad, a little embarrassed that he fooled me so easily. I make a lousy security guard."

He was dressed in his standard work uniform: khakis and a blue button-down shirt. I wore shorts and a festival T-shirt the aid station gave me because blood had soiled mine.

"Sanjay Kumar said the guy had an earpiece, that he was tailing you and talking to someone. Johnson?"

I shrugged. "I guess. Who else?"

"With the range of those radios he could have been miles away, nowhere near the park. Why would he hire someone to watch you?"

"I don't know. Maybe he wants to know what I'll do next. Maybe he's worried I'll figure out something else, something he wants to hide."

"Like what?"

"Maybe something from his past. Who he really is."

"How would you do that?" Rico squinted and pressed his lips together. "Do you know something I don't know?"

The only thing I knew that Rico didn't was that Sophie had invited me to her suite. Should I tell him?

He didn't wait for my answer. "You're done now, right?" he said. "The fraud investigation is finished. The security detail is finished." The question sounded more like a statement, like a coach lecturing a quarterback who tended to make up plays in the huddle.

"Well, she did invite me to the after-party."

"Hmpf. Figures."

I didn't want to take shit from Rico about my love life, so I changed the topic. "Have you made any progress on the investigation?"

He raised his eyebrows and nodded slightly. "Some. We still don't know who he is or where he comes from, but the LAPD found a woman at the apartment complex in Hollywood who recognized Sagebrush's picture. She said he ran high-end call girls in the early nineties. I sent a guy out this morning to work that lead."

"Spending precious money on this, aren't you?"

"Celebrity murders get special funding. The chief told me to do whatever was necessary."

After Rico left I tried to put myself in Johnson's place to guess at his next move, but I learned nothing from the exercise. He must have a reason for sticking around. Why? Why did he need to follow me?

CHAPTER 16

I NAPPED AND WOKE UP HUNGRY. It was nine fifteen.

While cleaning up I played one of Sophie's CDs with the volume high enough to hear in the bathroom. After showering I stood before the mirror to remove the bandage, humming along with the song. A red lump had grown on my forehead. The cut itself was small, considering the blood flow. The nurse had used two butterfly strips to pull it tight. I placed a new large bandage over the butterflies to keep the cut clean, and then pulled on jeans and a T-shirt.

I drove fast to the Four Seasons, taking the quick route on MoPac and Cesar Chavez. On the way I recalled listening to Sophie's music on my roof as a kid. If I could have, I would have sent a message back in time to that kid, the kid with few possessions but a head full of dreams, a message that told him one of his dreams would come true.

In the Four Seasons lobby a jazz trio kept the mood light, and lubricated guests crowded every table. As I hustled toward the elevators my eyes swept the room, and I recognized Halet Blevins at the bar. I slowed, my momentum toward Sophie interrupted by a new thought: Maybe I should ask Halet directly if he had told Johnson I was a CFO. Why not? Before I could consider the question he saw me and waved me over.

He wore a black silk shirt with the tail out, his long gray curls tucked behind his ears. He took a healthy sip of his drink and said, "I've wanted to ask you a question ever since Gwen Raleigh told me your real occupation: Why would a CFO pretend to be a security guard?"

I gave him the pitch that I took the gig as a lark. He smiled.

"Sounds like a load of crap. What's the real story?"

His cavalier attitude pissed me off. I stepped close so he could see my anger and spoke the words clearly. "Did you tell Johnson I was a CFO?"

"I should have mentioned you to Lieutenant Carrillo. I bet he'd write you down in his notebook."

It didn't surprise me that Rico had interviewed Halet. He would interview everyone.

"Did you tell Johnson?"

"No," he said. "But why does a CFO play security guard? Does it have to do with the bandage on your forehead?"

I couldn't tell whether to trust Halet. He held my gaze with steady eyes, his voice unwavering, but his lips formed a whimsical smile, as if he might be toying with me. Perhaps if I answered his question he would share some useful information. At that point I couldn't see the downside since Johnson already knew the truth.

"Sophie hired me to investigate a potential fraud."

His mouth dropped, and then he closed it and swallowed. After watching me for a few moments he said, "What sort of fraud?"

"Investment fraud."

The smile returned to his face.

"What?" I said.

"Nothing. I thought maybe Johnson was stealing from her. What did you find out?"

"There was no fraud."

Halet's smile grew wider. "No fraud, and yet Bryan Slater is dead, and Johnson is gone. Isn't that surprising?"

I still couldn't read Halet. As a talent agent he'd handled many negotiations. Whether he came by it naturally or developed it with experience I couldn't tell, but one thing I knew for sure: he had a great poker face.

"What do you know?" I asked.

"Plenty, but nothing about fraud against Sophie or this murder. I have problems enough of my own."

"What sort of problems?"

"No concern of yours."

I kept looking at him, trying to assess the truth. Meanwhile, he scouted the crowded room, his eyes landing on one table for a moment and then jumping to the next.

"Unless I'm mistaken," he said, not looking at me, "Sophie's waiting for you upstairs. She kicked us all out of her suite, and the rumor is she's found someone new."

I watched him for another minute, but he didn't say another word, and I walked away having gained little from the conversation. Before turning the corner to the elevators I looked back. His eyes had found something they liked. He listened to a cute blonde and her tall skinny girlfriend and then waved the bartender over.

I took the elevator to the seventh floor and found Adrian standing in front of the door to Sophie's suite, his arms folded across his chest, a sullen look on his face. His frown grew darker, his eyes cold. For a moment I entertained the wildest notion that Adrian was in cahoots with Johnson Sagebrush, that they had schemed to steal from Sophie, that something had gone wrong so one of them had to kill Bryan Slater, but an instant later I dismissed that theory as preposterous. Adrian had brought me into the deal.

"Everything okay?" I said.

He closed his eyes and held them closed for a long moment, as if trying to imagine something, and then I guessed at another motive for his sour mood. He'd had his chance with Sophie and turned her down, made the right decision, but maybe he had some regrets.

"She invited me to come," I said.

He took a deep breath, the sharp expression left his eyes, and he stepped out of the way. "I know. I'll take a break while you're here. Call me when you leave?"

"You bet."

I watched Adrian walk away and then knocked on Sophie's suite. She opened the door wearing a robe, her hair wet. My heart beat like it did when I lifted weights, fast and strong.

"Christ." She stepped close and reached to touch my forehead. "Does it hurt?"

"Not much. A dull throb. I took an Advil."

She stepped closer and pressed the robe against my belly, which sparked tingles of pleasure further down. The robe hung loose, the knot haphazardly fastened. I glanced to see the curve of her breast. She caressed my cheek. I tilted my head and her hand slid down my neck.

"Do you want something to eat or drink?" she said. "There's a feast here."

"Yes, please."

She fixed plates of food from the movable cart: lobster salad, thinly sliced beef, mangoes, grilled asparagus, and fresh bread. We ate on the balcony, candles on the table for two, iced champagne at the ready. I savored every bite: my teeth tearing into the beef with gusto; my mouth watering around the mango; my throat tickled by the champagne.

Sophie chattered on about the concert. I drank her looks and voice along with the sparkling wine. Yes, she was a rock star, but watching her, and listening to her, felt as natural as hiking through the woods.

"It takes me a while to wind down after a show," she said.

"I'll bet."

"Damn." With a confident smile she leaned back in the chair and pulled her hair behind her left ear. "We played so well today. If only it was always that good."

The air had cooled into the eighties, and the clouds had scattered to open the way for the stars. A few partygoers laughed on the ground-floor patio.

"I enjoyed what I saw. Nice tribute for Bryan."

"I felt like a hypocrite. Bryan came along when I needed someone to appreciate me. It was a fleeting affair between an aging woman and a young kid with a hard body. We both knew that."

She termed the affair with Bryan *fleeting,* but what about me? How would she describe whatever we were doing? I considered the question only briefly, then ignored it. We had only just begun.

I finished my glass of champagne and reached for the bottle. "More?"

"No, thanks. I had a couple drinks with the band earlier. Do you think that man who hit you today had anything to do with Johnson?"

"I think there's a good chance."

"Maybe it was unrelated. Could there have been someone else who wanted to hurt you?"

"It's possible."

She remained in denial about Johnson. I tried to put myself in her position. You had a trusted employee, a man who had worked for you for ten years, and then something went wrong and people told you that person was a thief and a murderer.

"I know you want to believe he's innocent," I said, "but truthfully, you don't know where he came from. What about your old manager? Could we ask him?"

She shook her head. "He died of a heart attack years ago."

How convenient for Johnson, another dead end.

She stood and walked to my side in her bare feet. "Do you think the paparazzi can see us here?"

A dividing wall separated our balcony from the next. Trees obscured the view of the water and Congress Avenue Bridge, but I could see the top floors of the Hyatt across the lake.

"Maybe."

"Take your time. Finish the food and champagne and meet me inside."

I finished the meal quickly, sipping wine between bites. I spread my hands on the tablecloth, smoothed it, my fingertips impatient.

When I entered the suite a few minutes later music played from hidden speakers; a woman sang a Nordic folk song, and a single candle lit the room. Sophie walked in from the bedroom carrying a second candle, her bathrobe untied. I glimpsed bare skin and pubic hair. She took my hand and led me back into the bedroom. She put the candle on the side table, turned to pull my hand inside the robe, and placed it on her bare breast. My thumb circled her nipple, warm and erect.

The robe fell from her arms and she stepped close to squeeze my back. My hands rested on the cheeks of her ass.

We swayed gently to the music, me fully clothed, her fully naked, her breasts against my chest, her face turned to the side. The music became part of the background, the candlelight surreal. I went through a strange transformation, out of the bright light of logic and into a world where mere money and possessions held no substance, a place where sound and light merged into one sensation, a deeper, subtler existence.

I lost sense of time and motion. In one moment we danced, and in the next I lay by Sophie, naked, our limbs entwined, her skin soft and moist, her curves and muscles perfectly proportioned, fitting seamlessly with mine.

Her lips caressed me, gently traversing my torso, my sides, and my upper thighs. She ignited a million nerve endings with her lips, softly, slowly, without aggression, as naturally as the music.

Our lovemaking ebbed and flowed like the natural rhythm of the moon and tides. At times we lay almost still, moving across each other like water flowing over glass, nearly one and the same. We grew more passionate, like mating animals, with thrusting hips, moans of pleasure, and shifting positions. We lost ourselves, she lying on her stomach with me on top of her, the sensation unbearably pleasant, my thighs pressed against her buttocks, my hands at her shoulders, her breath coming in short gasps.

Our lovemaking seemed to last forever. My mind slipped into and out of a state of alertness, my body at rest and then aroused again and then at rest again through the full hours of the night and on toward dawn. Finally my muscles relaxed, my bones settled, and I fell into a deep sleep.

I woke with the sun shining around the edges of the curtains. I lay on my side, pressed fully against Sophie's back and buttocks; her legs snuggled with the front of my thighs and shins. My arm curled over her torso, and my hand cradled the curve of her breast. Her diaphragm gently rose and fell as she breathed. I smelled her skin and touched my tongue to her shoulder, tasting her.

I lay like that for a long time, listening to her, wishing I could stay right there for days, knowing reality would soon interrupt our paradise. She moved her arm, and then she breathed more deeply and woke up. She reached to take my hand in hers. I backed away from her, allowing her to roll on her back and look at me. She smiled.

"I haven't slept that well in years," she said.

"I could watch you sleep forever."

"You get to see me in all my glory. Flabby tits . . ."

"Don't be silly." I reached to squeeze the left one. "Like a twenty-year-old."

"Fat belly."

My hand moved down her flat stomach to the top traces of pubic hair.

"Could have fooled me."

"Old-lady face."

"I'd like to kiss you all over."

Her cell phone buzzed from the next room. "That'll be Keri, or Adrian, telling me it's time."

"You're heading back to L.A." I tried not to sound disappointed. I'd known all along the night would end, but the end had come too soon.

"Yes. Keri and I must figure out my schedule. Johnson ran the whole thing."

"I'll get out of your way."

"Stay. Please stay . . . for breakfast, at least."

I let out a long slow breath. I'd stay for as long as she would have me.

We ordered room service and stepped into the walk-in shower together. We ran soapy washcloths across our bodies, familiarizing ourselves with elbows and clavicles and beauty marks and scars. My nerve endings rejoiced with every caress. We got carried away with our fondling and wound up on the bed again, half toweled off, taking sharp breaths, her legs aloft, hands on my backside, urging me to a quick finish.

Minutes later the room service arrived. I signed the check in hastily donned jeans and a shirt, while Sophie hummed brightly from the other room.

She sat across the table from me in the bathrobe again, buttering an English muffin. She smeared on marmalade and took a healthy bite. I ate scrambled eggs with link sausage and whole-wheat toast, and tried not to stare.

As the food filled my stomach my brain returned to the question of what Johnson feared I might discover. I had developed a hypothesis about the four hundred thousand dollars in his bank account, and I needed Sophie's help to gather test data.

"When we first met you told me you had lost money on a high-tech investment."

She nodded while chewing. Her tongue licked the corner of her mouth to grab a crumb.

"When did that happen?" I said.

She sipped her coffee and said in a flat voice, "Do we have to talk about that now?"

"Not if you don't want to." But in truth I *did* want to talk about the investment, and perhaps my tone of voice sent her that signal.

She gave me a half shrug. "In late 'ninety-nine I invested four million in an Austin-based software company. Everyone in Hollywood was making money in high-tech, everyone except me. I learned of this opportunity and jumped in.

"The company had grown in revenue from zero to eight million in three years. Nine months later they went bankrupt. I received forty-two thousand in liquidation proceeds."

I looked down at my plate. Four million was a lot to lose in a single investment, even for a rock star. With my game face on, I looked back at her, and tried to remove the sting from her loss. "You shouldn't feel too bad about that investment. A lot of people lost money the same way."

"Thank you, but I do feel bad about it, and stupid." She winced, as if wishing for a do-over on the decision.

"What else can you tell me about the company?"

"They called it Shareware. The software allowed friends to share documents, photos, and videos. The CEO planned to revolutionize how people interacted with one another. He had great vision but terrible timing. He said they needed only fifty million to reach profitability, but of course, when the Internet bubble burst no one would invest a dollar."

I had never heard of Shareware, but during the boom years technology companies came and went by the hundreds. So far her data was playing right into my hypothesis.

"How did you get introduced to the company?"

She cleared her throat. "That part is embarrassing." Her eyes watched her fingers as they fidgeted with her fork. "You know how they say you should never mix business with pleasure?"

"I've heard that."

"Well, I dated the CEO, Mark Cunningham. We met at a high-tech celebrity crossover party in early 1999." She swirled her head around and waved one hand in the air. "I got caught up in the whole thing: reinventing the world, new tech gadgetry, weekends in Vail. Mark was a visionary, but once he lost all the money the relationship fizzled. He couldn't look me in the eye."

"I see."

Sophie paused for a few moments, her head tilted to one side. "You seem a bit skeptical."

"Did you meet other investors?"

"Yes. Mark arranged the whole thing. He picked me up in San Jose and drove to the VC's office on Sand Hill Road. It was classy, subdued, with intellectuals in casual clothing."

"What about the actual company? Did you visit the office?"

She nodded again. "Mark took me there on a Friday. Forty geeky guys in cubicles in a trendy office: lots of computers, Nerf basketball, and beers in the fridge."

"Shareware."

"That's right. Are we finished discussing my crappy investments?"

"For now." I had heard enough to conclude that my hypothesis warranted further testing.

"Good, because I want to ask you something."

"What's that?"

"Will you be my manager?"

I leaned back to study Sophie's face, not sure whether she was joking. Images flashed before me: living among the palm trees of southern California, long walks on the beach with Sophie, business lunches at Spago. Her lips turned up in a smile.

"For a moment there I thought you were serious," I said.

"I'm perfectly serious." Her eyes held mine in a strong grasp. "You've got a good head for business."

"I know nothing about the music industry."

"You'll learn it. You're a good negotiator and I trust you."

"What about mixing business with pleasure?"

"Many couples work together in music."

Couples?

A one-night stand did not make a couple. Sophie had a relationship in mind, which sounded great, but we lived half a country apart and barely knew each other.

"Name one couple who works together in music," I said.

"Celine Dion and René Angélil."

I should have never given her that challenge; she had an advantage from living in the music world for two decades, but I had read something about a relationship that didn't work. "What about Mariah Carey and her manager? What's his name?"

"Tommy Mottola."

"What about them? That didn't work out."

"That's only one example."

"I don't know. . . ."

"Try it for a while. We'll take it slow . . . maybe the romance blossoms. Your business skills can rejuvenate my career." She leaned forward slightly, her arms on the table, closer to me. "I think you could really help me."

For a moment I thought she was trying to tell me something—that there was something she needed more than a personal manager—but after a few moments of silence she relaxed, and I knew my imagination had fooled me. First and foremost, she needed a manager. Given the requisite skills to do the job I would have risked mixing business with pleasure, but I knew she could find better candidates.

"The music sharks would eat me alive," I said.

She lifted her hands from the table with palms forward. "At least help me with the move to Austin. We could alternate weeks between here and there, a balance of both places. You'd have lots of time for Chandler and Callie."

What harm could that do? I could tidy Sophie's financial house, save her from the cruise-ship scenario. We'd have more time together. I liked the idea of being around her for hours a day. Even Warren Beatty went monogamous at some point. Maybe Sophie was ready to settle down.

"I'll think about it," I said.

She jumped up, a huge smile on her face. "Wonderful." She walked to where I sat. "Go home and pack a bag. You can fly with us today."

"No, not today. I've got a few things to do first."

She cradled my head in her hands and leaned to kiss my lips. "Then soon."

"Yes, soon."

CHAPTER 17

THE JEEP'S MARIGOLD COLOR captured my mood: carefree, brilliant, and alive. The leaves on the trees glowed an incandescent green. Sunlight glistened on Town Lake.

I tuned the radio to classic rock and listened to Fleetwood Mac. Stevie Nicks sang to me. Every note and lyric blended perfectly with the sights on the road. I cranked the A/C up and rolled the window down, wanting to feel a mixture of artificial coolness and natural breeze.

All my problems receded into the background. I lived in the moment, enjoyed the sensations of touch and sound and sight, and relished the Sophie afterglow.

Back at the condo I sat on the balcony to drink a Diet Coke and relive the night with Sophie. Of course, I couldn't recreate it, but I *could* remember it. But when I tried to remember the night of lovemaking I couldn't recall specific moments, only the feelings, the sensations, not the specific acts or order in which they occurred. The lovemaking in the morning felt more real. I could recall showering together, Sophie's hands on my torso, my growing excitement, the quick toweling off, and the half run to the bed. Those acts felt specific. Just thinking about them gave me a thrill. The overnight lovemaking session had lasted much longer; it stretched on for hours in a way I'd never experienced. I became a bit confused about what had actually happened. The only thing I knew for sure was that I wanted to do it again. I've never been addicted to drugs, but I imagined the lure felt something like that, a desire to re-create the initial experience, a desire so strong it became an overwhelming force. The analogy scared and excited me at the same time.

I went back farther in time to recall every interaction with Sophie since I'd first met her six days before. I replayed every conversation we'd had, tried to remember every time she'd touched my skin. I closed my eyes and watched a clip of her walking toward me the first time we met. I listened carefully and could hear her voice, her words. I tasted her lips on my lips, and could even smell her skin.

At some point I realized I had grown thirsty, and a little hungry, too. I checked my phone and learned, to my surprise, that I had thought about Sophie for three hours. It seemed like only a few minutes. Except for the thirst I would have happily stayed on the balcony and continued to think about her, tried to relive each moment with her again and again.

With some reluctance I went inside and fixed a sandwich. After eating I noticed a damp sensation on my back. While sitting on the balcony perspiration had soaked my shirt clean through. The temperature had climbed toward a hundred, the air breezeless on the balcony, and I hadn't noticed. I took two steps toward my sectional and almost sat down, realizing at the last moment that I intended to think about Sophie again. It took some effort to strip out of my clothes and take a cold shower.

Afterward I sat at my desk in the main room, a more business-oriented location. With my laptop before me I considered Sophie's investment in Shareware.

I began with two assumptions and their attendant streams of logic:

First, Johnson Sagebrush had conspired with someone else to defraud Sophie of her two-million-dollar investment in Second

Chance Productions. When I showed up the scheme was aborted and the money returned.

Second, this was not the first scheme Johnson had hatched to defraud Sophie of investment dollars. He had worked with the same coconspirator, and perhaps others, in 2001 to defraud Sophie of her investment in Shareware. Johnson's cut of that fraud was four hundred thousand dollars.

Conclusion: Johnson feared I would discover the Shareware scam.

I felt good about the first assumption. Something strange had happened with the money flows on the Second Chance investment. My conjecture about Shareware seemed a stretch, but two factors convinced me I should pursue the question further: First, the timing of Johnson's four-hundred-thousand-dollar deposit coincided with Sophie's losses. Second, a four-million-dollar investment in a software start-up was a big chunk of money. If a legitimate management team had run Shareware, they would have made the money last longer.

So I turned my attention to Shareware and Mark Cunningham.

My Internet search revealed no hits for a company named Shareware. I found SharePoint, Sharetime, Share-A-Fare, and even ShareTech, but no Shareware.

Next I tried Mark Cunningham. I found a journalist, a football coach, a fashion designer, and a mayor of a town in Vermont, but no CEOs in Austin, Texas.

I needed help from someone who knew the Austin high-tech market in 2000, so I called Sanjay.

"Hi, Joe. How's the head?"

"Only a little headache today, plus a lump."

"Sorry I abandoned you at the festival. Adrian wanted me close, and Keri promised to look in on you."

"Don't worry. It wasn't that bad."

I explained my theory that the investment in Shareware was a scam.

"I've never heard of Shareware," he said, "or Mark Cunningham, but there were a lot of start-ups in those days. It's possible I never came across them."

"Do me a favor and ping your contacts for anything on Mark Cunningham."

"A favor?"

"At the usual rates, of course."

"I'm on it. If he ever worked in Austin, I'll find him."

After the call with Sanjay I stepped out to the balcony. A cardinal sang from his perch in a nearby tree. The pool area was deserted. I inhaled the sunbaked air and felt the heat in my nostrils.

My cell phone rang, an unrecognized 512 number, just like the first time Johnson called. I hoped Rico's guys were paying attention.

"Hello?"

"How's your forehead?" said Johnson.

My hand clenched the phone.

"I have a lump the size of half a lime . . . thanks to you."

"I was afraid of that, but my guy had to smack you a good one to make you go down."

"Making excuses won't absolve you."

"No excuses. Only logic. As a finance type you understand logic. You wanted to catch him, and he didn't wish to be caught, therefore . . ."

My mind raced ahead. How could I best keep him talking? I took a deep breath and tried sitting down.

"Perfectly reasonable," I said. "Under the circumstances I might have done the same thing."

"You would have done *exactly* the same thing. But what is not reasonable is Sophie seducing you afterward."

I stood up again. How did he know I had been with Sophie? Had someone told him? Keri? Halet? Maybe he watched the Four Seasons.

"I'm not sure what you mean."

Johnson laughed a hearty laugh.

I looked at my hand as it closed in a fist. I pulled the fist toward my shoulder to flex my bicep.

"Let's not joke around," he said. "I lived with the woman for ten years. I know how she operates. You showed up bandaged and bruised, but instead of an after-party there's only Sophie, and she's half-naked. Am I close?"

"Not at all," I said.

How did he guess this stuff? It felt like he'd been in the suite with us. Had he bugged the room?

"That's what I thought," he said. "She's good. She's really good. I have to hand it to her: No one is more aggressive at getting what she wants than Sophie Tyler."

"What about you?" I asked. "What do you want?"

"Not that it affects me directly, but I want her to leave you alone. She is going to drag you down until you think of nothing else, not even your kids."

I couldn't get a handle on him. He bounced from topic to topic: Sophie, my family. My stomach tightened. I hated his talk about family.

"Why do you care about that?" I said.

"It bothers me. I told you about my dad. He was honest—I'll grant you that. He explained exactly how the world works, but it wasn't enough to save him in the end."

Something tickled the top of my foot. A huge centipede crawled toward my big toe. I swatted and missed. My second swipe brushed the bug to the concrete floor; it bounced and flew over the edge. I shook off the jitters.

"I take it your father is no longer living," I said.

"No."

"I'm sorry. How old was he when he died?"

"Forty-three. But that was a long time ago."

"How old are you?" I said.

"Why do you want to know that?" he snapped. "How could that possibly matter?"

I clenched the phone so tight it hurt my hand. I consciously relaxed my grip.

"Why are you following me?" I said.

"What makes you think I'm following you, because of the guy at the festival? You followed him . . . remember? Don't flatter yourself. I'm not following you."

Of course he was following me. I felt like arguing but didn't want to irritate him further. How long would it take for Rico's guys to get there?

"Let's go back to the question of what people want," he said. "Sophie wants you, at least for the moment. You want her, but you also love your kids. You'll have to choose between them."

"For the sake of argument," I said, "why is that an either/or choice?"

"Because she'll suck you in like a siren. You'll forget everything. You'll become addicted. She will starve your soul. The only food you crave will be Sophie: that voice, those words, her body, smell, and taste. When her arms and legs wrap around you and pull you in, she will hypnotize you. Every time you lunge inside her you'll become more addicted. And when she dumps you, like a dealer abandons a penniless junkie, you'll think of nothing else. Take my advice: Run from her. Run as fast as you can."

As he spoke I recalled the hours that passed like minutes. Something *had* happened to me, something I'd never experienced before. A door slammed on a nearby balcony, causing me to start. I clutched the railing.

"You're not a happy man," I said.

"You're wrong. I'm as happy as anyone else—more so, because I know the truth. I do what I want to do. So do you. So does Sophie. Every person does exactly what he or she wants to do. The difference is, I recognize that truth. I relish that truth. I don't hide from it, cowering under fabricated moral codes. I'm in the open . . . up front . . . with no disguises."

"No disguises? What about the name Johnson Sagebrush? That's false, isn't it?"

"I spoke metaphorically. You know what I meant. People are fake."

"You say you do exactly what you want, but why are you calling me? What do you want from me?"

"I want to be left alone."

"That may not be so easy with everything that's happened."

"You could do your part."

So he *was* concerned about me probing further. Johnson breathed into the phone like he had reached the top of a long flight of stairs. I pictured him with sweat beads on his bald head, smiling.

"I don't suppose," he said, "I could convince *you* to leave me alone."

"It's not me. The Austin police force is after you. You killed a marine. Half of those guys are veterans. They're after blood. The safest thing to do would be to turn yourself in."

A siren sounded in the background of the call, growing louder. Why would the police send a squad car?

"Are they coming for me?" he said. "What have you done? I just want to be left alone."

Damn the police. They might lose their chance to catch him.

I shook my head at no one and spoke in a rush. "You bastard. You've been stealing from Sophie for years. All along you plotted to steal from her."

"I'd love to have this debate now, but I'm short on time."

"Just because you want something doesn't make it right to steal."

"There's no such thing as right and wrong."

"Of course there is."

"Goodbye, Joe."

The line went dead, and I stared at the phone. A blaring siren? Idiots. I called Rico. All he said was, "Let me call you back."

As I paced the the condo, Johnson's vacuous chatter echoed in my brain:

There's no such thing as right and wrong.

CHAPTER 18

Rico wanted to compare notes in person. We surveyed the hills from the patio of the County Line BBQ on Bee Cave Road. Rico had an iced tea. I drank a Fireman's #4 draft. The sun set to the right, casting the patio into welcome shade. Rose would soon drop the girls off for dinner.

Rico told me the siren had been a coincidence. "Just bad luck, but it clearly scared him off."

"Where was Johnson?"

"A convenience store on First, just south of Ben White. The attendant recognized his photo. He thinks Johnson was in a white Toyota Camry."

To be honest, I didn't want to meet with Rico. I wanted to pack a bag and catch the next flight to Los Angeles. I had decided to run down the Shareware thing and then spend some time with Sophie.

"Are you listening?" said Rico.

"Yeah. Sure."

"My guy in L.A. found a prostitute who worked for Sagebrush in Hollywood. She said he went by the name Johnny and never had a last name. He was the nicest pimp she'd ever known, treated all his girls like royalty, never hit any of them, but he became ruthless with rude clients. She said a customer roughed her up once, and Johnson broke his arm."

"He clearly has violent tendencies."

"She said Johnson eventually traded up in clientele. He got off the street and into the high-end clubs, and eventually onto the A-list escort scene."

"Then what?"

"Then nothing. One day he disappeared. She never saw him again."

"Maybe that's when he began working for Sophie."

"That's our theory." Rico took a sip of his tea and glanced at the stunning view. He didn't appear to enjoy it. His face looked tense. "Tell me about the phone call."

"He wants me to leave him alone. He said that's why he called."

I left out the part about Johnson warning me to stay away from Sophie. Rico didn't know Sophie and I were lovers, and I didn't want to tell him, because I knew he'd tease me.

"Why does he think you need to leave him alone?"

"I don't know. He talked some more about his father. I got the feeling he might have killed him."

"Did he say that?"

"Not exactly. He said his father knew how the world worked, but it didn't save him in the end. He also said the guy died at the age of forty-three."

Rico sat straight and pulled out his notebook. "Okay. That's something to work with. We'll get back with Houston and look for unsolved murders of men in their early forties."

I looked into the restaurant and saw Rose and the girls threading their way toward us.

"Are we done?" I asked. "Rose is here."

Rico closed his notebook. "Yeah, we're done for now."

* * *

WE MET ROSE AND the girls at the hallway inside the patio door. They asked about my forehead and I made up a story, said I'd walked into a door in the middle of the night. Rico stayed long enough for a quick hello.

As soon as he left Callie tugged on my hand. "Daddy, come outside. Let's look at the view."

"You and Chandler go ahead. I need to talk with Mommy for a few minutes."

The girls rushed outside, and I turned to Rose, the pint glass still half-full in my hand.

"Like a drink?" I said. "We could sit at the bar."

She looked at her watch. "Dave's expecting me at six."

"The thing is . . . I need to tell you something. I'll make it quick."

We sat at the varnished bar off to one side of the main dining room. Rose ordered a glass of chardonnay. Diners waiting for open tables sat on bar stools and drank cocktails and draft beers.

Rose's wine arrived in less than a minute. She took a big sip and said, "So, what's up?"

I usually relaxed around Rose. We knew each other so well the words came easily, like falling asleep after a long day, but my mouth felt dry. I rubbed my hands down my pants legs and looked at the bar.

"Well, I'm going on a trip in a day or two. I might be gone a few weeks."

Rose frowned. "Really? Where are you going?"

I stopped rubbing my pants, took a breath, and looked at her. "California."

Her right eyebrow ticked up and then slowly fell to scrunch together with the left. "California?"

I nodded.

Her eyes narrowed, and she took another hasty sip of the wine. "Los Angeles?"

"I . . . Yes, Los Angeles."

"Sophie Tyler? Seriously?" She shook her head.

"I'm kind of feeling my way through this. Nothing's really happened yet."

"Oh, really? Nothing's happened?"

Her eyes seared mine, daring me to deny her accusations, and I had to look down. How did she know? Could she read me so easily after all this time?

"Damn it," she said. "I can't believe you."

I couldn't think of anything good to say. "What do you care?"

"What do I care?" Her voice rose higher.

A woman sitting on the other side of Rose glanced at me and then quickly turned away.

"Well, for one thing, this is going to confuse the girls. You just broke up with Alyssa."

"She broke up with me."

"Whatever. You're setting a bad example when you bounce from woman to woman."

"It just kind of happened."

"You idiot. It didn't just happen. She seduced you. She's a fucking—"

"That's not fair." I started to raise my voice, but then caught myself and tried to ratchet down the animosity. "Nothing is set in stone. We're taking it one step at a time."

Rose took two gulps in rapid succession. "Fine. That's fine. You want to get caught up in a Hollywood gossip story? Go ahead. Fine." She gulped again, the glass nearly empty now.

I loved Rose, and she was angry, but the conversation felt strange, as if I watched and listened to a dream. I should feel everything more acutely, react more quickly, but I couldn't spark my emotions any easier than I could run in the middle of a nightmare.

I said, "Wait a minute—"

"Go ahead." She set the glass down hard. "You want to fuck up your life with a has-been rock star? Great. I'm sure the kids will love it. 'Hey, Mommy, Daddy's shagging a singer who lives in Beverly Hills.'"

And then it occurred to me—the real reason for her anger. "You're jealous."

"No, I'm not jealous. I'm concerned about the girls. What are you going to do when they get all gaga about this, and she grows bored with you?"

"Yeah, you're jealous. I didn't see it before. You like watching me twist in the wind, strung out on you, playing the lackey around the house so I can see you on occasion. All the while you have the safe comfort of Dave's backing and the fat brokerage account with Morgan Stanley."

"Bullshit." Rose sat back and ran a shaky hand through her hair. She looked down, unable to hold my gaze.

I'd struck a nerve. I should have stopped. If Rose was jealous that meant she still had feelings for me, but now *I* was angry.

"Yeah," I said, "you like me coming by so we can eye each other over the kitchen counter and pretend we're still a young couple in love."

"No, damn it. I'm worried about the girls."

"The girls? Don't concern yourself. It'll be a thrill for them to see Hollywood."

Her lip quivered, and she bit down on the lower one. She brought the back of her hand up to brush away a tear. In an earlier time I would have reached for her, but now I saw her clearly. She had made the tough decisions to get what she wanted. But she sure didn't look happy.

"You don't have to be a shit, Joey." She stood fast, reached for her purse, and turned to leave. "Get the girls home by nine."

"Sure thing."

"Don't bother to come in."

"Wait."

She looked at me with disdain.

I hesitated.

"What is it?" she said.

"What did Sophie whisper to you at the festival?"

"Jesus . . ."

I immediately regretted asking the question. Sophie had said it was a secret. "You don't have to tell me."

Rose shook her head. "She said she knew I still loved you. Isn't that silly?"

As she walked out the nearby woman shot me a hateful look. I stared at her, not saying anything, my mind reliving the bitter exchange with Rose.

* * *

I GAVE MYSELF FIVE MINUTES to settle down and retrieved the girls from the patio. As they studied menus, I rewound the conversation with Rose. Maybe it wasn't as bad as it seemed at the time. What did she say? What did I say?

No, it was bad. We hadn't fought like that since before the divorce.

A kid waiter walked up. "Do you guys know what you'd like to order?" He gripped the order pad in his left hand, the pen poised in his right. He saw my face and took a step backward. "If you need a few more minutes I can come back."

I knew the menu practically by heart. I looked at the girls.

"I'm ready," said Chandler.

Callie concentrated on the page. "I can't decide between the brisket and the turkey."

Chandler clicked her fingernails on the tabletop and looked at the ceiling.

"You order one and I'll take the other," I said. "Then we can share."

"Okay," said Callie, smiling. "I want the Kids' Brisket Plate with lemonade."

Chandler and I placed our orders and the waiter left.

Focusing on the girls usually calmed me. Whenever I was stressed, hassled by the hectic pace of life, the girls' presence reminded me of what really mattered, and the other stuff settled down.

But I had to tell them of my pending trip to California and wasn't sure how that would go. I felt restless sitting and shifted my weight in the chair.

"Can we play the B.A.D. game?" said Callie, a sly smile on her face.

Chandler perked up. "Oh, yes. Let's play B.A.D."

"I don't think so, girls. We did that last week."

Callie giggled. "I really want to play the game."

"I *need* to play it," said Chandler. "You don't know what it's like, Dad. You really don't."

I shook my head, sensing danger. "Your mom would kill me."

While outwardly I showed the girls my disapproving face, secretly I wanted them to play the B.A.D. game, too.

"We won't tell," said Chandler. "We never tell."

Callie shook her head and pulled an invisible zipper across her lips.

"Okay."

Callie rocked up in her chair. "Yay!"

I looked at the tables around us. No one paid us any attention. A large group of kids and moms made a ruckus nearby. Two oversize men worked on plates piled high with ribs.

"Ten minutes only," I said. "That's it."

"Fine," said Chandler.

B.A.D. stood for Bitch About Dave. Starting a few weeks after the wedding, whenever I spent time with the girls, they invariably sprinkled the conversation with gripes about their new stepfather. I considered the griping unhealthy. Rose obviously had strong feelings for him, and even though it pained me to admit it, I believed she'd made a sound decision. In the areas of my shortcomings, an unsteady income and a penchant for trouble, Dave was pristine. He had no scars from bullet wounds, and on top of that he cared for Chandler and Callie.

I had told the girls they needed time to get used to Dave and asked that they stop complaining. That tactic backfired, because they immediately gave *me* the silent treatment, a torture I could not bear. As a compromise I invented the B.A.D. game. During an allotted period of time they could bitch all they wanted, but afterward they had to stop.

"Dave's too neat," said Chandler. "His sock drawer has an insert with separate compartments for each pair. He labels each compartment: 'black one, black two, brown one, running socks,' etc."

"Really?" I said.

"Dave can't cook on the grill," said Callie. "Mom has to grill the fish, and she burns it every time."

"Dave works too hard," said Chandler. "He comes home late almost every night, so we don't get to eat together; although I'd rather eat with you, anyway."

"Dave has never taken us camping," said Callie.

I viewed that complaint as a positive. I relished campouts with the girls and didn't want Dave to assume that role.

They went on like that for a while, offering up minor irritations that most women would happily tolerate in exchange for his strengths. At some point they veered into silly territory.

"Dave's ugly," said Chandler.

"Ding," I said. "Not true." I only allowed true statements during B.A.D. time. Three lies meant the game ended no matter how much time had passed.

"Okay," she said. "He's not ugly."

"Dave farts a lot," said Callie as she burst into laughter.

"Ding," I said. "One more ding and the game's over."

"Okay," said Callie, "but he curses all the time."

"He does not."

"Yes, he does," said Chandler. "He says the S-word at least twice a day."

Callie nodded her agreement.

Just then our hesitant waiter brought the food. The girls giggled as he sorted where to put the plates. I glared at them, which caused them to giggle all the more. I hardly ever cursed when around the girls. Rose slipped more than me, dropping the F-bomb on occasions when she burned a finger or did something similar. It would bother me if Dave cursed all the time, but I didn't believe the girls.

"I'm calling the third 'ding'. You girls are lying."

"He says, '*scheisse*'," said Callie.

"What?"

"*Scheisse*," repeated Chandler. "When any little thing goes wrong, he says '*scheisse*'."

Callie said, "It's German for—"

"I know what it means. Does Dave speak German?"

"No," said Chandler. "He took some in college."

"I'm not too worried about that."

Chandler shook her head. "It's a problem. A little *scheisse* here, a little *scheisse* there, next thing you know you've got a big pile of—"

"Knock it off. Eat your dinner."

The girls laughed again as they cut into the savory meat and dipped it in the tangy sauce. A little later in the meal the conversation drifted to Sophie. They reiterated how cool it was to meet her in person, and I mentioned that I planned to visit her.

"Are you still working for her?" said Chandler.

"Yes, sort of."

Callie put an unfinished rib on her plate and listened carefully. A smudge of sauce graced her cheek.

"I don't understand," said Chandler.

"Well, I am still doing a little work for her, but the real reason for going to Los Angeles is to get to know her better."

Callie's eyebrows furrowed. She had lifted a napkin to wipe her face but put it back in her lap unused.

"What does that mean . . . to get to know her better?" asked Chandler.

I hadn't planned to get into a big conversation about Sophie, but Chandler read clues as easily as a vampire novel. I needed to tread lightly.

"You know . . . to spend some time talking."

"Wait a minute," said Chandler. "You're dating Sophie Tyler?"

Callie adopted the concerned face of a much older girl. She looked at Chandler to gauge her reaction and then looked back at me.

"No. We're not dating, not yet."

"How long will you be gone?" said Chandler.

"I don't know. A week. Maybe two."

"Two weeks?" said Callie. "Why do you have to go for two weeks?"

"Nothing's definite yet. She might even come here."

"Here?" said Chandler. "Austin? Why would she come here? To see you?"

"She's thinking about spending more time in Austin. Look, don't freak out on me. Nothing's been decided. Eat your dinner."

The girls turned back to their food but a blue mood had settled over the table. I had no idea Chandler would react the way she did.

Callie took her cues from her sister. I had thought they'd be excited. Generally I could anticipate their reactions to news, but I had missed it, grown confused, momentarily out of touch with my own kids. How did that happen?

Gradually we began to talk again, and the conversation drifted to other topics. After the waiter had cleared the plates Callie left to visit the restroom.

Chandler stared at me without speaking. She fingered a bracelet I had given her as a birthday present.

"What is it?" I said.

"You're dating Sophie Tyler."

"I told you, nothing's—"

"I can tell when you hide things from us." Her chin trembled.

A heavy feeling entered my chest. The last thing I wanted to do was hurt Chandler. I switched chairs to be by her side.

"What's wrong?" I said.

She wiped her eyes with a cloth napkin. "I don't want to tell you." She shook her head. "You'll think it's stupid."

"No, I won't." I scooted the chair closer and put my arm around her shoulder.

She sniffled. "It's just . . . I always hoped that somehow, someday, you and Mommy would get back together."

"Oh."

Christ. What a bumbler I was. A catch grew in my throat as I recalled how many times I had hoped for the same thing.

She looked at me with glistening eyes. "Callie and I talk about it sometimes. We want it more than anything."

"I'm sorry, honey."

"But if you date Sophie Tyler I think you'll fall in love. You might get married."

I shook my head.

"And if that happens you'll never get back with Mom."

I held Chandler until she stopped sniffling. When she saw Callie returning from the restroom she stood to walk in that direction. My separation from Rose, and the subsequent divorce, had forced her to absorb emotional shocks, but she always tried to protect her younger sister.

After dropping them off, as I drove through the curvy hills west of Austin, I rehashed the conversations with Rose and Chandler. Then I thought about Sophie; her lips tasted of freshly picked fruit; her voice cooled the summer heat.

I loved Rose. I worshiped Chandler and Callie.

But Sophie pulled me like gravity. I considered driving to Beverly Hills right then, and if it hadn't been fourteen hundred miles, I might have done just that.

CHAPTER 19

Sanjay called a few minutes after I returned to the condo.

"Shareware exists, or at least it existed in 1998, and so did Mark Cunningham."

"Good. How did you find them?"

"I queried the Connection network."

Sanjay and I had both worked for Connection Software. During the high-tech boom the company had hired hundreds of brilliant engineers and moved them to Austin. When the stock market crashed most of the employees were let go, but many stayed in Austin. Three engineers had responded to Sanjay's query. Apparently, at the height of the boom, in early 1998, Cunningham had conducted a search for a VP of engineering for Shareware. Those three had interviewed with him face-to-face.

"Anyone I know?"

"Adam Preston, Jinwoo Hwang, and Janet Trask."

Faces popped into my head. "I remember them."

"I haven't spoken to them yet. I figured you'd want to do that, so I sent their contact information your way."

I walked onto the balcony, the phone at my ear. The setting sun had cooled the air into the high eighties. It was the last night of ACL, and R.E.M. played "Orange Crush" in the distance. Two loud couples partied down at the pool. One of the women laughed, a braying sound of unchecked hilarity.

"I've been contemplating your buddy's philosophy," said Sanjay. "Johnson's not that crazy when you think about it."

With his engineering mind Sanjay could analyze just about anything. He'd twist a subject this way and that to observe it from different perspectives, but sometimes he made simple issues too complicated.

"He's almost certainly a murderer," I said.

"True, but if you dial things back ten millennia, everyone behaved the same way."

"How would you know?"

"At that point in history a starving man would kill another man for a hot meal. Who would stop him?"

"The woman."

"She might try, but more than likely, after they finished dinner she would simply become the new guy's woman. Johnson argues that people today haven't changed: They still do what they want to do."

"Then where are the murderers and rapists and thieves? They should be everywhere."

"Go to Darfur. Anytime the fabric of societal control frays, the same thing happens: The strongest take whatever they want."

"This isn't Darfur. We have rules and laws, so no matter what the reason, if Johnson killed Slater, he has to pay the price."

Sanjay didn't answer. He'd taken Johnson's point of view purely for the intellectual fun, but Bryan Slater was dead and Johnson was still free, so I didn't feel like joining in.

"What are you going to do about Cunningham?" he said.

"I don't know. I need to think it through."

After Sanjay hung up I sat in a chair and listened as the couples continued their party downstairs. A splash sounded as someone jumped in the pool; a woman shrieked with joy.

I called Sophie to check in. They had just made it home from the airport.

"When are you coming to L.A?" she said. She didn't ask whether I would come. She made the assumption. "Tonight? You can still catch a late flight."

Her voice reminded me of an expensive cabernet, silky smooth. I could drink her voice. I walked to the wine fridge in the kitchen. The call with Sanjay had pulled me back into the search for Johnson, and then Sophie's voice pulled me westward. I considered her request that I rush to the airport, but the Shareware questions won the day.

"No. Not tonight. I have some things to do tomorrow."

A cabernet franc from Mendoza caught my eye. I retrieved the bottle and fumbled through a drawer for the wine opener. I put the phone on speaker to free my hands.

"You're looking for Cunningham, aren't you?" Her words formed a question, but her intonation made a statement, as if she knew the answer and didn't like it. "You think he conned me."

I didn't want to bring her into it yet. My conjectural theories demanded supporting facts, but she could save me time.

"Do you know how to reach him?" I asked.

"No. I haven't spoken to Mark in years."

"No problem." I dodged her last question by changing the subject. "Have you given any more thought to downsizing?"

"Yes, Keri and I have begun making a list. But I'm not sure I should move to Austin full-time. I love it there, but all my business contacts are here in L.A. What I thought we might do is rent a place in L.A. and divide our time between here and Austin."

We. Did she mean *we* as in Keri and Sophie, or Sophie and me? I closed my eyes and tried to recall the feel of her face nestled against my throat.

"The thing is," she said, "when I'm in Austin, Keri will stay with her folks. I wondered if I might stay with you."

Sophie was moving fast, but Chandler had shown me I must proceed with caution. Having Sophie stay at the condo sounded nice, but the girls visited often. I tried to sort through how all that would work.

"You've seen my condo," I said. "It's small."

"It's plenty big with you in it. You stay at my place out here, and I'll stay with you in Austin."

"That sounds logical. The thing is . . . with the kids and all—"

"Of course, of course. You have to do what works for the girls. I get that."

"Okay, you know, let's just—"

"Take it slow."

Sophie understood, her empathy a sixth sense, but my forward momentum had begun to slowly turn, like an aircraft carrier.

"Now will you *please* get your ass out here?" she said.

"Tomorrow. Next day at the latest."

"Hurry. Finish the work and come to me. Don't pack a bag. Don't shut the door. Come to me right away."

After she hung up I savored the buzz of our conversation—*Come to me right away*—for a few moments, but no longer.

The dream of being with Sophie, which I had always known deep down would never come to pass, now seemed within reach. Realization required only that I put everything else to the side: my girls, my love for Rose, and my desire to track down Johnson Sagebrush.

But I could never leave Chandler and Callie, not for any real length of time. I'd known that as soon as Chandler cried at the County Line BBQ. I'd go to California and spend a couple days with Sophie, maybe three, but then I'd come right back.

Neither could I abandon Bryan Slater. Rico had said the key was in Johnson's past. If I was clever and fast I might find something to help the investigation.

Johnson Sagebrush followed me for a reason. He wanted me to leave him alone, but he wouldn't leave me alone. Shareware had proven hard to find, and that fact alone convinced me I was on the right path.

* * *

In the morning I called Adam Preston and Jinwoo Hwang; they both gave me the same report: Cunningham had rented a few thousand square feet in an office building on south MoPac. The space was laid out in a typical start-up fashion, with twenty or so cubicles. They thought his idea for building a hosted file-sharing site was cool, but Cunningham didn't have his act together. He couldn't answer basic questions about funding, team size, and so on. After the interview they never heard from him again.

I tried Janet Trask but got her voicemail. I knew where she'd be.

* * *

Janet had left the software world two years before and bought a beat-up car wash on South First. The car wash occupied a corner lot about a half-acre in size, and had a side-street entrance with signage directing drivers to the hand-wash station on the left, the drive-through up the middle, and the self-serve area around the back. A small store with a cashier resided next to the drive-through. Customers could sit outside at picnic tables under a large tree and wait for their cars to be ready.

I found Janet working the post-drive-thru station. She and three others hovered around a Lexus, buffing and checking for anything the machine washer missed. She was tall and thin with long arms that moved fast when she worked. At the car wash she worked constantly. Janet did one last walk-around of the car and raised a rag-filled hand to signal to the owner that his car was ready.

She wore the same uniform all the other workers wore: a short-sleeved blue shirt with the car-wash logo, khaki shorts, and running shoes. Sweat had turned the back of her shirt a darker blue. She turned to me, wiped her brow with her hand, and smiled.

"Joe, good to see you."

"You, too, Janet." I glanced at the workers. They pulled the next car up and started working on it. "Business looks good."

"Thank God for sunny days."

"I can see you're busy and hate to bother you, but have you got a minute?"

"Sure." She turned to a small man who was buffing away. "Juan, you take the lead. I'll be back in a few."

We sat at the far picnic table. She had shoulder-length hair, a long chin, and a pointy nose.

"Where's Darin?" I looked around the site again in case I'd missed her husband on my walk-through.

"Gone."

"Gone where?"

I looked back to Janet. Her eyes and mouth had gone tight. A couple gray hairs sprouted at her temple; I hadn't noticed them before.

"Darin's done with me—and he's done with the car wash."

"Damn. I didn't know that. I'm sorry."

She shook her head. "I should have seen it coming. He grows infatuated easily but has a hard time with the follow-through. We dated off and on for eight years; then one day he became infatuated with marriage. We had a wedding, and he became infatuated with this business. Now he's lost interest in both."

"So . . . where is he?"

She shrugged. "He left a month ago. Last I heard he was scuba diving in Micronesia."

"Jesus."

"Yeah, it kinda blows. And the divorce will suck, too. We bought this place for nothing, but now it's worth something. Darin wants to sell, and I don't."

"Can you buy him out?"

"No." Janet bit her lower lip. "The bank won't lend me enough. Even if they did, I don't want that kind of debt. Do you know someone with three hundred thousand who wants to be a partner in a car wash?"

In point of fact I had three hundred and twenty thousand in cash in my safe at the condo. I had earned the money as an off-the-books bonus at the completion of a rather harrowing project eighteen months before. No one else knew about it.

I said, "I'll keep my eyes open for you."

"Thanks. What did you want to ask me?"

"I'm working on a project and want to learn about Mark Cunningham. Sanjay told me you interviewed with him for a VP of engineering job."

She laughed. "Mark Cunningham. Yeah, but we did more than interview. I actually dated the guy for a few months. Darin and I were 'off' at the time. After the interview Mark asked me out for dinner. He seemed like a nice guy, for a CEO, and he looked good, so I accepted the invitation."

Janet screwed her lips into a tight bunch pulled to one side, like she'd tasted a fruit that had gone bad.

"We had fun at first, but it turned out he wasn't that nice after all, sort of a dick, actually, so I ended it. Some months later I found out he was dating Sophie Tyler. Imagine that."

"What else can you tell me about him?"

"Not that much. Tall, blond hair, sort of a metro-Texan who aspired to be this rugged type, you know? Like he wished he was a cowboy or something. Fast talker. He knew nothing of technology, but he could spin a line of bullshit."

"Do you know how I can reach him?"

"No. I had no interest in keeping in touch, and then he started up with Sophie Tyler. Funny thing, though—about six months ago he called my cell. I didn't know who it was at first, because I'd deleted him from my phone. He said he'd bought a ranch about an hour out of town and invited me over for a tour. I was married by then, so I had a handy reason to decline his invitation."

"Did he tell you the location of the ranch?"

She shook her head. "All I remember is he said it was an hour from town."

"Do you still have the number?"

"Nope. No reason to save it."

That didn't leave me much to go on. You could drive an hour in any direction from Austin and reach land somewhat suitable for raising cattle. I'd already tried to locate Cunningham online with no success. He sounded a little sketchy. Maybe he'd bought a ranch and maybe he hadn't. If he had bought the property he might never have gotten a landline, or it could be under another name.

"Anything else, Joe? I hate to slack off too long. It sets a bad example."

"No, that's great. Thanks."

We both stood and walked around the table to shake hands. Janet hesitated for an instant and then leaned in to give me a peck on the cheek. She wore no makeup and smelled of manual work. She hustled back to her station, arms swinging hard.

* * *

County clerks in Texas were required to keep public records of real estate transactions. If Mark Cunningham bought a ranch within an hour's drive of Austin, one of the neighboring counties would have a record of it. I studied a map of Texas and decided his ranch could reside in any of the six neighboring counties: Burnet, Williamson, Bastrop, Caldwell, Hays, or Blanco. Lee County and Llano County were close enough to be in range, so I lumped them in, too. The home county of Travis rounded off the list of nine.

I visited the website of each county to learn the most efficient way to access their records. Travis and Williamson counties had online systems, and after fifteen minutes of searching I crossed them off the list. Unfortunately, the other seven counties required an in-person visit or an email request, with lengthy response times.

I studied the map further and plotted a clockwise circuit. I'd head east first to Bastrop, then farther out to Giddings in Lee County, then swing back south to hit Lockhart in Caldwell County, and then west to San Marcos in Hays County. If I hadn't found Cunningham by then I'd drive to Johnson City for Blanco County, then up to Llano and finally Burnet. The entire loop would take the better part of two days.

The Bastrop County courthouse had a searchable kiosk in the front lobby. In March of 2002, eighteen months earlier, M. Cunningham had purchased a hundred-and-twenty-seven-acre plot of land on County Road 192, about fifteen minutes away. I drove by the property twice but saw no sign of people, only an overgrown barbed-wire fence and a seldom-used dirt track. Trees and an unruly pasture filled the land across the fence. I stopped the Jeep a half mile down the road to knock on the door of a small house, but the man inside had never heard of M. Cunningham and wasn't aware of a house on that property.

I gave up on Bastrop and drove northeast on 21 and then east on 290 to Giddings, the seat of Lee County. They had not yet made the transformation to kiosks, but the clerk's assistant was quite helpful. Once she knew what I wanted she spent fifteen minutes on their antiquated terminal searching for grantees named Cunningham. She found several associated with sales in the last three years, but none with the first name of Mark or first initial of M.

I'd crossed off four counties and had five to go. From Giddings I drove southwest for an hour to Lockhart, the seat of Caldwell County. They had no ability to search records online, but the man invited me to fill out a form request, assuring me they usually responded within two weeks. I filled out the form. It was just after four o'clock. By driving fast I could make it to San Marcos before they closed.

When I parked in the side lot in San Marcos my phone said four forty-two p.m. Some county clerks stopped taking requests before five o'clock, so I trotted into the lobby to search for the right office. Sure enough, the sign on the front of the counter said, NO RECORDS REQUESTS AFTER 4:45 P.M., and the clock on the wall read four forty-seven. Fortunately, the woman behind the counter didn't care that government workers were reputed to provide crappy service. She listened politely to my request, frowned, and explained that their system was not organized that way. But then she asked if I knew when the transaction had taken place. I guessed between six and eighteen months earlier.

She told me to wait and disappeared through a side door for twenty minutes. I had begun to think she'd already gone home when she came back through the door with a sheet of paper. She'd copied the record of a transaction selling 232 acres and a residential building to a Mark Cunningham on County Road 312.

I drove west on State Highway 80 to Ranch Road 12 and then on toward the Devil's Backbone.

CHAPTER 20

THE LAND WAS HARD OUT that way: dry, white, crusty limestone rock; rolling hills; curvy, two-lane paved roads; lots of pear cactus; barbed-wire fences; and scrawny trees. A rich man could purchase a couple hundred acres, drop a million dollars on a home, and call himself a rancher. Several rich men had done just that, but they reaped little from the land. A few red Angus cows grazed here and there, but most of the area looked unproductive.

If Shareware was a scam, I envisioned it as a replica of the scheme used in *The Producers,* the Mel Brooks musical. With that scheme the fraudsters (Johnson and company) raised capital (Sophie's money) that exceeded the needs of the business enterprise (Shareware). Once they had her money in hand they drove Shareware into failure and split the proceeds.

When executed successfully the *Producers* con allowed fraudsters to net their profit undetected. They walked away clean. But for Johnson to have made it work with Sophie's investment, he had to be in bed with the CEO, which was why I wanted to talk to Mark Cunningham.

When I reached the intersection with Ranch Road 32, I pulled off to the side and consulted a map to confirm the directions. After another couple miles on Ranch Road 12 I took a right fork onto County

Road 312, a one-lane gravel-top drive, and drove through two miles of curves. I passed an old water tower and climbed a hundred feet in elevation before reaching an iron gate mounted between wooden posts. Cheap metal numbers tacked on the left post indicated Cunningham's address. I stopped and got out to swing open the gate.

Once inside I drove a couple hundred yards on a dirt road that wound through cedar, live oak, and cactus before reaching the cabin. Cunningham hadn't sunk a million dollars into his place. It looked like an old homestead with a wooden frame, and a roof that sloped down gently from right to left. A chain-link dog run peeked out from behind the left side of the cabin. The driveway petered out at the edge of the lawn, a good hundred feet short of the house. A faded blue Mercedes sat parked in the sun to the right of the cabin.

Ferocious barking came from the back of the cabin, followed by a man's shout and then nothing. I got out of the Jeep and walked toward the door. The covered porch was made of unfinished hardwood.

As I approached the porch a movement caught the corner of my left eye. I glanced that way and saw dark shapes moving across the ground, sleek, fast, and quiet. A low guttural noise came at me, interrupted by inhalations of air to feed the charge.

The Dobermans sprinted toward me, closing from a hundred feet away.

Pressure surged in my chest. I ran for the porch, my heart thumping as my toes dug into the dirt. My eyes tracked the lead dog, his teeth bared, his legs stretching fully with each stride. I stepped once more on a bare spot of dirt, and then leaped to the porch to grab an upright beam. I scrambled up the beam, sucking in huge gulps of air, my hands grabbing, slipping, and grabbing again.

I got a hand on the porch roof, the shingles tearing at my skin. The lead dog jumped, his jaws open, his body in full flight, and I shot a kick in his direction that glanced off the left side of his face. His jaws clacked shut on empty air, and he slammed into the beam. His mate ran behind him. She slowed her pace to study me. With eyes wide I pulled myself up, my other hand on the roof and legs wrapped around the beam. As my legs began to sag they fell into range. The bitch ran onto the porch and leaped from there, her jaws closing around my left shoe, pinching my heel. Her weight pulled my leg from the beam just as the male jumped again. I kicked blindly and clubbed him in the snout with my right foot. He whined and fell to the ground. The weight of the bitch stretched my arms as I kicked at her, finally landing a hard enough blow to loosen her jaw.

I wrapped my legs around the beam again, my chest heaving, while the dogs barked insanely. They took turns attacking, snapping jaws at the apex of their leaps. Each time they jumped my stomach tightened, my legs retracted, and I stared as their jaws snapped. My arms ached. Sweat stung my eyes. I had battled them to a temporary stalemate, but how long could I hold on? No more than a minute, maybe two.

A man laughed.

He strode toward me at a leisurely pace. He wore work boots, khaki pants and shirt, and a safari hat. A dog leash hung from his right hand. He shook his head as he continued to laugh, big chuckles that crashed against the cabin and thundered out to the hills.

"My, my. You're up a tree."

"Get your fucking dogs off me."

"Lady. Heel."

The bitch immediately left the porch and stepped to her master's side, silent. The male kept barking and jumped again, his jaws snapping as they closed on empty air inches from my leg.

"Brad. Stop that."

Brad barked again, coiled for another attempt. His master deftly looped a choke chain around his neck and pulled him from the porch.

"You can come down now," he said.

I eyed the female suspiciously.

"She won't attack unless I give her a command."

Unwrapping my legs, I dropped to the porch, exhausted and out of breath. My hands shook; I leaned to press them against my knees. I focused on breathing in and out, inhaling lungsful of air, until I could stand upright again.

"Those dogs are vicious," I said.

"They're protective. You're trespassing."

"You should post a sign on the gate."

"Yeah, I meant to do that."

The bitch sat obediently at his side, panting. The male growled low in his chest and struggled against the chain.

"Anyway," he said. "Why are you here?"

For the first time I studied the man carefully. Tall. Blond hair. He looked a little different without the fedora and sunglasses, but I recognized him.

"Hey," he said. "I know you. I'm not talking to you."

Suddenly, standing there, still breathing heavy, it all seemed worth it: the hours of driving on back-country roads, the frustrating answers from county clerks, even the mad scramble to stay clear of the dogs.

"You're Mark Cunningham. Johnson Sagebrush paid you to follow me, and you slugged me with a metal bottle."

"Bullshit. I'm not talking to you."

Lady began to growl. I didn't worry much about her so long as Brad stayed on the leash. One dog I could handle. Two were a problem.

"You'd better," I said. "You help me, and I'll put serious coin in your pocket. You don't, and I promise the police will be out here tomorrow."

Lady continued to growl. Cunningham considered my offer with a snarl on his face. If he made a move toward Brad's leash, I planned to run two steps and kick Lady hard in the stomach.

He smiled an ugly smile. "Or I could just let these dogs loose and watch them tear you to pieces."

"Do you really want to add murder to your résumé? Murder? Or would you rather make some money?"

He cocked his head to one side as if listening for something. For a moment I thought he was going to unleash Brad. Lady thought so, too, for she stood on all fours and growled louder. We remained like that for long seconds, with me ready to move on Lady, Lady readying herself for battle, and Cunningham trying to decide what to do.

"Lady. Heel."

The dog obediently returned to a sitting position. I inhaled deeply and exhaled slowly.

"Is there someplace we can talk more peacefully?" I said.

Cunningham put Brad in the pen and kept Lady at his side while he led me around to the back. The outdoor seating area looked nicer than the cabin. A stone fireplace stood at one side of the flagstone patio, and a built-in grill and bar ran along the outside edge. A trellis overgrown with vines provided ample shade, and a ceiling fan kept the air moving.

"Want something from the cooler?" He opened a half refrigerator behind the bar. "I have sodas, beer, or something stronger." He gestured toward a few bottles of liquor on the counter.

"Diet Coke?"

"Sure thing."

He grabbed a Shiner for himself, took off his hat, and sat at the end of a large wooden table that occupied the center of the patio. I sat on his right, two chairs away. Lady sat next to Cunningham. She eyed me with suspicion, still panting.

The fireplace was about twenty feet from the table, and next to it stood a large stack of wood. I eyed the firewood casually. No dog could outfight a man with a club, but I'd have to move fast to reach the pile in time.

"Smoke?" Cunningham held out a box of thin cigars.

"No, thanks."

"So you're working for Sophie Tyler." He snorted through his nose and shook his head. "I haven't heard from her in years."

He spoke with an air of resignation. His face was handsome, with sharp, well-formed features, and he had a full head of long blond hair, neatly groomed. With strong hands he pulled a wooden match from a box.

"I'm working for myself," I said. "I see Sophie Tyler purely as an opportunity. Have you seen the news lately?"

He eyed me with suspicion. "I don't have much use for the news out here." He struck the match and leaned forward to pull on the cigar. A pleasant aroma crept across the table.

"Your buddy Johnson Sagebrush—"

"He's not my buddy." Cunningham's voice rose with anger. "Johnson's an asshole. He paid me to provide a little reconnaissance—nothing illegal about that—but after our run-in at the festival I told him no more."

"I was about to say Sagebrush is wanted by the police for questioning about a murder."

His eyebrows stitched together and he scratched his jaw. "Murder?"

"That's right. Someone murdered Bryan Slater."

He quickly shook his head. "I never heard of Bryan Slater. Murder. Really? And the police think Sagebrush knows something? I'm only a little surprised. He always struck me as wired too tight, and I never understood why Sophie allowed him to manage her affairs."

"Let's cut the crap. I know you and Johnson conned her out of four million in the Shareware scam."

A low rumbling noise came from Lady's chest. Cunningham reached to pat her on the head.

"Is that what you think? You think I stole from Sophie?" He stared at me, incredulous, as if I had accused him of a more serious crime, like terrorism or pedophilia. He opened his mouth to say something, but I cut him off.

"Don't try to deny it. I can prove in an afternoon that you scammed her, but that's not why I'm here. I'm after Sagebrush."

He took another long pull at the cigar as if thinking through his options. "Why?"

"Because he knows who got the lion's share of the money. I've seen the wire transfers through his bank account." I glanced back at the cabin. "Judging by this place, I'd say you spent your proceeds a long time ago."

"I have nothing to say."

I leaned forward.

The rumbling noise from Lady grew louder.

"Let's not go through that again," I said. "If you don't talk to me, I'll have to tell the police about the scam. They want to learn anything they can about Sagebrush. And when they hear you two conned Sophie together they'll get a subpoena for your records."

He shifted uncomfortably in the chair. I couldn't get a good read on him. He seemed confused. He said nothing for a long while and then must have reached a conclusion, for the trace of a smile came to his lips. "What did you say about making some money?"

"Tell me what you know about Sagebrush. When I find him I'll put the squeeze on him and share what I get with you. You'll make a lot more than he paid you to follow me around."

"How much?"

"I'm going to hold him up for two million. When he comes through I'll give you five hundred thousand."

His eyes opened wide when I mentioned the money. He took a long time to respond again; perhaps he weighed the upside of working with me against his other alternatives.

"How do I know you won't cheat me?" he said.

"You can come with me. I could use the help."

Cunningham's face fell. I didn't think he had an appetite for shaking down Johnson Sagebrush, but if he could sit in the background and take money, he'd do it.

"That's not good enough," he said. "I don't want any part of the violence."

"Sure. Then I'll give you my address." I reached into my wallet for one of my business cards. "If I screw you over, you can tip off the police. That would create a world of hurt for me, and you'd be no worse off than you are now."

He sat silent for half a minute, looking alternately between my card and me. I began to think he would turn me down, but then he said, "What do you want to know?"

"Start at the beginning. When did you first meet Sagebrush?"

He frowned, sucked on the cigar, and blew the smoke out slowly. "Thirteen years ago, in 1990. He introduced himself as Buddy Wantannabe. Back then he worked as a bouncer for a strip club in Houston called Club Paradiso. I went there regularly when I attended Rice University. Buddy still had hair then, and he tried to comb it over, you know? He had this big smile, real nice to all the girls. They loved him, too."

Cunningham shook his head, as if he still couldn't fathom what the girls saw in Buddy.

"He could kick ass when somebody got nasty in the club. I once watched him beat up a huge drunk. This cowboy thought Buddy was nothing, but Buddy moved fast and punched with ferocity and power. The guy dropped to the floor, and Buddy hit him twice more, then stopped. Buddy didn't even breathe hard, and he looked the same as always. He smiled at the cowboy, helped him to stand, and then walked him politely out the door. I never saw anything like it."

"Did he tell you anything about his past?"

Cunningham scrunched his nose and shook his head, but then his eyes opened as he remembered something. "He told me he came from Oklahoma. He'd had a few beers that night. Some small town. But he said he would never return."

"What was the name of the town?"

"I can't remember."

"Think hard."

Cunningham closed his eyes. He leaned back in the chair and took a deep breath. "Nope. Either he never told me or it's buried under so much crap I can't pull it out."

"Okay. Keep going."

"There's not much else from the Houston days. Buddy dated one of the dancers for a while. Cute girl. Blonde. Nice legs. It was kind of weird. They went on vacation together and never came back."

"What do you mean?"

"They just disappeared. I came to the club one night and asked a dancer about Buddy. She said they never returned from vacation."

"What was the girlfriend's name?"

"You mean like her stage name?"

"No, her real name."

"You gotta stop asking the detail questions, man. I drank a lot in those days . . . drugs, too."

"Try."

He closed his eyes again, and this time he pulled it out. "Marci."

"Last name?"

"Nobody used last names much."

"Okay, so what happened then?"

Cunningham got up from his chair and walked back to the fridge for another Shiner. "Need another Coke?"

"I'm fine. Thanks."

He pulled the top off, took a pull from the beer, and sat against the counter. Lady moved to sit next to him.

"I didn't see him again for seven years. In 'ninety-eight I had raised three hundred thousand dollars for a start-up here in Austin. In those days anyone with a pitch could raise money. I burned through the cash in about six months and was out of options when Buddy called me out of the blue. Only he no longer went by Buddy Wantannabe. Now he was Johnson Sagebrush, Sophie Tyler's manager." Cunningham shook his head. "I was stunned. I would sooner have believed that Bush Senior was gay. But Johnson pulled it off. He acted like a personal manager."

"Yeah. So tell me about the scam."

He didn't answer right away. He looked at the ground, like he was trying to sort something out, and then he looked up at me again.

"It was Johnson's idea," he said. "He called me up. We met for beers at an old bar on South Lamar and talked it over. He believed that with the hot high-tech market, there should be a way to scam a gullible investor. The idea was to bring in the dumb money, fake the expenses, have the company go belly-up, and keep the difference. I had the company ready to go with Shareware, but Johnson did the heavy lifting. He brought the target. He brought Sophie.

"Johnson set me up for success. He made me get in shape first. I worked out like a maniac for two months. Then he told me what to wear, what to say, and what to order on the menu. He knew exactly what kind of man would attract Sophie."

As Cunningham relayed his story I recalled Johnson's confidence in predicting Sophie's actions. Tightness gripped my stomach. My right thumb rubbed my left palm over and over.

"Sophie and I became quite the couple," he said. "My picture made it into a celebrity magazine. They caught us dashing into an L.A. nightclub. I led the way, holding her hand. She wore a slinky dress with a lot of sequins." He tilted his head and a twinkle came to his eye. "You know what the best part was?"

"I can guess."

He threw his head back and laughed. "I know what you're thinking. You thought I would say sex was the best part. Well, the sex *was* great. In no time we were fucking like porn stars. Sophie loved to fuck. She went for me like no woman ever has, before or since."

"I don't need those details."

"I bagged a rock star. How many guys can say that? But what I planned to say, before your dirty mind interrupted me, was that I never met *anyone* remotely like Sophie Tyler. Johnson and I set her up, just like I told you, but if I had known her beforehand, I would have never . . ."

Cunningham stopped talking. He took a deep breath, frowned, and swallowed hard. I thought he might actually tear up, but then he moved his head to stretch his neck and took another drag off the cigar.

"How did you work the fraud?" I said.

He shrugged. "We kept it simple. I already had the office and a few employees. We brought her in for a visit, pulled her into a conference room with a bunch of diagrams scrawled on the whiteboards, and she was hooked. A lot of start-ups fail so we knew the endgame from the outset, but the market crash allowed us to pull the trigger early. 'Sorry, Sophie. We almost made it.' By that time she'd grown tired of me, so the breakup was easy."

He said the last line wistfully, as if Sophie had stolen something from him at the same time that he and Johnson stole the money from her.

I almost felt sorry for him, but then I caught myself. He was just another corporate thief. I've always hated fraudsters; we should lock them up with the blue-collar thieves. And he made love to Sophie under false pretenses.

"What else can you tell me?"

Lady must have detected an edge to my voice; she tensed up and the rumble turned into a low growl.

"Nothing. That's it."

"Tell me something to help find him, something from the Houston days. Nobody disappears like that."

"No . . . that's about it." But then his eyebrows lifted and he straightened his shoulders. "There is one thing that might help you find him. One night at the club Buddy asked me how to get a fake identity. I didn't know, but I'd heard a rumor about a pawnshop."

"What pawnshop?"

I asked it too forcefully. Lady rose to her feet, the hair on her back bristling, and Cunningham held her by the collar.

"I don't remember."

Then something changed with Cunningham. His eyes went flat and his lips drew tight.

"What's your relationship with Sophie?" he asked.

"I . . . I told you. I see her as an opportunity."

"No," he said, "I think it's more than that. You're with her, aren't you? Maybe you should go," he said. "I hate to keep Brad in the pen too long."

"Tell me about the money. What happened to the money?"

He nodded. "That much I do remember. I sent four hundred thousand to an account in Johnson's name, and three-point-six million to an unnamed account in Mexico. I earned a pittance, only a hundred thousand, but the time with Sophie made it all worthwhile."

"Who else was involved besides Sagebrush?"

Cunningham shrugged. He either didn't know or wouldn't tell me.

"It's time you left," he said as he stood straight. "Don't make me snap my fingers. You don't want to know what Lady does when I snap my fingers."

I got up and casually walked to the woodpile. I picked up a piece of mesquite eighteen inches long and two inches thick.

"Thanks for the Coke."

Lady squirmed against Mark's hand on her collar.

"My pleasure. Watch your step on the way out." He had a weird grin on his face. I didn't trust him any more than he trusted me.

"Don't sic that bitch on me. If you do I'll beat her to death with this hunk of mesquite."

I walked carefully around the cabin to the Jeep, a constant eye over my shoulder, watching for a low dark shape moving at speed.

CHAPTER 21

I HAD NO INTENTION OF HONORING my promise to Cunningham. As I reached Dripping Springs, cell coverage returned, and I called Rico. I gave him everything I could remember from the conversation: Club Paradiso, Buddy Wantannabe, the stripper Marci, the pawnshop, and the high-tech scam.

"Why did you go out there in the first place?"

"I had a hunch about the money that flowed through Sagebrush's account in 2001. I thought it was a long shot, so I didn't mention it to you."

"Uh-huh."

"You wouldn't believe what I had to go through to find Cunningham. I finally found him at the Hays County Courthouse. I thought I'd try his ranch on the way home."

"You should have called me before you went to see him."

"I thought about it, but . . . I . . ."

The Jeep hit a bump on 290, and I jostled in the seat.

"You sound kind of edgy," he said. "Is there anything you haven't told me?"

How much should I tell Rico? I'd just provided him with new information, fresh meat to feed his investigative machine, but I still retained one secret.

Few cars drove on my side of the road, but returning commuters crowded the opposite lane. They drove directly into the setting sun.

"Well . . . I . . ."

"Yes? You what?"

"I slept with Sophie Tyler."

"Oh, shit. Here we go."

"It was her idea." As soon as the words passed my lips I realized they sounded stupid. "It just kind of happened."

"No, it didn't 'just kind of happen'. That's how teenagers get pregnant. You're supposed to think about these things."

"It bothers me that Cunningham slept with her. You know? He's an ass."

"Christ. You got it bad. So what now? Are you moving to L.A.? Will I read about you in the checkout lane?"

"No. No way. Well, I'm going out for a short visit."

Rico gave me a little more shit, but I could tell he wanted to get off the phone.

"Okay," he said. "Thanks for the info. We've got work to do here on the Houston stuff. Call me if you hear from Sagebrush."

"Sure."

Once back in the city limits, I detoured off MoPac to Highway 360 and stopped at a Thai spot for dinner. I lingered over Tom Yum soup and Panang curry. I had given Rico a boost. His team would work their magic and catch Johnson soon.

After dinner I drove back to the condo, poured a glass of wine from the bottle I'd opened the night before, and called Sophie.

She picked up immediately.

"Speak," she said. "Let me hear your voice. I'm desperate."

I breathed quickly. I could see her face, her bluish-green eyes, flowing hair, and high cheekbones.

"Hi, babe," I said.

"Oh, that's it." She talked fast, her voice eager. "All day long I've wanted to call but resisted. Keri's got me going through old shit from the storage closet. Throwing things out. She's grabbed hold of this downsizing project. I had to insist we stop at five o'clock. For Pete's sake, we're not day laborers. Not yet anyway."

I wanted to be with her, to share an everyday experience, something as mundane as shopping for groceries.

"I'm drinking wine," I said, squinting at the bottle in the fading light. "Pulenta Estate cabernet franc from Mendoza."

"Never heard of it."

"It's all the rage in the wine section at HEB."

"Oh . . . HEB. To hear those letters warms my heart. I can't wait to shop at HEB."

"Whole Foods is the high-end place now."

"Whole Foods, Central Market, HEB. I love them all."

"You'll be mobbed."

"I'll wear my hair in braids. No one will recognize me."

I laughed. We hadn't spoken in twenty-four hours. The long drive through the hill country had dimmed the Sophie afterglow, but listening to her banter revived the warm feeling in my chest.

"When are you coming?" she said.

"Tomorrow, I think. It's too late today, and I'm tired."

"Tomorrow then. I'll go to bed early and dream of you, of wrapping my arms around your neck and my legs around your hips."

I closed my eyes and saw Sophie in bed with Cunningham, going at it like a porn star. I shook my head to clear the image away.

"Cunningham cheated you on the investment in Shareware," I said.

"Shit."

"Johnson organized the whole thing. They stole four million dollars from you."

Sophie didn't respond. What was she thinking? She had called herself stupid when we talked about the Shareware investment. I thought her biggest mistake was trusting Sagebrush, but I didn't say anything more about it. She couldn't reverse that decision now.

"Don't talk about money," she said. "Talk about something else."

We ended up discussing her move in L.A. She was considering a change of neighborhood, maybe a condo near the beach in Santa Monica or Malibu.

After we hung up I noticed something: Her words affected me but not as intensely. I wanted to see her also, but not desperately. We were magnets whose attraction grew strong when close together, but weakened with distance.

Then I recalled Johnson's words: *When her arms and legs wrap around you and pull you in, she will hypnotize you. You'll become addicted.*

Bullshit. I would spend a few days with Sophie in California, and she'd spend a few days in Austin with me. No big deal. I would always put Chandler and Callie first.

But a small doubt nagged me, a question about my strength of will. Would my conviction waver as I spent more time with Sophie? Could I resist her?

I pushed the question away, told myself I had other things to do.

The sun had almost set. As I sat on the sectional in semidarkness, my mind returned to the conversation with Mark Cunningham. I didn't see a next move for me. I sifted through the new data and cross-referenced it with everything else I'd learned, trying to find a loose end or a logic stream to pursue. I had just poured a second glass of wine when it occurred to me: I forgot to tell Rico about Oklahoma.

After a few beers one night, the bouncer Buddy Wantannabe had told Cunningham he came from a small town in Oklahoma. Earlier,

I had gotten the impression from Johnson that he might have killed his own father. If so, he had escaped undetected.

I stepped to my desk and woke up the laptop; the white screen glowed in the otherwise darkened room. I typed a search into Google: "unsolved murders in Oklahoma". A number of websites popped up: one organized by the state, a site for the Tulsa Police Department, and a long list of private sites.

I spent time on the state government site researching open cases with posted rewards but found nothing related to Johnson Sagebrush. The Tulsa site had summary facts of a number of cold cases, but nothing seemed to fit. A television news site from Norman had an old unsolved murder of a housewife. The subsequent Google hits seemed random: a media article on a single case, several missing-persons sites, and various crime-statistic sources.

But on the third page of the search I found a low-traffic, true-crime site called UnsolvedHomicides.com. Ten minutes later I stared at a high school picture of Johnson Sagebrush.

Dewey Couple Found Murdered; Son Missing

On a warm spring morning in April of 1986, June Sprinkle walked to the Wannamakers' house next door to borrow a cup of sugar. She could see her friend Olive's car in the driveway and was surprised when no one answered the doorbell. After ringing twice June walked around to the backyard thinking she'd find Olive tending her garden. Once there she noticed the back door slightly ajar. She feared Olive might have fallen sick, so she walked up the steps to knock.

"Olive," she called. No answer. June took three steps into the kitchen and screamed. Olive Wannamaker lay on the floor in a pool of her own blood, dead of multiple head wounds from a blunt instrument.

June continued screaming as she ran from the house, afraid for her life. The police found Brownie Wannamaker in the garage in a similar condition. They discovered the murder weapon, a crowbar, in a trash can in the garage. Two days later Brownie's 1982 Dodge Ram D-150 was found in a Target parking lot in Tulsa, forty-five miles away.

The Wannamakers' eighteen-year-old son, Charles, had gone missing. Initially the police believed the murderer had killed or abducted Charles, and an organized search of neighboring areas was conducted; however, other factors have led Charles to become a suspect.

For most of his senior year Charles Wannamaker had sexual relations with one of his schoolteachers, thirty-five-year-old Annabelle Poteet. A single woman, Ms. Poteet resigned her position soon after the affair became public knowledge. Apparently the Wannamaker couple had discovered the affair and reported it to school officials. Ms. Poteet has cooperated with police in the investigation but has refused to speak to anyone else about the matter.

Charles Wannamaker was considered a polite student by his classmates, always smiling, never offensive; however, he appears to have had no personal friends. In his junior year Charles was charged with a misdemeanor for public disturbance when an altercation initiated by two football players ended with both of them in the hospital.

The murder remains unsolved, and Charles Wannamaker has not been found. The state of Oklahoma offers a reward of ten thousand dollars for information leading to the arrest of a suspect.

I pushed back from the computer and closed my eyes.

Charles Wannamaker had become Buddy Wantannabe and then later changed into Johnson Sagebrush. Four years elapsed from when he abandoned the truck in Tulsa to when he met Cunningham in Houston. What had transpired in those four years? Were there other aliases? Were there other victims? I feared the stripper Marci's life had come to a gruesome end. If so, Johnson had killed at least four people.

Johnson claimed that everyone acted only in his own self-interest. He saw the world as Sanjay's primitive man: There was no right and wrong, only strength and weakness, primordial rules. The strong took what they could take, and the weak suffered the consequences.

I thought of his parents. What was his mother doing as he walked into the kitchen holding the crowbar? Perhaps she cooked pancakes, relieved that Brownie had not assaulted her that morning as he did so many other times. What had she done to earn her son's brutal justice? Had she reported the affair with Annabelle Poteet to school officials? Had the affair with Annabelle been the one thing Charles cherished?

I imagined Charles swinging the crowbar as his mother screamed on the floor. My throat ran dry. A sinking sensation invaded my chest. Sanjay's mention of Darfur came to mind. What had he said? *Anytime the fabric of societal control frays, the strong take whatever they want.* I shuddered at the thought of living in such a place, ruled by the instincts of primitive men.

I had much to tell Rico and had promised to call him, but before doing so I had to step outside to breathe fresh air, to shake those terrible notions from my head.

Standing up, I stretched and moved toward the balcony. My fingers flipped open the lock and I slid the door across. As I stepped over the threshold a gentle breeze blew and brought with it a rich, deep, earthy scent: sandalwood.

I instinctively stepped backward into the room, and a rushed movement flew through the spot where I had stood.

Kutchiiiittssszzzzzz.

An object collided with the sliding door. Shattered glass fell.

I shuffled farther into the darkened room and almost tripped, my heart pounding. I gasped for air.

I saw him. His silhouette framed the doorway, his bald head dark, his solid frame heaving, and the crowbar hanging loose in his hand.

"Damn it," he said. "You're a tricky bastard."

The open laptop threw off light for him to see by, and I reached to shut it. Visibility collapsed. I blinked hard, twice. My eyes discerned only dark shapes of furniture, light fixtures, and Johnson standing at the door.

I needed a weapon.

A block held knives on the counter, of limited use against a crowbar-wielding monster. Four chairs surrounded the circular oak table. I stepped back toward the counter and opened an upper cabinet door.

"I'm here to kill you," he said. "I can feel your breath on my neck, and I don't like it. You might as well come here and get it over with."

"My Smith and Wesson says different."

"A gun? I believe you have one, but not in the open. Your daughters come here. You'd never risk a gun falling into the wrong hands."

I grabbed a heavy water glass and threw it at him. I was still jittery, and my aim went wide; the glass flew through the open door and crashed against the balcony rail. I took a deep breath.

"What was that? Did you throw something at me?"

I grabbed two more glasses and flung one at him. It cleared his head and crashed into the doorframe.

"Damn it. Stop that."

I threw the third glass, my aim true. It landed with a thud against his body. Johnson ducked.

"Damn you."

I pulled a six-inch knife from the block and stuffed it blade-first into my back pocket; then I hauled a stack of plates from the cabinet and held them in my left arm. I took one and spun it like a Frisbee. The plate narrowly missed Johnson on the left and shattered against the sliding door. He dived behind the sectional.

I could just make out the sofa and the television on the other side. I hurled another plate, aiming six inches above the back of the sectional. The plate crashed into the television. I hurled another plate and heard the *thwack* of porcelain against flesh. He groaned.

"Hold up now. Jeez. You got my heart thumping."

I threw another plate. From the sound I imagined it bounced off the flat-screen and landed on the floor.

"Give it up," I said. "The police will catch you. They know everything now. They know all about your parents, Charles."

He didn't respond. I stepped to the oak table with four plates left and slowly pulled a chair back.

"Or is it Charlie?" I said.

"Don't call me Charlie. My dad called me Charlie."

"They know about Houston, too. What happened to Marci?"

"Marci? They know about Marci?"

"You need help. Drop that crowbar. We'll call the police together."

"I didn't want to kill Marci. I liked her, but she knew about Johnson Sagebrush. She got nosy, went through my billfold."

"So you killed her?"

"I left all that shit behind when I went to California, just like I'll leave it all behind now. You think I need help? I don't need anyone's help. I know what I'm doing."

His frame moved up behind the sectional, and I spun another plate at him. It hit him below the head.

"Damn you."

The room was darker on my side. I could barely make him out. I threw another plate at him and then threw the last two in quick succession toward the sliding door. They crashed against the wall and the doorframe, making a huge racket.

I lifted the chair and rushed forward, spinning it behind me. Johnson rose from his crouch, and I bashed his head with the chair. I nearly fell over the sectional. I backed off, gathered my balance, and wound the chair up for another blow. Johnson rose at the same time. I saw his right arm swinging forward and slammed the chair toward it.

Caleeeinng.

The crowbar hit the floor. I clambered over the sectional and punched at Johnson's form.

He sagged. I punched him blindly, again and again, hitting him on the shoulder and chest. He sagged farther. I kept punching him, driving him down to the floor.

He spun around to get leverage under his legs and pushed. His shoes caught me at the chest and hurled me over the sectional. My head banged into the table. I shook it and turned to see him flying through the air. He landed on hands and knees, and then scrambled on top of me on the floor. I punched at him wildly, hitting the side of his face and his neck. He raised his arms together high, his hands locked, and thrust them down. I jerked and the blow landed on my shoulder. Pain shot through muscles and into the bones in my back. I shouted and spun my legs around, trying to knee him in the side. He grabbed my shoulders and thumped them against the floor and then his hands reached for my throat. I hammered at his arms, but he was too strong. He choked me, cutting off all the air. I spun my hips left and right, trying to throw him without success.

My brain slowed, the wheels grinding. Blue images flashed. I struggled to pull the knife from my pocket.

Get it out. Turn it. Yank it.

Finally I got the handle free and extended my arm to the side.

He sat crouched above me, his feet on the ground and his massive thighs wedged against my chest. He grunted with effort as I slammed the knife into his thigh.

"Aaahhhh."

He let go and grabbed for his leg. I stabbed again and got his forearm.

"Yyyaaaaa."

He stood and held his arm while I crab-walked away from him.

"Shit. You bastard. You fucker."

He stumbled toward the sliding door, his left arm at his thigh. I scrambled to my knees and then stood. As he stepped out to the balcony I walked around the sectional and picked up the crowbar. I approached the balcony carefully, looking left and right around the open doorframe.

Johnson had disappeared. I glanced up to make sure he didn't cling to the ceiling, like Spider-Man. He was gone. My chest heaved.

I stepped to the balcony rail and looked down. Johnson hung from the floor of my balcony by his hands, his legs swinging.

I swung the crowbar at him.

Paannngggg.

But before the crowbar hit the rail he dropped and landed neatly on the balcony below. It took him only a few seconds to climb over that railing and drop another eight feet to the ground. He stood there and looked at me. He didn't say a word, but a spotlight from the corner of the building shone on his face. He smiled and gave me a mock salute; then he turned and limped past the pool and down the path toward the tennis courts.

CHAPTER 22

"CHRIST, THIS PLACE is a mess," said Rico.

After calling 911 and Rico, I'd left everything in the condo untouched. Scattered chairs littered the kitchen. The chair I'd used to beat Johnson lay next to the television with a broken leg. The floor across the back wall was covered with shattered bits of sliding door, glasses, and plates.

"It was dark," I said. "I kept throwing shit at him to keep that crowbar away from my head."

The squad car with two officers had arrived in minutes. They wore sidearms and radios. The big one walked down to the tennis courts with a flashlight while I gave his partner a summary and suggested we save further details for Rico.

Rico finished surveying the fight scene and shook his head. "He used a crowbar?"

I nodded, leaning against the kitchen counter with a glass of water. He studied me, his eyes lingering on my throat, all the humor gone from his face.

"You're lucky," he said.

"I don't feel lucky."

I had already recounted the conversation with Johnson but hadn't yet shown Rico the true-crime article. I led him to the laptop. He studied the text and photos for several minutes.

"This is Johnson Sagebrush?" He pointed at the yearbook picture.

"That's him."

"Damn. He's a serial killer." Rico said the words with respect, as if we were dealing with a different kind of murderer, a specialist of a higher order, like a neurosurgeon or a microbiologist. "A serial killer crossing state lines attracts a lot of attention. The FBI will triple their resources." A vein bulged in his temple as he studied his notebook. "By the way, the stripper Marci turned up in a Houston missing-persons file."

"He told me he killed her."

"Yeah, the description of the boyfriend matches Sagebrush."

Two men in plainclothes walked through my front door. Rico greeted them briefly, gave some instructions, and then turned back to me.

"Are you close to catching him?" I said.

Rico gave me a bitter smile. "The name Johnson Sagebrush hasn't turned up anywhere. He's not using his cell phone. I think he's paying cash for everything and staying in places that don't ask questions, or he has another identity."

"Another identity?"

"Sure. If you buy one fake identity, you might as well buy two. But why did he come after you?"

"He said he could feel my breath on his neck."

Rico pulled on his earlobe. "Why? Because you went to see Cunningham?"

"I don't know. Maybe."

He scanned the apartment again. "Christ, what a mess."

"Can I start cleaning up?"

"We've got the crowbar for fingerprints and the knife for DNA. Did he touch anything else?"

"Only the railing . . . and my throat."

"You can clean the condo, but you might want to spend tonight somewhere else."

"I doubt he'll come back. He's got to do something about that leg."

Rico silently studied my face, his eyes deadly calm. "Look . . . buddy . . . I've hunted serial killers before. They're different. They don't fit easy patterns. Some go years without killing. They kill a few people in one place, disappear, and then surface somewhere else and kill more people. Sometimes they have psychological issues, but not always; sometimes they kill without compassion, which seems to fit his profile."

"I'm okay here. He won't come back."

"Well, all right, but keep your gun handy."

* * *

RICO'S DETECTIVES STAYED awhile to further examine the crime scene. After they left I spent two hours cleaning up. A flying plate had damaged the flat-screen, ruining the television. I also needed a new glass panel for the sliding door, and the chair looked irreparable; otherwise, the damage was superficial. Lucky indeed.

I called Adrian to give him an update. He said he'd stay with Sophie until the police caught Johnson.

The air conditioner struggled against the heat coming through the broken door, so I disassembled two cardboard boxes and taped them across the opening.

By then it was ten o'clock. I drank another glass of wine, took a hot shower, and examined myself in the bathroom mirror. The attacks were taking a toll. In addition to the lump on my head, a bruising discoloration had appeared on part of my throat. It hurt to swallow.

I climbed in bed but slept fitfully. Disturbing images woke me: fast-moving Dobermans, Cunningham laughing, and Johnson bashing his mother on the kitchen floor. At four thirty I gave up and made coffee.

I glanced at the balcony door. Would Johnson dare return? Could he scale the floors with the wound in his thigh? I grabbed the Smith & Wesson from the bedside table and carried it outside. From my balcony I could see across the lake to downtown and beyond to the UT Tower. The revolver and the quiet of the early hour soothed my nerves, and I thought about why Johnson tried to kill me.

Had Cunningham called him after I left the cabin? If so, Johnson would know I had unraveled the Shareware scam. Now he was afraid I'd discover something else.

If I kept digging I'd figure it out.

Cunningham had said he wired three-point-six million to Mexico. Johnson's cut, four hundred thousand, had gone to the Wells Fargo account in Houston. Who got the rest?

Something bugged me about Cunningham. During our conversation he had paused for long spells, his face buried in thought. At the time I thought he was debating whether to double-cross Sagebrush, but perhaps he was hiding something else—the identity of whoever received the bulk of the money: Johnson's coconspirator.

Had Rico's men or the FBI already questioned Cunningham? I had called Rico late in the day and given them a lot to research: the Oklahoma connection, Marci's murder, and the unidentified pawnshop. They might not have alerted Cunningham yet, but they would contact him soon.

If I drove to his ranch right then I'd get there by daybreak. I could make another run at the man, interrogate him about the identity of a coconspirator more forcefully this time.

* * *

THE HUNK OF MESQUITE still lay on the passenger floorboard of the Jeep. For added comfort I brought my Smith & Wesson. Ninety minutes later I opened the gate of Cunningham's ranch and heard a Doberman barking, a relentless, crazed noise. As I drove through the scrub oaks and pear cactus I saw them: circling vultures.

Lone vultures are a common sight in the hill country, floating high on the wind, their keen senses of sight and smell searching for a fresh meal, but these had already found the carcass. A half dozen circled lower to assess the situation.

As I pulled to the edge of the tired lawn I saw the source of the vultures' scrutiny: a dark, lifeless shape lay on the grass to the left side of the cabin. Back in the pen the male dog, Brad, ran to and fro, warning the vultures with his constant barking.

I grabbed the revolver and the hunk of mesquite and cautiously approached the cabin. I moved in close, glancing at Lady forty feet away. Blood had soaked the yellow grass around her skull. The vultures circled lower, growing less fearful of the dog in the pen.

I walked lightly along the left side of the cabin to the back, breathing slowly and steadily. Brad grew frantic, running back and forth in his pen, stopping to bark at me, and then returning to focus on the vultures. I flipped off the safety.

The patio looked undisturbed, the chairs neatly arranged around the large table in the middle, the ashtray nearly full with thin cigar butts. The back door stood open six inches to the inside, which caused hairs to rise on my neck. I peered through a window to the right of the door and saw a countertop and sink. The faucet dripped. A crude table sat in the center of the room, and a stove and a white refrigerator occupied the opposite wall.

I stepped across the doorway to look through a picture window, my heart rate jacked up. A commercial for a hair product blared inside the room. I moved closer, trying to see under the pull-down shade. The lower half of a couch was visible, facing the window about eight feet away. In the unlit room, on the left of the couch, I could barely see two legs wearing khaki pants and work boots. I watched the legs for a full minute, but they never moved. I feared it was too late to ask Cunningham questions.

I returned to open the door, my finger on the trigger. A hallway ran from back door to front door, with an opening to the kitchen on the right. I glanced in the kitchen, then made my way down the hall. A door on the right opened into a small office. A doorway on the left led to a second hallway. Two doors on the right of the second hallway led into small bedrooms. I checked them quickly to verify that no one else was in the house. A large framed opening on the left led to the living room.

The show was an infomercial for hair transplants. The spokesperson yammered away about the efficacy of the procedure.

Mark Cunningham sat on the right side of the couch, motionless, a crowbar rudely protruding from the top of his skull. Johnson had swung the crowbar with its curved side down. The point had lodged deeply in the brain matter. Blood had seeped out of the wound and through Mark's hair to the back and sides of his neck. My stomach felt queasy. I looked left and right to make certain no monsters lurked nearby.

A nearly empty bottle of Jim Beam sat open on the table in front of Mark. His glass lay on the floor to the side. I stared at the planted crowbar, my heart still pounding, and imagined how it happened. In Mark's drunken state he had turned the volume so high he didn't hear Lady's shriek of pain; nor did he notice as Johnson crept in the door and through the halls to his living room. Johnson hadn't bothered to turn off the television. I grabbed the remote off the table and pressed mute.

A landline phone sat on a small table to the side of the couch. I called Rico to report the murder. He gave me shit for going to see Cunningham again, and then said he would drive out with the FBI.

It would take them about an hour, so I walked into Cunningham's office to have a look around. A desk faced the front window, and three filing cabinets stood next to the side wall. An empty docking station sat tethered to a large monitor on the desk. I looked under the desk but saw no computer there, either. Johnson must have taken it.

Cunningham had neatly labeled the three file cabinets: PERSONAL, RANCH BUSINESS, and SHAREWARE. I flipped through the green Shareware folders. The financial statements showed only the initial three hundred thousand dollars of start-up capital; Sophie's four-million-dollar investment was not recorded.

The rest of the Shareware cabinet contained standard information for a small company: human resources, supplier records, legal contracts, etc. I spent twenty minutes going through the files, thinking Mark might have hidden something interesting, but found nothing.

Inside the right-hand drawer of the desk was a thick stack of loose papers waiting to be filed, random stuff, bills, old letters, and articles on ranching. I wasted more time going through that stuff.

Thirty-five minutes had passed since I called Rico. It would take all day to review every file. I needed a more analytical approach. What single piece of data could help me discover Johnson's secrets? In early 2001 Sagebrush had received his cut from the Shareware scheme. Cunningham would have received his share at about the same time.

In the Personal filing cabinet I found Chase bank statements for the past three years. Cunningham used Chase for his everyday checking account. Every month seven thousand dollars transferred in from a Fidelity brokerage account, and every month he spent it all.

A quick glance at my phone told me that Rico would arrive soon. I looked out the front window but saw no cars.

Next I looked through the Fidelity statements. I expected a cash infusion of some kind in early 2001. I tore through the 2001 statements: January, February, March. Nothing. The balance steadily declined from thirty thousand dollars toward zero. My eyes flew across the pages: April, no; May, no; but in June of 2001 Mark Cunningham received a wire for a hundred thousand dollars from an unnamed account in Mexico.

Who owned that account: Johnson or the other partner? Johnson had routed the other money through Houston to Belize. Why the account in Mexico?

Looking through the window, I still saw no dust from approaching cars, but Rico and the FBI would arrive any minute. I rushed to the kitchen and grabbed a hand towel to wipe the places I'd touched on the desk and filing cabinets.

I found an empty washtub lying against the back wall of the cabin. Brad's barking had devolved to high-pitched whines. As I cleared the corner of the house I beheld a gruesome sight. I banged the tub with the mesquite, louder as I drew near, until the vultures reluctantly took flight. I placed the tub over Lady and weighted it down with rocks from a nearby pile. Then I put the revolver into the glove box and sat in the Jeep to wait for Rico.

CHAPTER 23

RICO AND AN FBI AGENT named Baronski questioned me for ten minutes. At the same time a forensics team examined the cabin. Baronski asked me to wait in case he had more questions; then he and Rico went inside.

I spent the interval watching the vultures circling high in the sky. I had no doubt they would return when everyone had left. Vultures are determined creatures.

In my view either Keri Theroux or Halet Blevins was Johnson's partner in crime.

Keri knew from the start that Adrian had engaged me to review Sophie's finances. She could have tipped Johnson off my first night in Beverly Hills. That might have led Johnson to unwind the Second Chance scam. Later, she knew I'd gone to see Sophie at the hotel.

Okay, so let's say I assumed she was dirty. What was the endgame? Suddenly she was inclined to return to Austin to start her own life. Johnson took off. Keri got her cut and lived happily ever after.

Halet had guessed early on that I was there to do more than provide security; he could have called Johnson. He also knew I'd gone up to Sophie's room at the Four Seasons. But what was Halet's motive? He had money problems ten years ago. Did he still need extra money?

How could I find the other coconspirator? Mark Cunningham couldn't tell me. Neither could Bryan Slater. Bank records? Maybe, but that would take time. What about email? I still had Johnson's passwords.

Rico walked around the corner of the cabin, a serious look on his face. "We don't have any more questions," he said. "You can take off." He chewed a piece of gum and raised his eyebrows, not saying anything.

"What?" I said.

"We may not catch this guy soon. We've run Wannamaker, Wantannabe, and Sagebrush through the search engines and come up empty. If he's got a clean passport in another name all he has to do is book one flight, fade into the landscape of a remote location, and he's home free."

What a miserable outcome. My face grew warmer.

"You can't give up yet," I said.

"Oh, I'm not giving up. I'll never give up. I'll find this fucker if I have to chase him across the world." Rico said the words as someone taking a sacred oath, as if the brotherhood of marines took their obligations to heart.

"Will you release his picture to the press?"

"Definitely. This story will make the national news, and he'll try to find a place to hide until things calm down. Meanwhile, you go to L.A. I'll keep you posted."

"Great. Thanks. But I've been thinking this through and came up with a possible wrinkle."

"What's that?"

It took ten minutes to explain my conjecture about Keri and Halet to Rico.

As I spoke he narrowed his eyes and pursed his lips. After a long moment of silence he said, "Maybe you ought to leave this alone now, head out to L.A., and wait for the all clear."

"I will, but if I can figure out who is working with Johnson I might be able to get some of Sophie's money back."

Rico stepped closer. His jaw muscle bulged, and he gestured toward the cabin. "You saw that, right? The crowbar? This guy's really fucking dangerous. You know?"

"I don't have a death wish."

"I mean it. You were lucky last time. If you get in a tangle with him, I won't be around to bail you out."

"I have no intention of trying to catch him myself."

He nodded and took a step back. "Okay. Good." He kept nodding. "That's good. You know . . . just go out to L.A. Hang with Sophie for a few days. Stay away from here until we get this sorted out."

"You bet, but can you do me a favor?"

"What's that?"

"Get someone to bury the dog."

• • •

BACK AT THE CONDO I packed a suitcase and called Sophie. It was only eight fifteen on the West Coast, but she still answered. She said she wanted to hold me, and sing to me, and make love all night. She told me things only lovers tell each other. I didn't mention Cunningham's murder. I'd be with her soon enough and could tell her in person. She said she'd grown weary of Adrian and Keri. Adrian acted paranoid, and Keri acted strange. They needed a fourth person around to balance things out.

"Acting strange? What has Keri done?"

"She keeps harping on about moving back to Austin. Says with you coming maybe I don't need her to be around as much."

Why did Keri say that? Was it part of her endgame? Did she have an account in Mexico?

"Sounds like there's tension in the air," I said.

"Let's not talk about this anymore. Come out here. We can discuss it then."

"All right."

"Text me your flight information. We'll pick you up."

"Sure thing."

We ended the call soon thereafter, and I sat still to think it through. Something strange had happened on that call with Sophie. I didn't completely understand it. It was as if I'd been wearing heavy earphones, the kind that completely envelop the ears, muffle all other sound, and someone had removed them.

Forty-eight hours earlier my every thought, no matter where it began, ended with Sophie. Even now I could summon the taste of her lips. But the fantasy had dissipated. Distance and time sharpen the analytical mind. I was a CFO, the skeptic on the team, the glass-is-half-empty guy. Infatuation was not the basis of a long-term relationship, and Sophie Tyler had established an unmistakable pattern.

Joe Robbins: notch thirty-four.

* * *

I CHECKED THE TIME. I had at least two hours to search Johnson's email before leaving for the airport. He had opened a Yahoo account in 1994. I started by searching for messages to or from Keri. There were hundreds of them. I read a few dozen. Nearly all had to do with schedule logistics.

We have to get Sophie here by nine o'clock.

That dinner conflicts with the charity event.

She can't do the interview so soon after landing from London.

I tried searching on Halet and ran into the same problem. I gave up. I had to narrow the search. What about the bank account in Mexico?

I searched for emails to or from Keri with "Mexico" in the content. There were about twenty, and I read each of them carefully. About half had to do with Johnson informing Keri of his plans to vacation in Mexico. The other half had to do with Sophie taking trips to Cabo San Lucas.

That's right—Sophie had dated someone from Mexico. I'd learned that from the research I'd done before first meeting her. What was his name? I couldn't remember.

In any case, none of the emails implicated Keri or Halet as colluding with Johnson. I'd burned an hour and learned nothing.

But by then I had grown interested in Mexico itself. Mark Cunningham had sent the majority of the fraud proceeds to Mexico and received his cut from the same account. Johnson liked to travel there. Maybe he controlled that account as well.

The search on "Mexico" by itself returned over a hundred emails. I started with the oldest. For thirty minutes I learned what Johnson liked to do on vacation. He booked hotels, fishing trips, golf outings, and dinners at nice restaurants. A number of emails came from women, and by the spicy content I deduced that Johnson did more at night than eat fancy meals.

I read a one-line email that appeared to come from a fellow carouser.

When will we see you again? Las mujeres *are asking about you. H.R.*

The date was March 23, 1997. The sender's email address told me nothing, but the message piqued my interest, because it came from someone outside Sophie's circle who had known Johnson well.

The initials caught my eye. What was it about H.R. from Mexico?

I pulled the research I'd done on Sophie before I met her, clicked on the link that listed her paramours, and found the one from Mexico, a real estate agent named Hector Romero. There was a picture and a blurb similar to the write-ups of all her lovers:

From 1993 to 1996 Sophie sporadically dated Hector Romero, a celebrity real estate agent in Cabo San Lucas. Here they are relaxing after a snorkeling trip at the Cabo Pulmo Marine Reserve in the Sea of Cortez. Sophie was so smitten with Romero that she bought a beach vacation home. Of course, Hector acted as her agent.

I pulled up Continental's website to look at flights. Luckily, they had a departure at twelve forty-five p.m. with a connection to Cabo San Lucas. After rebooking my flight, I called Sanjay and asked for his help in ferreting out another fraud.

CHAPTER 24

My itinerary called for a connection in Houston. By then Sanjay had found what he could, not everything I asked for, but most of it. He relayed the data in a quick conversation between terminals.

I had lots of time to think on the flight to Mexico. Hector could have moved on from Cabo. He might be dead for all I knew, but I had no better idea.

With the time difference the plane landed around five. I fought off a heavy feeling as I walked across the clear-paneled jet bridge and through the corridors to the immigration line. They had changed the terminal in the last thirteen years, made it bigger, shinier, and more efficient. I longed for the old design, because it was simpler, sort of like my life the only other time I'd been to Cabo, on my honeymoon with Rose.

I zipped through customs, rented a car, and made it downtown before the agency closed at six o'clock.

• • •

Cabo Dream Realty dealt in high-end second homes from an office on Avenida Lázaro Cárdenas. Outside the office they listed their registered agents; Hector Romero's name was not among them.

I pushed open the door and walked into the cool air-conditioned space. Plush carpeting covered the floors, and three glass-front offices occupied the back wall. Through the open door of the middle office a woman sat at a nice desk and typed while watching her monitor. Panoramic photos of El Arco, sandy beaches, and golf courses graced the walls of the waiting area. A cute receptionist in a white dress shirt frowned at me.

"I'm sorry, sir. We're almost closed."

I had dressed to fit the part, with pressed khakis, a nice polo shirt, and cowboy boots. "That's all right, honey. I don't need much time. I'm shopping for an agent who can keep my wife inside the ten-million-dollar budget we agreed on."

The receptionist raised her eyebrows. The woman in the middle office looked up from her monitor.

"You see, when we bought the place in Telluride we agreed on seven million, but dang it if she didn't find a way to spend nine. I asked her, 'What would happen to the dealership profits if we spent more than budget every year?'"

The receptionist nervously reached for the handset at her side. The woman in the middle office pushed back her chair.

"But if you folks are closing shop I can check out some of these other guys. The sign on one place said they were open till seven."

The receptionist picked up the phone and rapidly pushed buttons, but the woman in the middle office had already made a move. She strode confidently toward me, her hand outstretched to shake mine.

"That won't be necessary. Welcome to Cabo Dream. I'm Gigi Juarez."

"Joe Robbins. Nice to meet you."

Gigi looked about fifty. She wore a dark pantsuit with a coral-and-blue shirt. Her hair was brown and full, cut to shoulder length, with a tinge of gray. She was a bit overweight but carried it well.

"Would you care to sit down?" she said, gesturing back to her office.

"I don't want to keep you, if you're about to close."

"It's not a problem." She had a pleasant smile, not overtly salesy—a helpful trait for someone who wants to inspire trust.

"Good, good. You know, what would really punch the ticket is if we could have a drink. I had a long flight today and could use one."

"Well, I, uh, we could arrange that."

"I walked through the marina on the way here and saw this nice restaurant. Maybe you know it. It's got an open-air deck on the roof and looks over the yachts. Just beautiful."

"Um, let me think." She clasped her hands and pressed her lips tight as she concentrated.

"The tagline says something about a lobster house."

She snapped the fingers of both hands. "Lorenzillo's."

"That's it."

"A wonderful choice, Mr. Robbins. Let me get my purse."

* * *

Our waiter wore black pants, a white shirt, and a red tie. He recognized Gigi instantly, and they chattered in Spanish. We ordered wine and a light appetizer. I was partial to Lorenzillo's, because Rose and I had dined there as a young couple in love. I would have happily sat alone, wandering through the bittersweet nostalgia, but I had reached out to Gigi for a reason.

She gave me a sales pitch for the business. Her father owned the agency but no longer worked in the office. They had been the leading agency in Los Cabos for twenty years. She assured me that for ten million dollars there were wonderful properties she'd be delighted to show me herself.

"I have a confession to make," I said, losing the drawl I'd adopted in the office.

She stopped pitching, and the brightness fell from her face. "What?"

"I'm not here to buy a house."

She frowned. "I don't understand."

"I need your help. I want to talk with Hector Romero. I want to ask him questions about a transaction your agency handled seven years ago. Detailed questions."

Gigi's eyebrows fell to create a line above her eyes. She held her shoulders straight and her chin steady. "That sort of information is confidential."

"Hector conspired with another man to convince my client to sell her house too cheap. That man is now wanted by the police, and I need to talk with Hector about him."

"Who is your client?"

"Sophie Tyler."

"Sophie Tyler?"

"That's right. She purchased and sold a home through Cabo Dream. Hector Romero acted as her agent."

Gigi's expression softened. Her shoulders fell. "Hector and Sophie were lovers."

"Yes, I know."

She drank from her water glass and looked over the marina. The breeze lifted strands of hair above her head.

"I don't understand what women see in him," she said. But then she paused, and her eyes lost focus as she looked at nothing. She raised one eyebrow as she thought. "No, actually, I do understand. I was half in love with Hector myself when we first hired him. Some men . . . they have the perfect combination of charm and looks." She tapped her chest. "They may have little inside, little substance, but women find them hard to resist."

"I've known a few men like that."

She drew a deep breath and then lifted the wineglass to drink. She sat straight in the chair and pulled her shirt down at the sides. "Cabo was on fire. Sophie bought the house at the absolute peak. The market began to weaken soon after she made the purchase, and then we suffered a triple blow. First the local government passed new zoning restrictions. Then the state threatened to double property taxes. Those hits were bad enough, but the real killer was a drug-related crime spree, including two murders and a kidnapping. The cartels had made a mess of Tijuana and other places. We thought they might come here.

"Panic set in. Buyers disappeared and nothing moved. I remember it clearly: We cut back our staff, had to fire three longtime workers, and then Sophie's house went on the market. I told Hector she should wait." Gigi grimaced. "You can always sell a house if you lower the price enough. She sold it for thirty-five percent less than she paid."

"Did she get a fair price?"

"I didn't think so, but according to Hector she needed money right away. He told me if I had a higher offer he would be glad to take it. But there were no other buyers."

"Where is Hector now?"

"I fired him six months later." She shrugged. "I trained him myself. When he started he knew nothing, but he learned fast and brought a lot of clients to the agency, mostly women, some single, some not. A husband came to the office one day and shouted at me. He claimed Hector had shown his wife a lot more than real estate."

"Where can I find him?"

Gigi sat back in the seat. I sensed she was struggling and thought she might go quiet on me.

I leaned forward. "I'm not after Hector. The man he worked with is a murderer. I need to learn more about that man."

Her eyes grew wide. She looked at my shoulders and arms. "Will you hurt Hector? I don't want you to hurt him."

"I'll make you a deal. Cabo is not that big a place. In a day or two I can find anyone here, certainly Hector, but if you help me I won't touch him, not if he tells me the truth." I tried a smile to encourage her.

Gigi made a decision and reached for her cell phone. "I'm going to make a call." She speed-dialed from her chair and spoke in Spanish. I heard her say Hector's name. She kept the conversation light, laughed twice, and thanked the other person multiple times before signing off.

"According to my friend, Hector frequents the bar at Los Cabos Royale. He has an arrangement with the manager. I understand that Hector has a different dinner companion almost every night."

"Thank you."

She finished the glass of wine, placed her hands in her lap, and adopted a look of quiet acceptance. "When Hector first joined the agency he worked hard. He came from a modest background and wanted to better himself. I liked him. I wanted him to succeed, but at some point he found an easier way." Her eyes looked at mine carefully, concern on her face.

"Don't worry. I won't hurt him."

As Gigi walked from the restaurant I signaled the waiter to order another glass of wine and a main course. Sailboat hardware clanged against masts in the marina. The sun had lowered past the point of burning, and a pleasant breeze touched my skin. I sipped the wine.

I would have given almost anything to relive that one night. Rose had just turned twenty-two. I was twenty-four. She played footsies with me under the table. We had little money in those days, and the dinner was our big splurge for the trip. On other nights we ate fish tacos from street vendors and drank cheap beer. But on that night we had cocktails and wine and lobster. We dreamed big. One day we'd have enough money to travel the world, experience new cultures, and taste the best food and wines available.

Chandler was born eleven months later, and for ten years I worked like a slave to build a career. Just when we seemed to be on track I made that fateful trip to Vegas, and it all fell apart.

After dinner I drove ten miles up the coast in search of Hector Romero.

CHAPTER 25

I ARRIVED AT LOS CABOS ROYALE a little before eight, just in time for the rush at the bar. A soft blue light filled the room, while live plants and the open air created a tropical feel. Large aquariums with exotic fish separated the bar from the seating area. Jazz music played softly and mixed with the happy chatter of vacationers.

Hector sat at the bar talking with a well-dressed blonde. He looked about forty, with jet-black curly hair combed back from a high forehead. He had thick eyebrows, a dark complexion, a strong nose and chin, and wore a black shirt with lightweight slacks. They both smoked cigarettes.

Hector's right hand waved in the air while he told a story. She listened raptly and wore a delicious smile.

I stepped between them at the bar and put my hand on his shoulder. "Hey, Hector. Long time no see."

He frowned and said in a challenging tone, "I'm sorry. Have we met?"

I turned to the woman. "Hi, sweetie. Am I interrupting something?" I stuck my hand in her direction. "Joe Robbins."

She shook it nervously but didn't respond. I guessed her age at high forties. She wore a black cocktail dress and diamond earrings and looked frustrated.

Hector persisted. "Where did we meet?"

I leaned toward him and whispered, "Johnson Sagebrush sends his regards." I turned back to the woman. "I didn't catch your name."

"It's . . . uh . . . Diane."

"My pleasure. By the way, Diane, you look great in that dress. It's a killer. Hector and I worked together in real estate."

I spoke in Hector's ear again. "I'm not trying to mess up your gig with Diane, but I need ten minutes. I'll pay you a thousand dollars."

I turned back to her. "Look, I'm sorry as can be, but Hector and I need to talk about an old deal. Ten minutes. Tops. I'll bring him right back. Here, have a drink on me." I put two twenties on the bar and signaled for the bartender to bring Diane another round.

I smiled big at Hector. "Ready?"

He didn't look ready. He looked pissed, but he couldn't make a scene at the bar. His manager friend would disapprove, so he smiled and looked at Diane.

"*Mi amor*, you must excuse me. I had no idea Joe would be here. Wait for me, please."

Diane looked like she'd been stood up for the prom. "We have a reservation in fifteen minutes."

"I'll have him back in no time," I said. "Promise."

We walked to the open-air entrance of the hotel. A circular fountain in the courtyard sprayed water under a fading sky. People walked by constantly, back and forth between the guest room hallways, the lobby bar, and a crowded restaurant.

"You interrupted my date," he said as he blew an angry plume of smoke.

Hector was tall and broad-shouldered. I guessed that his physique and charm would slay any number of women.

"I said I'd pay you."

He nodded noncommittally. "Yes, but Diane is worth more than a thousand dollars."

"This can be quicker than Diane."

"So you are a friend of Johnson's."

"He tried to kill me, so I wouldn't call us friends."

Hector's eyebrows shot up. "Kill you?"

"Yes."

He took a long drag on the cigarette, his eyes squinting. "What do you want to talk about?"

"Sophie Tyler and real estate. You and Johnson stole from Sophie. I want to know all about it."

His eyebrows fell right back down again. He pressed his lips together and kept them closed, not saying anything right away. While he thought, a young couple walked by us on the way to the restaurant.

"All right," he said, and then he flipped his hand to the side to indicate the matter was of little importance. "It's history. But I didn't steal from Sophie. Lots of investors lose money on real estate. I don't mind talking about it, but not here. Too many people. Let's go down by the pool. It's quiet there."

Hector walked to a winding staircase between the lobby bar and the restaurant. He glided down the stairs, light on his feet. I imagined him charming clients on the dance floor. At the ground level a sidewalk coursed through lush landscaping, tropical flowers, and giant ferns. Smalls lights on low fixtures lit the way. Fountains on either side featured porpoise figurines.

The landscaping gave way to a huge pool surrounded by lounge chairs. A couple made out on one twenty feet away. The man groped the women openly, and she seemed to enjoy it.

Hector leaned toward me and spoke in a hushed tone. "They should get a room, right?"

All of a sudden he was my friend, cracking a joke about the lovebirds.

"Come on," he said. "This way."

He walked around the pool and then off to the left toward a wing of the hotel. A sitting area with a bench opened on the right, and Hector stopped. He looked around, no one in sight.

"We can talk here. Did you notice the full moon? Beautiful, eh?"

I *had* noticed the full moon—it looked larger than normal. I did a head fake in that direction while Hector prepared to sucker punch me.

I turned back to Hector, but instead of stepping into his punch I rocked back and let it go by. He shuffled to keep his balance. Frustrated, he threw a second punch with the same hand, his right, but I dodged that one as well.

He pulled his fists up like he thought he should and jumped back and forth on his feet. My left fist rose automatically to the front of my face, the right behind it and lower. My feet began to move. I threw a left jab that clipped his forehead. His head popped back.

"You're in trouble," I said.

Hector tried a wild punch with his left. I let it go by and threw a straight right to his body, a lot of power behind the punch. He grunted, doubled over, and struggled to breathe. I gave him time to recover. When he straightened up I faked a right and hit him in the body with a left. As he doubled over again I slammed three right punches into his side.

He fell to his knees, unable to breathe. After a few more seconds he gasped for air.

I said, "Why do you pretty boys always think you can fight?" I pulled him up to sit on the bench and gave him a minute to recover. My breathing was easy, my blood pressure steady.

"I don't care that you're a prostitute," I said. "Hell, everyone has to make a living. But you set up Sophie Tyler. You and Johnson manipulated her into selling her house at the wrong time."

He shook his head. Perspiration shone on his brow, and he struggled to catch his breath. "No. I never . . ."

"Bullshit. You convinced her to sell her house at a million-dollar loss to a shell company. Three years later the house sold again for two million more than Sophie's original price."

Sanjay had determined all that from his Internet searches. I thought my knowledge of the scam mechanics would impress Hector, jar him into helping me fill in the blanks, but instead he looked at me as if I spoke a foreign language.

"You're going to tell me everything," I said, "or I will hit you again. This time I'll punch your face, and it will show. You'll lose your date with Diane. You'll be out of business for at least a couple weeks."

His eyes squeezed shut in pain. When he opened them he gave me a nod. "What do you want to know?"

"How did you meet Johnson Sagebrush?"

"Here . . . in Cabo . . . he was on vacation. I met him in a bar downtown." Hector paused to rub his side and take a few breaths. "He said he wanted to meet a couple nice girls and didn't have a lot of time. I set him up with some local high-end women. They loved him. They said Johnson was their best client. He took them for fancy meals, was polite, and an excellent tipper."

I sat on the bench and looked at the moon, waiting for the rest of Hector's sordid tale.

"That became a routine. A couple times a year Johnson came down with a wad of cash, and we'd party."

"Tell me about Sophie Tyler and the real estate."

He shook his head and smiled, which took me by surprise.

"I fell in love with her the moment we met. I'd never met anyone like her, so open, so free. Her voice sounded of paradise. I found her a wonderful house with a fantastic view of the ocean. We spent long weekends together, just the two of us. In my entire life I never knew such joy."

The conversation had taken a surreal turn. I wanted to learn about Johnson's past and the first con against Sophie, how they had convinced her to sell the house cheap and then flipped it for a three-million-dollar profit, but Hector was stuck in a dreamy recollection of his love affair.

I remembered the photo of Hector and Sophie on the snorkeling trip, the genuine smiles on their faces. He may have played a con on her, but on that day, sitting in bathing suits in the sunshine, they had both been happy.

Whatever. I knew the outline of the con anyway, so I tried a different tack.

"How did you first meet Sophie?"

"Halet Blevins introduced us at a yacht party."

"Halet Blevins? Her talent agent?"

"Yes. I met Halet through Johnson. They go way back together. Before he was Sophie's manager, Johnson used to provide Halet with escorts and cocaine. They'd come down here together to party, but Johnson wasn't there when I first met Sophie."

Bing!

Finally I knew the identity of the coconspirator.

Halet Blevins and Johnson gave Sophie all her advice. They had played off each other for years, coordinating tactics, scheming about the Cabos play, the dot-com con, and the fake movie.

Johnson had known about my investigation from the start. Halet had learned I was not a security guy from Gwen, and then he had warned Johnson about me. Later that night Johnson watched the security videos and saw me search his computer.

I sat back on the bench and looked at the moon again. What more could I learn from Hector?

"Did Johnson ever go by another name?"

He frowned. "Not that I know of."

"You sure?"

"Positive. Johnson Sagebrush. That's it."

Maybe Halet knew Johnson's other alias. I would ask him that question, among others, like why he'd arranged to have Johnson work for Sophie in the first place. I'd ask him those questions as soon as I could get my hands around his throat.

"If you don't mind," he said, "I hear Diane calling. She . . . well, we've done this before."

"Hold on. How much did you make from the con?"

Hector spit in the bushes off to the side and glared at me.

"What's your game, anyway?" he said. "You know damn well it was Sophie's idea to sell the house."

What nonsense. What did he hope to gain with this tripe? I might have to hit him again.

Then Hector's muscles tensed up, and he jerked his head farther away. "Now I understand," he said. "Johnson sent you, didn't he?"

I stood up and made a fist, my heartbeat pounding in my ears.

"You're here to steal from Sophie," he said, his voice climbing.

I drew back to punch him. I'd make it a solid blow and aim to break his nose.

"Go ahead," he said. "Hit me all you want. I won't tell you another thing. I'll die first."

It wasn't so much his words as his expression that stopped me. Hector meant what he said. He would take the punch and many more, more than I was prepared to give.

"I don't understand," I said.

When he realized I wouldn't hit him, Hector lit another cigarette. He struggled to stand, then turned to me and said, "You and Johnson Sagebrush can go straight to hell."

I stared at the empty space where Hector had stood long after he'd gone. A hundred yards away the surf ran up the beach. A soft wind rustled the fronds in the palm trees. I walked to the beach and sat in a lounge chair. The surf broke to create gleaming foam in the moonlight.

I kept thinking about what Mark Cunningham had said when I first accused him of scamming Sophie:

"Is that what you think? You think I stole from Sophie?"

He had almost said something else, but I cut him off, gave him time to fabricate a story to go along with my preconceived theory.

Mark had worn the same expression as Hector when he talked about Sophie, a mixture of wonderment and desire. If I looked in a mirror would I see the same face?

She had seduced Mark and Hector just as she had seduced me. Or did she? It hadn't felt like a seduction, more like an irresistible pull, like the swirl of a maelstrom, the outcome preordained.

Between planes in Houston I had studied the online maps of Cabo. Sophie's former house was a mile up the beach. I took off my boots, rolled my pants, and started walking.

CHAPTER 26

THE HOUSE STOOD ON THE SIDE of a hill that rose up from the dunes. Similar high-end homes occupied the surrounding hills. Sophie's old house had two floors, a tile roof, and floor-to-ceiling windows across the back. A pool deck area overlooked the ocean.

I had half expected the home to be dark; many around it were, but bright lights shone in Sophie's place, and on the ground floor a person walked from room to room behind plate glass windows.

Sanjay had learned that the shell company that bought Sophie's house had flipped it two years later to a Graham Whitaker. The house was part of a gated community with an unlisted phone number. I had guessed that my best chance to meet Whitaker face-to-face was with an old-fashioned knock on the door.

As I climbed the dunes to get closer the going got tougher. Fine grains of sand, whipped by the wind, stung my face. I grabbed at sea grasses that clung to the dunes. The terrain changed from dune to hillside, and I ran into rocks, cactus, and native shrubs. At the top a six-foot concrete wall formed the back edge of the pool deck. I reached for the upper edge of the wall and heaved myself high enough to grab the lower railing of the patio barrier.

Large potted plants and four palm trees framed the deck area. The wind rustled the leaves and made ripples on the water in the pool. Behind me the waves crashed and rolled up the beach. I clambered over the rail, crept halfway to the house, and crouched behind an outdoor bar.

The ground floor was one great room, with the kitchen and dining area on the left and a living space to the right. A woman stood in the kitchen leaning against a counter, talking on a cell phone. She wore slacks, a sweater, and had short gray hair. A man sat reading a book in a big chair in the living space, his legs resting on an ottoman. He wore a sweatshirt, running shoes, and had reading glasses. They had left the sliding doors open, and the soft sounds of a Steely Dan song carried out to the patio.

The woman continued to talk on the phone as she watched a coffeemaker on the counter. She closed the flip phone and put it down; then she poured coffee into two mugs and walked into the living space. She handed a mug to the man, leaned to kiss him, and sat in a nearby chair.

Lurking outside the windows, watching the older couple, I felt like a peeping Tom. Climbing the dunes had been harder than I expected, but I had made it that far, and they seemed harmless enough, so I pressed forward.

I stayed in the shadows and walked to the side of the house. A narrow strip of smooth gravel stones separated it from native foliage. I walked along the strip of gravel, past two central-air units, and came out to the front yard. From there I crossed the small lawn, climbed two steps, and looked at the front door—no doorbell. I knocked twice.

After twenty seconds of no response I knocked again. A shadow moved behind the glass at the side of the door.

"Who is it?" said the man.

"Joe Robbins. I'm a neighbor."

I waited in silence. The lie was an attempt to induce him to open the door.

"Just a minute. Be right there."

Footsteps walked away. After a short interval they returned. A dead bolt clicked and the door opened. The man stood about six feet. He had removed his reading glasses and wore a windbreaker with his hand in the right pocket.

He hadn't worn the windbreaker in the back room, and his hand looked funny in the pocket, as if he held something.

"Sorry to disturb you," I said.

"We've been coming here for years, and no one's ever knocked on the door at night."

Whitaker spoke in a flat tone and eyed me with a steely gaze. My blood pressure jumped ten points. When Keri Thereaux held a gun on me I hadn't felt threatened, but with this man I needed to tread lightly.

"Let's take it easy," I said. "I'm going to raise my hands." I lifted my arms until my hands were face-level, palms forward.

"Sure."

"Sorry I lied. I'm not a neighbor."

"You have dirt on your hands and a lump on your forehead. I figured you weren't here to borrow sugar."

Whitaker seemed calm, which gave me comfort; he wouldn't casually shoot me or accidentally pull the trigger.

"As I said, my name is Joe Robbins . . . and you're Graham Whitaker."

"How did you know my name?"

"The Internet." It felt like I was standing in front of a rattlesnake trying to avoid making a stupid move. "You want to take the gun out? It will shoot straighter that way."

"Why not?"

Graham pulled the gun from his pocket and pointed it at me. It looked every bit a serious pistol, large-caliber.

"Why are you here?" he said. "Were you planning to steal from us?"

"No, I only want to ask a question."

"Graham," shouted a woman from the other room, "is everything all right?"

"Just a minute," he said. He stared at me with unemotional eyes. I thought perhaps he was trying to decide on a course of action.

"The way I see it," I said, "you have three choices. You can shoot me, you can let me go, or you can hold the gun on me and have your wife call the police. Shooting will create problems for you, and letting me go sounds risky."

"Yeah, I guess I'll go with number three." Then he shouted, "Honey, call the police."

"You have every right to," I said. "I lied to you and I sneaked onto your property. On the other hand, calling the police will create a lot of hassle, and I'd like to point out that if I wanted to cause you harm I could have walked straight through the back door."

He frowned.

"The doors are open, right? Screens only? I heard Steely Dan playing. You have good taste in music."

"What's the question?"

I looked back to the street. If a car drove by they'd see me with my hands up and Graham with a gun. The police would show soon thereafter. Graham looked out with me, and I guessed he was thinking the same thoughts.

"We'd be more comfortable inside," I said. "I'll keep my hands up. You keep the gun pointed."

He nodded and stepped to the side to let me through. We walked down a short hall and into the main room.

His wife stood nearby, cell phone to her ear, her eyes bright. She spoke in a shrill voice. "Jesus, Graham, what the hell is going on?"

"Did you get through to the police?"

"No one's answered yet."

"Don't bother. This young man appears to be a friendly prowler with a question. I suggest we listen to what he has to say and then decide what to do."

The three of us stood in the middle of the great room, me with hands up, Graham with gun pointed, and his wife trying to sort out what she thought. She relaxed her shoulders and closed the phone.

"Well," she said, "I suppose you could always shoot him if we don't like what he says."

I chuckled.

"Would you like some decaf?" she said.

"Yes," I said, "thank you."

"You take cream or sugar?"

"Just black, thanks."

"By the way, I'm Sandy."

She reached to shake hands but then changed her mind.

"Joe Robbins."

While Sandy went for coffee Graham pointed with the gun to an armchair. "You can sit there."

I sat in the chair with my arms still raised.

"Put your hands on the armrest," he said. "I'll keep the gun pointed."

"Thank you."

We sat in silence. I sensed Graham wanted to wait for Sandy. She seemed the more talkative of the two. She soon returned, handed a mug to me, and then sat in the chair next to Graham.

I took a sip.

"How's the coffee?" Graham asked.

"Delicious, thank you."

Sandy warmed her hands with the mug and smiled at me.

"Okay," I said. "Sorry I lied. I just have a couple questions."

Graham kept the pistol pointed at my midsection.

I decided to keep the story short.

"My client sold this house to the person who sold it to you. That man tricked my client into selling her house too cheap. I'm trying to find out more about him."

"Who's your client?" said Graham.

"Sophie Tyler."

"The musician?" said Sandy.

"That's right."

Graham had a blank look on his face, but Sandy perked right up.

"She's famous, dear. Been famous for twenty years. Someone told me she used to own this house."

"Are you a detective?" said Graham.

"Not exactly. I'm a freelance CFO. I do short-term assignments for companies. This is kind of a one-off deal."

Graham lowered the pistol slightly. "How much did your client lose?"

"She bought the house for three million and sold it after fifteen months for less than two million. Two years later you bought it for five million."

"Ouch. She got skinned."

"That's awful," said Sandy.

"What do you want to know?" Graham laid the pistol on the arm of his chair, his finger outside the trigger guard.

I put the mug on the side table and leaned forward. "Anything you can tell me about the seller."

"Weird deal," said Graham, warming up now. "I found the house on an Internet site and called the number. He had a strange name, Robert Fanciful. A real estate venture owned the house; Fanciful acted as representative. I had a lawyer look into it, and it checked out fine, so we bought it clean, using only attorneys for the paperwork."

"What did Fanciful look like?"

"I never saw him. Sandy went to the closing."

"I remember him," she said. "He was bald and wore a bright yellow shirt. He had great manners: opened the door for me, kept calling me ma'am, and ran down the hall to buy me a Coke."

CHAPTER 27

I CHECKED INTO AN OCEANFRONT room on the third floor of Los Cabos Royale. After turning on the room light I called Rico.

"Hello?"

"It's Joe." I tossed my bag onto the bed and opened the minibar.

"Where are you?"

"I'm in Mexico . . . Cabo San Lucas." I reached into the fridge for a Pacifica. I could imagine Rico's face, the sectoral heterochromia growing with his anger. "Robert Fanciful."

"What?"

"Johnson's other identity . . . Robert Fanciful. I took a long shot coming down here. Sophie lost money on two investments before the independent film she hired me to investigate. The first was a house in Cabo. Johnson used the Robert Fanciful alias to buy the house."

"Holy shit."

"Yeah." I took a big gulp of the beer and opened the door to the balcony. The smell of salt air came in with the breeze.

"Robert Fanciful? You sure?"

"Yep."

"Okay. I'll feed it to the FBI. They have awesome systems. Anything else?"

"Catch the fucker, will you?"

"Will do. Bye."

I had dirt on my hands and scratches on my arms, but a beer never tasted so good. I'd leapfrogged Johnson Sagebrush. If he were hiding behind the Robert Fanciful alias then the full force of Austin's finest and the FBI would now crash on his head.

I showered and changed. Then I sat in a chair on the balcony and called Sophie. I had already decided I would not make the list in the next article on Sophie Tyler's paramours. She had a strong pull on me, stronger than any I'd ever experienced. I didn't know how it worked, some strange amalgam of beauty, voice, and outsize personality, but I could resist her. My family came first, and Sophie had a lot of explaining to do.

But then she said just one word, "Hello?" not in her bright and bouncy way, but in a hollow, toneless voice, as if she'd had one hell of a low day, and I began to waver. She needed my help.

"Hi, it's Joe."

"I didn't recognize the phone number. Where are you?"

My cell had grabbed a signal from a local service, and the source number got lost in translation.

"In Dallas. I had to come for a minor family crisis—my sister. I forgot my charger, so I'm using Dad's calling card."

"Is she all right?"

"Fine. It's a long story. I'll tell you tomorrow."

"The line sounds funny."

"Yeah. It's one of those cheap networks. God knows where the call is routed."

After a long pause she said in a soft voice, "We heard about Mark Cunningham." Then she spoke more loudly, as if she didn't wish to sound afraid. "It's all over the news. So is Johnson's picture."

She finally had to give up the pretense and accept that her erstwhile manager was a killer.

"Is Adrian still there?"

"Yes. He barely leaves my side. Stands outside the door when I go to the bathroom."

"Good."

The offshore wind picked up and blew against my face. The air caught the top of the bottle just right, creating a low whistle.

"We got some awful news today," she said, her voice cracking.

"What happened?"

"Halet Blevins has pancreatic cancer. He's not expected to live more than a couple months." She whimpered, unable to speak for several seconds, and then said in a tearful voice, "H-He's been with me for twenty years."

"I'm sorry."

Halet had referenced having personal problems in the lobby bar of the Four Seasons. What an understatement. I let her cry without interruption; it was the only medicine I could provide. When she was ready we talked about Halet, nothing to do with the fraud schemes, but the early days, which is what she wanted to talk about. She gave him much of the credit for her success.

I wanted to ask her about her affair with Hector, and to also discuss our plans as a couple, but it didn't seem the right time. Still, I couldn't resist asking one question.

"Is there something you haven't told me?"

The surf pounded the sand on the beach below, and the breeze cooled my skin. The full moon had crossed overhead and begun its descent. I could sense Sophie thinking.

"I don't believe so."

"Nothing at all?"

She hesitated for a long time. I tried to guess her facial expression. Confusion? Indecision? I could have shared the origin of my question, but chose not to, because I had not told her of my trip to Cabo.

"I'll be there tomorrow," I said. "You can think about it overnight."

"Do you love me?"

There they were, the big words. I'd fallen in love with Sophie in high school, a crush, or perhaps idol worship, nothing more. But how many kids got to meet their idols the way I'd met mine? Humans know many kinds of love: romantic, passionate, conditional, spiritual, platonic, and others. Surely at least at least one of them fit my feelings for Sophie.

"Yes, I love you."

The second beer was half gone. After the call I went inside to search the minibar for something stronger. On the way back my phone rang. I answered without thinking, expecting Sophie again, which made no sense because I'd just told her my phone was dead.

"Hi, Joe."

I froze in the doorway. A tingle crept along my back and shoulders. My left hand clenched in a fist.

"Johnson . . . you bastard . . . you tried to kill me."

He let out a long slow breath. "Yeah, you gave me no choice."

"What the hell does that mean?"

"Where are you?"

What should I tell him? Not Mexico.

"I'm in Austin."

"Your phone ring sounded funny, like you were in another country."

"The only place I've been to lately is Mark Cunningham's ranch."

He paused. "Had to happen. I hated to kill the dog, though. She didn't give me a choice, either."

I stepped fully onto the balcony. The wind had settled down. A long wave crested and crashed and rolled to shore.

"What's that sound?" he said. "Is that the surf? Are you at the beach?"

"That's the wind on my balcony." I stepped into the room and pulled the door closed.

"Are you in Mexico?"

How did he guess that? Had Hector called him?

I laughed and tried sarcasm. "Yeah, right, Mexico. I needed a vacation."

He dropped the subject of my location as if it were a settled question. "How's Sophie? You two getting along like lovebirds?"

All this time he kept coming back to Sophie as if he sought to keep tabs on her.

"Actually, it doesn't look like it's going to work out."

"The heck you say."

"She's kind of old, and like you said, she's in a different league."

"You say that now. You sound like you mean it, but she'll draw you back in."

"I don't think so."

"Remember Odysseus? He had his men tie him to the mast and stuff their ears with wax. Well, you don't have a crew, and you're going to crash hard."

"Have you spent a lot of time with the classics?"

"I try."

As the conversation pinged back and forth the vision of a plan came to me, a lie that might get Johnson off my back. What I wanted most was for him to relax, to stay put in one place long enough for Rico to catch him.

"I want to make a deal with you," I said.

I looked through the window, watched the moon's reflection bobble on the waves, and waited.

"What kind of deal?"

"I admit it. I've been tracking you down, trying to find a way to get Sophie's money back. In fact, I'm in Mexico now."

"I knew it."

"But I've given up on you. You've got this all planned out. I'm willing to bet the money left Belize long ago. You've combined it with the Cabo winnings and moved it through three different countries, am I right?"

Johnson was quiet, but not for long. "Go on."

"I can get money from Halet Blevins." I paused a second to let him process that. "Halet must have made more than two million out of the scams, and I think he'll return it to keep the story secret. Don't you?"

"He might."

"Sophie gets two million back, and you sail away clean. She might even pay me a bonus."

"What about the police?"

"I won't say a word. That's my offer. Leave me alone, and I leave you alone. I just want to go back to my kids and forget all this."

"And Sophie?"

"I already told you. It's over."

I gripped the phone tight, praying he'd go for it. It was true that I wanted no more to do with Johnson, but mostly I wanted him locked up or killed. It took me a second to recognize the sound, because I'd rarely heard Johnson laugh. He sounded relieved, like I'd set him free.

"That sounds so sweet," he said. "I just want to be left alone. I never wanted to kill you. I never wanted to kill anyone. I always had a reason. You know that."

"Sure."

"I do have a plan, and now I can implement it. I can leave this craziness behind and start over."

"Solid plan, Johnson. Solid plan."

CHAPTER 28

THE STORMS ROLLED IN OVERNIGHT. By the time I dropped the rental off a tropical depression had settled over the airport. I dashed through pouring rain to the terminal only to learn they had canceled my flight. The wind prevented aircraft from landing for two hours, ruining the airline's schedule.

I tried to relax. I ate breakfast, drank extra coffee, read a magazine, and thought through my plan. One more trip to L.A. I'd meet with Halet Blevins and then have a long conversation with Sophie.

A few big questions remained. Why did Johnson monitor me? Was he concerned I would discover his alias, Robert Fanciful? Did he worry that I would track the diverted money? More importantly, what role did Sophie play? It now appeared that she might have arranged the theft of her own money.

The puzzle was a Rubik's Cube, with different pieces of data tied together like colored squares. When I turned the data in one direction the orange squares lined up, but the rest of the colors became jumbled together. With a few more twists of the cube most of the blues aligned, but the greens and yellows and whites were all mixed with the reds, and the oranges came apart again. My mind kept resorting the data but nothing worked.

I tried lateral thinking, watched passengers go in and out of shops across the concourse. A young couple studied jewelry at a kiosk. An overweight tourist in a flowered shirt came out of the liquor store holding a large shopping bag. I had time to kill and went shopping myself. I walked through stores in search of something for the girls but had trouble finding the right gift. I finally selected two Swatches with colorful bands. As the woman finalized my duty-free purchase I had a new thought for the Rubik's Cube.

My mind raced as I walked back to the snack bar. I ordered a bottle of water, my nerves too tight to handle more coffee. I closed my eyes to sift through all the data, looked at the cube from all angles, and was stunned that the colors lined up perfectly. I sat still for twenty minutes, hoping for a different answer, and then called Marco Ruffini.

"Yes," he said. "Sophie got a large tax refund in 1997 when she applied her investment loss from the Cabo house." A few minutes later he said, "Yes, because of the Shareware losses Sophie paid no income tax in 2000, 2001, or 2002."

I stared at my shoes with my shoulders slumped. The advice I had given Gwen Raleigh and the Connection employees kept ringing in my ears:

Don't fuck with the IRS.

* * *

I DOZED ON THE FLIGHT, my head nodding. An image of a crowbar smashing glass shocked me awake.

Would Johnson keep his end of the deal? Would he leave me alone? He should. He'd assess the situation logically. Danger threatened: a massive manhunt, his picture on the Internet, and a thousand pairs of searching eyes. I offered him the best chance: *You leave me alone, and I leave you alone.* Johnson would hide, wait for the noise to settle, and Rico would find him.

We landed a thousand miles north at the end of a beautiful day. I called Gwen to get Halet's address and then rode the shuttle to the rental lot. On the way I listened to a voice message from Rico.

"Johnson rented a car in Austin last week using the name of Robert Fanciful."

I called Rico from the car.

"Did you catch him?"

"Not yet, but we're about to. The FBI put twenty people on the phone and found his motel, an independent motor court in Dripping Springs. They take cash, apparently, no credit card required."

From La Tijera Boulevard I turned left for the on-ramp to the 405. "How can you be sure it's him?"

"Only one Robert Fanciful. I'm sitting in my car across the street looking through binoculars at his rental car. The FBI is preparing to rush the door. He's got the Do Not Disturb sign hanging on the knob." The sound of someone knocking on Rico's window came through the phone. "Gotta run. I'll call when we have him."

While driving I thought about Halet Blevins, the talent agent with pancreatic cancer and a penchant for high living. By then I suspected he wasn't involved in the Shareware and Second Chance schemes, but I still wanted to talk with him. He might help me understand how everything got started: Johnson, Cabo, and the tax fraud.

Night crept in as I continued north to the correct exit. I followed Wilshire through a section of office buildings and began climbing into the hills. I found the address just short of Beverly Glen Boulevard.

Halet's condo building stood ten stories high. I pulled into the drive and noticed flashing lights. Three patrol cars sat parked outside the lobby, the nearest car emitting dispatch calls through an open window.

I ground my teeth and hoped for a coincidence. My stomach churned.

Well-groomed landscaping surrounded the building. Each floor had four units, two facing the front and two on the rear. Residents gathered on balconies of higher floors to watch the spectacle.

I walked to the lobby door, but a policeman blocked my path.

"I'm sorry, sir. No one is allowed in the building for the moment."

"What's going on?"

"I can't say, sir."

"Any idea how long it will take?"

"Hopefully soon." He smiled and shrugged, as if he'd like to help me but had no idea how to go about it.

I walked beyond the patrol cars to where a couple stood watching.

"Do you know what's happening?" I said.

The man stood with his arms crossed and stared at the patrol cars. "No idea."

The woman showed more interest. "We've only been here a few minutes. I saw some people walk around the corner." She pointed to the left. "Maybe we should check it out."

The three of us followed the parking lot to the side of the building. A cluster of people had gathered at the far end of the lot; everyone looked across the back of the condo. The police had strung yellow tape to block off a small section of the lot, and two officers stood guard to keep onlookers out.

I edged my way closer to the front. A man my height stood with his hands in the pockets of his jeans. He wore a leather jacket. A woman in high heels and a skirt stood by his side.

"What happened?" I said.

"Jumper," said the man.

"You don't know that," the woman said. "Maybe he fell."

"Nobody falls from a high-rise balcony."

I leaned right to look over another woman's shoulder. Two men in plainclothes stood talking in the center of the garden fifteen feet from the building. Shrubs and flowers obscured the view of their feet.

"Who was it?" I asked of no one in particular.

Several people shrugged, and a woman said, "Don't know."

Then a man in front turned to speak to us all. "One of those guys said, 'Blevins.'"

Damn it.

I looked over my shoulders. My hand twitched.

"Oh, my God," said the woman in the high heels. "Halet Blevins? I spoke to him in the parking lot yesterday."

"Halet Blevins?" said someone else. "The agent? Jesus. Why would he commit suicide?"

"I heard he had cancer," said a man, shaking his head. "Pancreatic."

A woman next to him nodded, and the conversation turned to gossip.

I slowly stepped out of the crowd and walked to my rental, searching the edges of the parking lot.

Maybe Halet *did* jump. He had chatted up girls in the lobby of the Four Seasons, knowing full well his time was running out. Maybe he'd struck out with them, or worse yet, maybe he got one upstairs but couldn't perform. Feeling depressed about that, he had returned to L.A., considered the bleakness of his remaining life, and taken the easy way out.

Or did he? Could Halet have known about Robert Fanciful?

I imagined Johnson on the balcony of Halet's condo. He scanned below to check for onlookers and then stepped inside. Johnson returned with an unconscious Halet over his shoulder. With a little effort he heaved Halet over the side and watched as he fell to his death.

Johnson had called me in Cabo twenty-two hours before. It took twenty hours to drive from Austin to Los Angeles, eighteen if you hauled ass the whole way.

I turned on the car, opened the front windows, and rubbed my eyes. Johnson had me thinking in circles, growing dizzy, like a kid riding twice on a Tilt-A-Whirl.

I called Rico's cell but got voicemail. They were conducting the raid right then. I sent him a text to call me. As I turned on Wilshire toward Beverly Hills I called Adrian. The phone rang only once.

"Adrian Williams." He sounded normal: crisp, confident, in command.

"Hey, it's Joe. I'm glad to hear your voice. Is everything okay?"

"No problems here. Are you on the way?"

"Halet Blevins is dead."

"What?"

I told Adrian it looked like suicide, but I also relayed my paranoid notions that it could be Johnson's work. Adrian laughed at me, told me I was silly, but he sounded a little nervous. We stayed on the phone for a while, neither of us saying anything, and then he told me to be careful.

Next I called Sophie.

"Hi, Joe." She sounded tired. "Where are you?"

"Fifteen minutes away."

"I didn't sleep last night. I kept thinking about what you asked me . . . you know . . . if I had anything to tell you. I do. I want to tell you something, but we have to do it in person, and it's going to take a long time."

So she would confess her sins after all, relate the whole story. How she had realized that selling a rental property for a loss in Cabo would reduce her taxes in the U.S. How selling the house to a shell company allowed her to flip it later and keep the gains offshore.

I guessed about some of the details. These kinds of structures could be done in many ways. Hell, it might even be legal, but the Shareware scheme, that wasn't legal—that was tax fraud.

"We've got all night," I said. "I'll be there soon."

I fought traffic on Wilshire for ten minutes and thought about Sophie's mess. That was the only way I could line up the colors on the Rubik's Cube. Sophie and Johnson had worked the Shareware scheme together. They generated fake business losses to offset her real income. I'd run some rough numbers. Between the rental house and Shareware she had avoided paying four million in taxes.

She would give me all the details, but I assumed that the tax benefit of the Cabo losses had left her wanting more. Johnson had found the target company in Shareware, and Sophie had done the rest. She had seduced Mark Cunningham, pulled him into her web, and convinced him to create the fake P&Ls. Then they routed the cash to the shell company in Mexico.

The Second Chance deal was a mistake from the start, poorly structured. Perhaps she got greedy, but she realized her mistake when Ruffini raised questions. She tried to cover herself by hiring me and unwinding the investment, but that went wrong, too.

Poor Mark Cunningham. He sat on that ranch all alone and thought about his time with Sophie. He grew resentful about his take. He'd been used and paid little for his risk. When I showed up he sold Johnson out, but he couldn't sell out Sophie.

I guessed the part about Cunningham, too, but I thought it a good guess for one reason: I couldn't abandon Sophie, either. I wanted to help her. She'd broken the law and would go to jail for it, most likely, but with a bit of work on my part and some help from the right lawyers she could cut a deal with the IRS.

Sophie's real problem was that she'd partnered with a serial killer. I doubted that she or Halet knew about Johnson's violent past. As Rico said, serial killers vanished for years at a time.

I turned left on Santa Monica and then left again on North Canon Drive. At the intersection with Sunset Boulevard the road became Benedict Canyon Drive. A quarter mile short of Sophie's place my cell phone rang. It was Rico.

"We missed him." He sounded anxious, breathing heavy. In the background I heard others talking fast. "Hold on." He muffled the cell and yelled something. Someone else yelled back.

I turned right on Tower Road and slowed to a crawl.

"I don't know," said Rico. "The bed's made. They say the Do Not Disturb sign's been on all day, so the maids never went in. The towels are dry, never touched. He might have left yesterday."

Acid rose from my stomach to my throat. Pressure grew behind my eyeballs, pounded at the back of my head. I looked in the rearview and at both sides of the road.

"I think he's here," I said. "Halet Blevins is dead. It looks like suicide, but I think Johnson killed him."

"Shit. What about Adrian?"

"I talked to him ten minutes ago. Everything was fine." I veered right onto San Ysidro Drive, barely moving now.

"Okay. Call Adrian again. Give him an update. I'll get the local police to send some units over there."

I called Adrian's number but got voicemail. Then I saw the truck on the right curb, a white Toyota with Texas plates. I did a Y-turn on the street, sped back to Tower Road, and parked.

By the time I made it to the back wall the sun had nearly set.

CHAPTER 29

THE WALL STOOD EIGHT FEET HIGH. I jumped to grab the top, hoisted my legs up and over, and dropped lightly amid the junipers. A high wind rustled fronds in the fan palms. As I walked toward the house a thrashing noise came from the ferns beside me.

I turned that way, my nerves on edge.

It was only a small animal. I took slow, measured breaths to steady my heart rate.

At the edge of the patio I crouched behind a flower bed to survey the backyard. The outdoor spots lit the pool and deck area. Bright lights shone in every room in the house, but I detected no movement.

Rico's words rang in my ears.

But Sagebrush is a serial killer.

I ignored the words and flexed my shoulders to stretch the muscles in my back.

I crept from chair to chair on the patio, pausing often to watch the windows. The bamboo wind chimes rang on the back porch. The palm trees swayed. I looked behind me, and all around the yard. I made it to the back right corner of the house and tiptoed up four stairs to the side door.

It stood open. Forced. Johnson had a new crowbar.

He might have watched my every move from the security room inside. Had Rico reached the local police? I pulled out my cell and dialed 911. When they came on the line I whispered, "I'm outside Sophie Tyler's residence at 1102 Benedict Canyon Drive in Beverly Hills. A serial killer is inside the house. Tell the police to be careful. He could have hostages."

"What is your name, sir?"

"Joe Robbins. I'm a friend of Sophie Tyler's."

"Please stay on the line while I contact the police."

Seconds could mean everything.

I hung up and rose to look through the door window. The mudroom on the other side was empty. I had to be silent now. Luckily, the door opened without squeaking. I stepped inside and searched the room for a weapon. I found an umbrella, not much use against Johnson's crowbar.

I opened the door to the kitchen, every nerve alive, the umbrella held at the ready. The overhead lights shone brightly. I heard faint human voices. It sounded like an argument, but I couldn't discern the speakers. My chest tightened.

A broken plate lay wedged in the corner at the far edge of the floor. In search of a better weapon I quietly opened a drawer on the left and saw odds and ends: spatulas, mixer attachments, can openers. I took another step into the kitchen.

A pool of blood seeped from the edge of the butcher block.

I stopped breathing and froze.

My eyes shut, not wanting to see. I willed them open, took two steps, and saw Adrian Williams crumpled on the floor. His nose was pushed to one side, his jaw crushed. The blood looked fresh but had stopped flowing from his skull. Light shone on the pool of blood. An empty shoulder holster sagged against his armpit.

A heavy sensation swept me, threatened to overwhelm me, but I suppressed it, pushed it off to the side. I would grieve for Adrian later.

I looked in all directions. No immediate threats.

Voices argued in the distance, a man and a woman. It sounded like Sophie. A second drawer contained a rack of razor-sharp knives. A knife had saved me once before, but this time Johnson had Adrian's gun. I grabbed one from the rack and walked around the blood to the hallway. The argument continued. It came from a distant room of the house, possibly upstairs.

As I turned the corner to the music room a prone body came into view.

Another corpse. My stomach ached. I stared . . . unable to breathe.

But the body moved.

I rushed to her side. Relief flooded me with a lungful of air. Keri struggled against the bonds, eyes terrified, duct tape across her mouth, loud breaths coming through her nose. Johnson had bound her hands behind her and secured her feet to the heavy sectional.

I leaned to her ear. "Shush. Be quiet." I cut the bonds at her feet and hands, the knife sawing loudly at the fibers in the tape. I helped her stand and quietly pulled the tape from her mouth.

She began shaking. I held her steady.

"Where are they?" I whispered.

"He moved so fast." She shook her head. "I tried to fight but he laughed and threw me onto the floor."

Johnson shouted something, and Keri glanced through the door to the great room.

"We have to help her," she said.

I shook my head. Keri couldn't help me through the next part. "Where's your gun? The pistol."

"In my bedside table."

"Is it loaded?"

"Yes."

"Where's your room?"

"Upstairs, opposite side of the house from Sophie's suite."

"Good." I gave her my cell phone. "You run to the street. The police should arrive soon, but call them again to be sure. Don't come back here."

I watched Keri enter the hall and go to the door. She opened it with little sound and looked back at me. I nodded, and she stepped outside.

I walked softly from the music room to the great room. From there I could hear the argument clearly. They were on the second floor.

"Where is it?" he said. Johnson sounded calm, as if he were negotiating a simple transaction. "Give me the numbers. Make the call."

"No," she said, her voice unsteady. "You're a murderer. You killed Bryan and Mark."

"Don't believe the media. Thieves killed Bryan; it was a random mugging gone wrong. The thing with Mark was an accident. *He* tried to kill me, and you never liked him anyway."

They kept arguing, with him making requests and Sophie growing more urgent.

I climbed the stairs at the far end of the great room, careful to make no noise. At the top I turned into a hallway.

"Where's Adrian?" she said.

"He's downstairs. He's fine."

I stopped at the door to the voices, holding my breath; it appeared to be the entrance to the master suite, but I couldn't see into the bedroom. I felt exposed, ill equipped to face Johnson. I needed that gun.

"Did you kill him?" she said.

"No, I like Adrian. I tapped him. He's sleeping on the kitchen floor."

Fucking liar. Energy surged in my legs, and I fast-walked away from the suite, past a second bedroom to the hallway, where I turned right to cut across the front of the house. It took only a few seconds to jog to the opposite wing and find Keri's bedroom. I took her pistol from the table, checked to make sure it was loaded, and flipped off the safety.

Back in the hall I stopped; no more words came from Sophie's suite.

My jaw clenched. I trotted down the hall, my chest heavy. Had he killed her?

I paused at the suite's entrance, the pistol held steady in a two-handed grip.

Sophie mumbled something low. She was alive.

"Keri's fine," Johnson said. "I promise. Just give me the numbers and make the call."

"No, you killed her," Sophie said, her voice shaky. "I know you killed her."

"I swear . . . she's fine."

"Show me." She grew defiant. "Show me she's okay, and I'll give you the combination."

"You want Keri. I'll show you Keri. Stay right here."

He appeared in the hallway, walking. He carried the crowbar in his right hand, swinging it casually, with his left hand empty. Surprise jumped onto his face when he saw me. I raised the .22.

"Damned if you don't show up at the worst times."

"Don't move."

He turned left, and I pulled the trigger.

PEAUHHH!

The sound hit the walls and reverberated, jarring everything.

He disappeared.

I'd missed him. I knew it. When he turned his body the target shrank. He moved, and my shot went wide on the left.

I ran into the suite. He'd gone through the door to the bathroom. I followed him.

The overhead lights were on in the master bath, shining on a white marble counter with two sinks, a sunken bath, and a walk-in shower. The bath entered the main bedroom on the left. Where did he go? The mirror above the sinks gave me an angled view into the bedroom. I saw an empty chair.

"Sophie?"

I walked softly to the bedroom, the pistol pointed straight ahead, and heard her sigh.

The room was brightly lit, the doors to the balcony open, a cool breeze blowing in. A faint fragrance of sandalwood hung in the air. Hardwood beams ran from floor to ceiling on each wall of the white room. The bed was against the back wall.

Sophie stood next to the bed, staring through the balcony door, perhaps in shock. I didn't see Johnson. I imagined him sneaking up on me, the crowbar raised high. I spun around to point at the hallway. Sophie continued to look out the door, hugging herself tightly, shaking. I knelt on the floor to look under the bed—all clear.

"Where is he?" I said.

Finally she looked at me. Her arms came unfolded, and she took a deep breath. "You came. I knew you'd come."

I pointed back through the door to the bathroom. I pivoted to the balcony door. My eyes moved constantly. I ran to the left of the room and looked back down the empty hallway.

"He's gone," she said.

"Where?"

"Over the side of the balcony." She pointed out the door.

I ran to crouch at the entrance, the gun still held ready. I looked from the left of the door to the right of the balcony, and then crossed the door to look left. I stepped outside, my head turning left and right; then I spun around again to look back down the hallway. I tiptoed to the balcony rail and looked over the edge. I turned back and looked at the roof.

I walked back into the bedroom, more confident that Johnson had fled. The police would arrive soon. They'd cordon off the neighborhood, bring in helicopters, and hunt him down.

When I lowered the gun Sophie came toward me, but I put out a hand to stop her.

"No. Not yet."

She spoke in a low voice, "What's the matter?" but as soon as she asked the question another thought seemed to cross her mind. "What about Keri?"

"She's fine. I sent her out the front door. The police will be here soon."

She raised her arms toward me, but I shook my head. I couldn't let her off so easy.

"All this mess to avoid paying taxes," I said.

I had lingering concerns about Johnson, so every few seconds I glanced at the balcony and the hallway. I'd feel better when he was in chains.

But we didn't have much time. The police would soon join us, and I wanted a chance to talk with Sophie first, so I laid it out in a few sentences: the shell company, the Shareware fraud, and why she hired me.

She drew up to her full height, growing indignant, and straightened her shoulders. Here it came—the fraudster always had a justification.

"I've paid fifteen million in taxes in the last twenty years. Isn't that enough?"

A siren sounded in the distance. The bamboo wood chimes played as the breeze from the open door chilled my arms. I looked back to the empty hallway again.

"How much did you promise Johnson?"

"Twenty percent of the savings. Nearly a million dollars now." She looked away from me, her arms hanging loose by her sides. "I first got the idea from Halet. Without investment losses he couldn't have paid his taxes. That was a long time ago."

"Halet's dead."

"What?" She cried, her voice higher.

"Johnson killed him this afternoon."

"Why? Halet had nothing to do with it." She closed her eyes and grimaced, as if to shut out the latest tragedy. "N-n-no one was supposed to die. It was just a tax strategy." She crumpled, her knees collapsing.

I rushed to grab her by the arms. As I touched her, a tingle ran from my hands to my shoulders.

Tax fraud involves numbers and money. When you steal from the government, you either get away with it or they put you in jail. Nobody dies.

But Sophie had hired a serial killer.

"Sophie," I said. "Listen to me. I can help you with the police and the IRS. You had nothing to do with the murders. That was all Johnson."

She looked at me again, the saddest face I'd ever seen, her lively eyes lifeless, no trace of a smile.

Feelings rushed me, as they had the morning after we'd made love—desperate longing. My heart banged in my chest. My eyes consumed her: hair carelessly about her shoulders, bluish-green eyes, and perfect nose. I saw only her, felt only her, everything else crowded out. But somewhere in the deep recesses a small voice struggled to be heard.

"No one was supposed to die," she repeated. "I wanted to tell you about it. I tried to tell you at the Four Seasons, but I couldn't."

The small voice grew louder, clamoring to break through. I blinked and remembered the danger. I looked away from Sophie to the balcony and then to the hallway.

"Why did Johnson come back here?"

She didn't answer, her eyes nearly vacant. I squeezed her shoulders.

"What was Johnson asking about? What numbers?"

She shook her head, as if to wake. "He wants more money. I have two million in cash in a safe in Mexico."

I paused for a second, connecting the dots. A safe in Mexico with a lot of money that Johnson could steal; it all made sense.

"Hector has the safe," I said.

"Yes. It's huge . . . immovable. Hector doesn't know the combination, but if I call him and give Johnson the sequence, Hector will give him the money."

I held her in my arms, her body warming mine. I pulled away and looked at her, trying to memorize her. Her face changed, becoming less desolate. She almost smiled.

"Okay," I said, "sit on the floor by the bed. We'll wait for the police."

Then I heard a noise. I began to turn, my hand rising, finger on the trigger of the .22.

Sophie's face froze.

Keri yelled from the hallway, "Leave me alone, you miserable fuck. Leave me alone!"

Johnson strode toward us, carrying Keri as easily as a throw pillow, her arms and legs flailing. He held his left arm tight across her chest and constrained her legs by wedging his right arm through her crotch. He gripped the crowbar in his right hand, but I didn't see Adrian's gun.

"You asked for Keri," he said cheerfully. "I found her sneaking around outside."

Keri continued to struggle. "You dick. I'm going to kill you."

He shielded himself with her body.

I focused on breathing, the target close, face-to-face with the killer. Everything faded away: Sophie, the room, leaving only Johnson and Keri and me. Sooner or later he'd give me a chance, and I'd shoot that fucker dead.

He laughed. "I tell you, girl. Keep twisting those boobies against my arm and I'm liable to get excited."

More sirens had joined the first. They drew nearer.

While Keri squirmed and cussed, Johnson watched my gun hand. He moved his head constantly.

Keri twisted her shoulders free for an instant. I adjusted my aim. She turned toward Johnson and clawed at his face. I almost squeezed the trigger, but he scrunched behind her, pulled his right arm from her crotch, and rapped the crowbar against her skull.

She collapsed.

Sophie gasped.

I stayed focused on Johnson.

He hoisted her body higher and ducked.

"Drop that gun," he said, "or I'll smash her skull. You know I will. You've seen my work."

"No."

"Okay, then, here I go." He adjusted the crowbar in his hand and made ready to pull his arm back.

In that moment I saw Mark Cunningham on his couch, the crowbar protruding from his head.

"Wait," I said.

I dropped the .22 onto the floor two feet from me. I could reach it and fire in a few seconds.

"Kick that gun farther away, won't you?"

"No." Instead I took a step toward Johnson. If he moved his arm, I'd rush him.

He smiled and held Keri carelessly in his arm. "Okay. Have it your way. Sophie, dear, I don't have a lot of time. Give me the combination."

He said nothing about the call to Hector. Maybe he figured there wasn't time. Maybe he planned to kill us all.

Sophie's face had turned white. She stared at Keri.

"Sophie!" said Johnson.

"It's in a hidden compartment," she said, and stepped toward the bureau.

"You won't get away," I said. "The police are here. They'll shoot you."

"Heck. I can climb a wall same as you."

Sophie returned from the bureau with an envelope. Her hand shook. I took the envelope from her and pushed her off to the right.

"Let Keri go," I said. "And drop the crowbar. Then I'll give you the envelope."

"All right." He dropped Keri to the floor. She fell like deadweight. He stepped away from her and moved the crowbar to his left hand, but Johnson wasn't left-handed.

"Now drop the crowbar. That was the deal."

A broad smile came to his face. "Yeah, that was the deal, but—"

I had no time.

I ran toward him as he reached behind his back. It took me three steps to get there. In his haste to reach the gun tucked in the back of his pants he let the crowbar stay at his side. I reached him so quickly he didn't have time to ready either weapon.

I grabbed both of his wrists.

He fired the revolver.

PEAUHHH!

My ears rang. Sophie screamed. My adrenaline surged. We began a crazy dance, him swinging my weight around, and me tightening my grip on his wrists.

PEAUHHH!

The noise rattled the windows.

PEAUHHH!

Glass shattered in the bathroom.

He flung his gun arm down, trying to force me to turn it loose.

PEAUHHH!

Splinters flew as a bullet tore through the floor at my foot.

I tripped over Keri's body, started to fall, and pulled Johnson on top of me. I slammed his hand into the floor and he lost his grip. The revolver bounced. I kneed him in the side and scrambled to my feet.

He stood slowly, the crowbar in his hand, a creepy smile on his face.

I reached to the floor and picked up Keri's .22. As I stood he rushed me.

He came at me quick, his eyes ablaze, his knees lifting high. He shifted the arc of the crowbar to intercept the pistol as I aimed. The crowbar rapped my knuckles, and the .22 flew from my grasp, landed with a clatter on the floor, and slid under the bed.

Everything slowed down. Pain shot up my arm. Johnson's swing pulled him to the left. The two of us took a moment to adjust, regain our balance, and face each other again. As Johnson raised the crowbar I planted my left foot and swung my right leg in a roundhouse kick to the back of his thigh. He groaned and shifted his weight. I replanted the left foot and kicked him again.

Johnson's left leg collapsed, and he fell to his knee. I lunged for the crowbar, grabbed it at both ends, and twisted it against his grasp, trying to break his fingers. He wrapped his left arm around me as the crowbar fell to the floor.

He pulled me down in a bear hug, his arms squeezing the air from my lungs. I spun hard left to break his grip, scrambled to my knees, and punched his face. I jumped back before he could grab my head with those powerful hands.

Sophie had left the room. She shouted for help from the balcony.

I needed distance from Johnson. Up close he'd kill me. In a boxing match I could pick him apart.

He got to his knees and then his legs, breathing heavily. He held his hands outside his face with open fists.

"You dumb shit," he said. "She'll wreck your life."

"Fuck you."

He came at me slowly, circling. Each time he got in range I threw a jab at him. I leaned in close enough to lure a swing from him, rocked back to let it fly past, and hammered him with a straight right to the face. He kept looking down at the crowbar, trying to get on top of it. Every time he looked longer than a second I punched him again.

I miscalculated, threw a hard left punch he expected. He sidestepped me and swung his left arm against my head.

Pain pierced my ear . . . shocked my brain. I fell to the ground but rolled to my feet an instant later. He had his hand on the crowbar. As he brought it up I kicked at it with my right foot. I made solid contact, and the crowbar smashed against a mirror on the wall.

Johnson ran toward me, his arms outstretched, his eyes bulging. As he reached me I hunched down and grabbed his shirt at the top. His hands closed on empty air. I pulled down on the shirt, got hold of his thigh with my right hand, and let his momentum carry him forward as I flipped and then slammed him into the wall.

I backed up a step, expecting him to fade, but he scrambled and landed on his left foot and right knee. He charged me again, staying low this time. I feigned right, stepped left, and threw a hard hook to his face. He paused only an instant, then spun around and kicked me in the midsection.

I doubled over, all the air gone from my lungs. Johnson pushed me at the shoulders. I tried to backpedal, began to lose balance, and he hurled me at the wall. I bounced off and raised my fists. He batted them away, grabbed my upper arms at the sides, and cracked my head on one of the exposed beams.

My ears rang. My vision blurred. Johnson reared back, preparing to butt me with his head. As he reached the farthest point back I kicked blindly with my right foot and got him in the balls.

He fell to his knees, his left hand across his genitals, pain etched on his face.

I gasped for air, an eerie tune playing in my head. I sank to the floor. Johnson crawled toward the crowbar against the mirror.

Through the corner of my eye I saw Sophie run in from the balcony. I tried to shake my head, to will her away from the fight, but she leaped on his back.

"You bastard! You murderer!"

I spied Johnson's revolver four feet from me and scrambled toward it. Glancing back at Johnson and Sophie I watched him reach behind to grab her arm. He flung her away. She slid across the floor, knocked her head on the doorway to the balcony, and fell unconscious.

I reached the gun as Johnson grabbed his crowbar. He stood, looked at the envelope on the floor, and I shot him twice.

The bullets knocked him backward into the mirror, but he didn't fall. His mouth dropped, and his eyes looked dazed.

I kept pulling the trigger, but the gun was empty.

The first shot got him on the outside of his arm, causing little damage, but the second shot hit him inside the shoulder, almost to his chest. The small black hole on his shirtfront turned red and grew larger. He swayed on his feet and stared at his wounds, still alive, still a threat. He turned toward Sophie, looked at her lying on the floor.

He took a step toward her, the crowbar in his hand, and I dove for the bed. I slipped under but Keri's gun had slid farther than I thought. I clawed at the floor to pull closer, wasting precious seconds, my hand finally grabbing the .22. I backpedaled out from the bed, put my finger on the trigger, and swiveled to shoot Johnson.

They were gone, both of them. What happened?

The sirens stopped outside. Lights from the street flashed against the high palms in the backyard.

The crowbar lay on the floor. I rose to my feet, looked around the room, and saw a smear of blood near where Sophie had lain.

My breath came in big gulps. I held the pistol with two hands, pointing forward, and stepped gingerly onto the balcony. Shouts came from downstairs. Flashlights bounced their beams against the trees in the woods.

I edged my way farther onto the balcony and glanced in both directions. Where did they go? Then it dawned on me.

I ran to the rail and saw them lying together on the patio, limbs entangled, heads apart. In the faint light I couldn't distinguish Sophie's hair from the blood.

I held the rail with all my strength, unable to look away, unable to feel the loss even as darkness gripped my heart.

CHAPTER 30

THE POLICE SIRENS draw closer.

The noise swirls as it rises and falls and grows louder. Someone is crying, a wail of unrelenting grief.

I raise my head and then sit and gradually stand. There is the balcony. The palm trees sway in the distance. I walk toward the rail and see the swimming pool and patio below. As I come closer the patio changes color, first to yellow, then purple, and finally to black.

The sirens and the crying merge into angry music, hateful urban lyrics of violence and abuse. My heartbeat matches the drum in my head. All is lost.

I woke up. I was in the condo. Weeks had passed. The clock read three seventeen a.m.

In the bathroom I splashed my face and looked in the mirror. My eyes were sunken, my cheeks thinner.

I walked to my desk in the main room, sat before the laptop, and stared at the screen, my fingers on the keys. After ten minutes I typed a single line: "I can't write and I can't sleep."

I put on running clothes and took a glass of water to the balcony. A neighbor's wind chimes stirred in the breeze. The notes formed incessantly random music.

My mind returned to the same questions. What if I had done this instead of that? What if I had been faster or smarter or better, my aim truer? What if I had left it all alone?

I kept remembering what Johnson had said when he called me on the morning after Sophie and I made love:

I don't suppose I could convince you to leave me alone.

What if I had complied with his request? Would Cunningham still be alive? Adrian? Halet?

Would Sophie be alive?

I finished the water and walked outside.

I ran on Spyglass to the MoPac bypass and then down to Zilker Park. I picked up the trail and started around Town Lake. I ran steadily, my shoes beating a familiar pace on the packed-dirt path. I focused on the effort, the stress on my lungs and muscles and joints, the perspiration streaming down my back. I ran all the way to I-35, across the pedestrian bridge to the north side, and returned to MoPac, a seven-mile loop.

Back at the condo I sat on the balcony, exhausted, and drank glass after glass of water. The capital shined in the distance.

I put in earbuds and turned on the music. An acoustic guitar was her only accompaniment. Sophie's voice began low and slow, and then steadily rose to the soprano range. Her voice and lyrics carried me to when I was young and sat on the roof above my bedroom.

In Cabo I had thought Sophie's charms had run their course and that I could resist her in person, but now I'd never know. Tears formed and trickled down my face. I didn't bother to brush them away.

* * *

AFTER SOPHIE WAS MURDERED the police asked me to stay in L.A. for a couple more days. I checked into a cheap motel and met with no one except the detectives. I ignored the media, seldom left my room, and when the police released me I sneaked away in the middle of the night to catch an early flight to Austin.

I called Chandler and Callie once, so they could hear my voice and know that I was okay, but I couldn't summon the energy for an in-person visit.

I turned off the phones and neglected email. I worked out two or three times a day but never seemed to get hungry. I drank water constantly but never desired anything else.

Rico stopped by to check on me one day and knocked until I answered. He invited me for dinner with his family, said Alma's cooking could mend anything, but I declined.

He walked me through details of the investigation, asked about some loose ends. I answered what I could, but had no questions of my own. On the way out he stared at me for a long time, searching for the right words, but I assured him I was fine.

Every day I sat on the balcony for hours. I noticed things I never had before: the length of the shadows, the smell of the late-summer heat, and the frequency of the birdcalls. When I sat still long enough a black-throated hummingbird came to the feeder four feet from me.

One day the hummingbird darted away, startled by a knock on my door. I stalled for a full minute, hoping they would leave, but the knocking persisted, so I finally walked inside.

She looked the same but not the same, beautiful round face, shoulder-length brunette hair with highlights, shapely body, but something was missing: a feeling that had been alive and strong was now lost. The feeling had died with all the others.

"Rose."

She looked at me without speaking for a long moment, her eyebrows tense, her lips pressed together. "Can I come in?"

I tried to process the question, standing still, not sure how to line up the pros and cons, not sure of anything.

She pushed past me into the condo. She wore black dress pants, modest heels, and a chartreuse short-sleeved top. I guessed she had stopped by on the way home from law school.

"I left you eight voicemails," she said.

"I'm behind with those," I confessed.

"Your voice mailbox is now full, so I decided to check for myself."

A sharp pain entered my forehead. I ground my eye with my palm.

"Can I have something to drink?" she said.

"Uh, sure." I looked at the refrigerator, knowing I was being impolite. I wanted her to leave so I could go back to watching the hummingbird.

"Christ, I'll get it myself."

I tried to rise to the occasion. "There might be a beer in the fridge. I wouldn't drink the open wine. It's likely gone bad by now."

She pulled the cork from the bottle and sniffed. "How long has it been here?"

"I'm not sure. A few weeks."

She looked at me strangely.

I gave up on the conversation and returned to the balcony. I sipped from the water glass next to my chair.

Rose came out with an open bottle of Heineken. She pulled a chair from the round table and positioned it next to mine. She drank from the bottle and angled it toward me. "Do you want some? We can share."

"No, thanks."

"I talked to Rico."

I nodded.

"He's concerned about you."

"Rico always has concerns."

"How long have you been back from L.A.?"

"Two weeks, more or less."

Why did she have to come? I was better off alone, content to observe the world in silence, happy to work out often and just sit the rest of the time.

"What are you doing out here?" she said.

I blinked slowly, twice, while I tried to think of an answer. "Watching the day."

Rose looked puzzled again. Her visit had ruined my concentration. I no longer noticed the subtle sounds of late afternoon, and the hummingbird would stay away so long as we talked.

"When did you eat last?" she said.

"I don't know. Breakfast, maybe." My stomach ached, not from hunger, but from emptiness of another kind, a loss that could not be replaced with food.

"I can fix you something," she said.

"Thanks, but I'm not hungry."

She looked at me, her eyes performing a careful search. She leaned back in the chair and stopped talking. Both of us watched the late afternoon in quiet, and soon the sensations came back to me: traffic on MoPac a half mile away, the flapping wings of a fat mourning dove, the sun on my feet.

Rose drank the beer in casual sips. When the bottle was empty she put it on the table in front of us. "It's not your fault."

"I don't know. I think maybe it is my fault."

"You didn't kill Adrian and Sophie. Johnson Sagebrush killed them."

"Yes, but—"

"Rico told me if you hadn't gone to L.A., Johnson would have killed Keri, too."

"Maybe."

"If you hadn't helped the police find Johnson, he would have gone on killing people. God knows how many, so you can stop blaming yourself."

"I don't know."

She stopped talking again and sat silently. All of her thoughts had occurred to me earlier as I reviewed and re-reviewed the ten days I had known Sophie Tyler. I had relived key moments a dozen times and rethought my decisions a hundred times. Why had I misread Cunningham? Why had I answered my cell phone in Cabo? Why had I dived for Keri's gun instead of protecting Sophie? I had made mistakes, serious mistakes.

After another ten minutes the hummingbird returned to the feeder. He dipped his beak into the nectar and drank greedily. His wings made a clear outline as they kept his body perfectly still.

When the hummingbird left Rose put her hand on mine. Her thumb ran up and down the tops of my fingers. She stood before me suddenly, stooped, her hands on my face, and leaned to kiss me.

"What are you—"

"Shhh. Stop talking."

She pressed her lips against mine and put her hands to the back of my neck. I recalled the smell of her skin. At first I felt nothing, a numb moist pressure, but Rose let the kiss linger, breathing through her nose, and then pressed harder, more insistent, until finally my lips came alive.

I kissed her back, the memory of our love rushing over me like water over rocks in a fast-moving stream. When we finally broke off the kiss, Rose grinned. The love of my life stood before me, her hands on my chest. I took her hands in mine and kissed her palms.

"I've wanted to do that for a long time," she said.

I wasn't sure what to do next, aware only of my desire to be with her.

"Unfortunately," she said, "we can't do what I really want to do. We can't make love."

"It would confuse the kids."

"Yes, it would. Not to mention Dave."

She knelt before me and came in close for another kiss.

"Chandler and Callie need you," she said. "They know you were there when Sophie was killed, and they're scared."

She said the words gently and without judgment, trying to help me understand.

For the first time since L.A., I wanted to see my children. I wanted to hold them close.

"I love you," she said. "I'll love you forever, and you'll love me forever. Nothing can change that. We can't be lovers, but that doesn't mean we can't love one another." She smiled sadly. "That's not perfect, but so long as we touch base once in a while, I think we can make it."

I pulled her closer and kissed her again. "You're right. I think we can make it."

CHAPTER 31

THE NEXT MORNING, I woke up ravenous and went straight to IHOP. I ordered the Grand Slam Breakfast, a large orange juice, an extra side of sausage patties, a Belgian waffle with strawberries and whipped cream, and a pot of coffee.

Back at the condo I sat at the laptop and wrote for four hours.

For the next three weeks I spent as much time with the girls as they could spare. They were quiet around me at first, but regular visits restored the ease of our interaction, the banter, the joking, a few minutes of the B.A.D. game, and the occasional exchange of raw feelings.

In her will Sophie left everything to Keri. I met Keri for lunch last week. She was devastated, of course, but found that focusing on Sophie's estate helped her deal with the grief. She'll work with Sophie's attorney to reclaim assets from Mexico and settle with the IRS. Once that's completed and she's sold the mansion, Keri will move to Austin and manage Sophie's legacy from here.

The conversation with Keri prompted me to attend to my own financial affairs. After a minimum amount of due diligence, and some shuffling of funds, I became the silent partner in a car wash on South First.

• • •

I HAD PROMISED TO TAKE Sophie to Krause Springs, a promise I could never keep, but I had a plan for the next best thing.

Last week I invited Sanjay and Mandi to go on a picnic with the girls. For foodstuffs we stopped at Opie's Barbecue in Spicewood and selected smoked meats from the open grill. The girls urged me to order more, saying I still looked too thin.

Krause Springs was nothing fancy, an old campground with a spring-fed swimming pool, picnic area, and natural springs. It was a hidden gem of Austin, forty-five minutes from downtown, far enough to remain unspoiled by the sprawling metropolis.

We selected a table beneath tall cypress trees. The summer heat had broken a few days earlier, and the sun could only warm the air to the high seventies. A half dozen other groups recreated near us, some swimming in the pool, some eating lunch. The aroma of grilling hamburgers made me hungry.

Mandi stood a little over five feet and was thin. She had dark hair cut in bangs that ran straight across her eyebrows. She wore red lipstick and yellow-framed sunglasses. Chandler and Callie thought she was cool.

Mandi took charge. "Joe, you sit at the head of the table. The girls can sit on either side of you. Sanjay, get drinks from the cooler, please. We have beer, lemonade, and iced tea."

"Can I have a beer?" said Callie, a smirk on her face.

"Ha," said Mandi. "Not for a decade at least, but you can help me spread this tablecloth. Chandler, you can put out the food."

"Everyone has a job but me," I said.

"You sit down," said Mandi. "You paid for lunch, so you get to be lazy."

"I would have paid," Sanjay protested, "if I'd known it would buy me a chance to be lazy."

"It's too late now," said Mandi.

Sanjay accepted her logic without debate and set about taking drink orders. We had a mountain of food: brisket, ribs, smoked turkey, link sausage, barbecue sauce, slaw, creamed corn, beans, and Texas Toast. We did our best to consume it all.

"Daddy," said Chandler. "Have some more brisket."

"I'm about full." I put my hand on my stomach, stuffed with food. The other emptiness remained, the gnawing tightness that stemmed from the loss of a lover, but it wasn't as sharp. Sometimes I almost forgot it was there.

"Get some beans, too," said Callie.

"I'll grow fat soon eating like this."

"We'll worry about that later," said Chandler.

Mandi looked on and smiled while Sanjay stifled a laugh.

The picnic area and swimming pool were on a flat piece of land below the parking lot. After lunch we walked down a metal staircase to explore the namesake springs.

The bottom of the staircase brought us to a natural pool. We crossed the stream at the top of it and left our towels in the sun. After a brief swim Sanjay and I climbed from the water to lounge on the flat rock and watch the girls play on a rope swing.

I let the sun dry my skin. The light breeze felt good.

Mandi was in her late twenties, but with her wispy figure and two-piece suit she could pass for late teens. The three of them took turns on the swing, trying different stunts as they released the rope and crashed to the surface.

Sanjay laughed. He was a serious thinker, an engineer by training and an introvert by personality, but as he watched the girls on the rope swing, he kept laughing to himself. He couldn't take his eyes from them. He'd wipe the smile off his face, try to look at something else or make an intelligent observation, but then he would hear a splash, and his head would snap to the girls, and he would laugh again.

"How are you and Mandi getting on?"

"Wonderfully." He turned to me, the smile still on his face. "She's such a good person, kind, intelligent, and funny."

"That's great. I'm happy for you."

"We're going to be married."

It took me by surprise. The last time we'd discussed their future he had sounded pessimistic. "Excellent."

"You look puzzled."

"No. It's fantastic news . . ."

"But what?"

"Nothing. You two make a great couple, really. It's just that when we talked before you had differing views about having kids."

"Oh, that," he said, as if the matter were no longer relevant. "That won't be an issue."

"So you convinced her not to have kids."

"Yes, well, no, we compromised. We're going to have one child."

"What happened? You were adamant about the danger of overconsumption."

"Yes, I was adamant." Sanjay turned to look at me, his brown eyes thoughtful. "Sometimes I devise extreme solutions to problems. Mandi pointed out that if every woman has only one child, the population will decline. I ran some numbers. In fifty years the population would shrink to half the current projection."

He looked back at the rope swing.

Chandler shrieked as she released the rope at its furthest extension. She formed a perfect cannonball and made a big splash.

Sanjay smiled again. "My father once warned me not to let my head rule my heart. I look at you, Joe. I see what you have with Chandler and Callie. Your children love you like no one else. I want that. In my heart I want a family."

"Good for you. Having children was the best decision Rose and I ever made."

Sanjay nodded as if he knew that already. After another minute he stood and waded into the pool to swim toward the girls.

The heat of the rock warmed my feet. Playtime with family rejuvenated the soul. Modern society made it difficult to enjoy the luxury of laziness. The race to do more, experience more, and acquire more left us with little time for slow leisure. The gadgets called to us. They summoned us with instant rewards and fantastic views, but they also stole our ability to relax, to let the mind perambulate, to settle down.

As I watched through my sunglasses a redhead emerged from the water. I had noticed her swimming earlier but paid little attention. She wore a black bikini and had fair skin. She wrung her wet hair as she came closer. Her body was toned but not overly muscular. I resisted the urge to watch as she walked to my left, but I glanced over as she arranged her towel to sit down, and listened as she brushed her hair.

"It's such a gorgeous day," she said. She had a big smile and gestured with her hands to indicate the sky, the sun, and everything else. "Isn't it?"

"Beautiful. Now that the heat has broken we can enjoy the outdoors again."

"Amen to that."

She was bold enough to talk with a stranger while layering sunscreen on her limbs, shoulders, and stomach. I guessed her age at midthirties. She reminded me a little of a girl I dated in high school.

"Is that your family swimming by the tree?" she said.

"The two youngest are my daughters. The others are friends."

"They sure are having fun. I almost tried the rope swing, but with this bikini top, I thought better of it."

I couldn't think of anything to say. She reached into a backpack and pulled something out.

"You mind if I turn on some music?" she said.

"Be my guest."

She plugged her iPod into a miniature boom box and pressed a couple buttons. She adjusted the volume to a pleasant level, loud enough for me to hear but not so loud as to disturb others. The band played a folksy rock tune I had never heard before. The guitar, bass, and drum players were good, and the female singer made the sound come alive. With a bouncy snap to her voice, she reminded me of Cindy Lauper, and she sure could hit the notes.

"You know this band?" the redhead asked.

"I don't think so."

"The New-timers. I guess they're suggesting they're the opposite of old-timers."

"Clever name."

She raised her eyebrows. A dusting of freckles graced the high part of her cheeks and the bridge of her nose.

"They just released their first CD," she said. "Based right here."

"Austin's a great town for music."

"That's why I moved from Chicago two months ago. That and this." She pointed to the sky with her index finger. "Chicago's fine if you love winter." She shook her head. "I don't care if I never see another snowplow."

"How did you find Krause Springs? This is a bit out of the mainstream."

"A guy at work. He offered to bring me and then bailed out, so I came on my own."

I glanced across the pool to the tree. The girls showed no sign of growing bored with the swing. Sanjay swung far out on the rope but lost his balance and fell on his stomach. Ouch.

It occurred to me that if I waited much longer, they'd stop playing on the swing, and I'd forever lose my chance to join them.

The redhead put on sunglasses and leaned back on her elbows. Her toes tapped to the music.

On the other hand, if I chatted a bit longer with the redhead I might learn her name, might even ask her out for dinner.

Life is full of choices.

I stood up. "I think I'll try that rope swing."

THE END

ACKNOWLEDGMENTS

A HEARTFELT THANK YOU to friends and family who read early drafts and gave me great feedback: Steve and Melissa Baginski, Wayne and Corinne Wallshein, Wade Monroe, Susie Kelly, Ryan Cush, Tom Kelly, John Price, Patricia Little, and Melanie Howard.

John Reiter and Gene Sutter helped me with international and domestic banking questions, Bill Bohls gave me advice on tax rules, and Alex Kelly provided sorely needed assistance on website design and construction.

Derek Murphy of Creativindie designed the book covers for the entire Joe Robbins series, Michelle Josette copyedited the final manuscript, and 1106 Design did the print layout and eBook formatting.

As always, Tiffany Yates Martin of FoxPrint Editorial provided a mixture of encouragement and straightforward critique that enabled me to write a better book. Thank you, Tiffany.

ABOUT THE AUTHOR

PATRICK CONDUCTED extensive research for the financial thriller genre by working as Chief Financial Officer for six different companies. He lives and works in Austin, Texas, with his family and two lazy but lovable dogs named Pete and Sheila.

Hill Country Siren is the third novel in the Joe Robbins Financial Thriller series. Patrick is currently writing a novel outside the series and will return to Joe Robbins as time allows.

If you have a few moments to spare, please post a rating and/or review on Amazon, Goodreads, or whatever review site strikes your fancy.

Go to www.patrickkellystories.com to peruse photo galleries of scenes from the Joe Robbins thrillers. You can track Patrick's writing progress on the website or at www.facebook.com/patrickkellywriter

59231055R00183

Made in the USA
Charleston, SC
31 July 2016